TRIGGER POINTE

A NOVEL BY

Carlos Harleaux

TRIGGER POINTE

Published by 7th Sign Publishing

peauxeticexpressions.com

Book Cover Design by Ethionel Hernandez Ramos
Interior Design and Typesetting by Stewart A. Williams
Photography by Chris Booth

ISBN – 13: 978-0-578-36407-0

INTRODUCTION

Halston's blood trickled down his arm. The alley he stumbled through was narrow, dank and smelled of rancid sewage. His feet felt like lead structures and his head spun vigorously. He realized he hadn't eaten all day. Nevertheless, the adrenaline from his rage kept him going. He replayed the video again on his phone as he ignored his phone's five percent battery warning. A sense of euphoria covered him like a warm blanket on a cold winter night. He grinned as he finally made his way back to his car, with his body weight pressed against the side of the door.

"Is he bleeding?" he heard a woman ask the man she walked beside.

Halston was usually more socially aware, but tonight he couldn't have cared less. As he slumped into the driver's seat of his car, he pushed the ignition and reviewed the video once more. Halston let out a sinister chuckle as he recounted his actions in his head. The antics weren't a part of his nature but he felt powerful rebelling against his expected persona.

However, this wasn't the way his life was supposed to turn out. He exhaled deeply.

The car provided a haven for his chaos. He sat silently, with the headlights on. The quiet hum of his engine was barely audible against the loud clamor of his thoughts. Halston finally put his car in gear to leave the scene before anyone could find out what he had done. Dammit. He accidentally liked her Instagram video. He quickly recanted the 'like' and threw his phone on the passenger seat.

Halston sped home in a frantic rage despite the residue of the night's earlier rain, driving an average of 95 mph. Luckily, he didn't get pulled over. That could have really been the tipping point to an already horrible period in his life. At least it would have all been worth it if he got caught.

Sharon quaffed the top of her freshly cut auburn hair with her fingers before her 11:00am appointment. She pulled out her iPhone, the latest version, and turned the camera towards her to make sure her lipstick was fresh. She reapplied one more coat for good measure. 10:50 am. Many first-time patients arrived early, perhaps to make a good first impression, in an attempt to show that they really didn't need therapy after all.

Nonetheless, she was nervous for first-time patients. Don't ask why: she had no idea, other than the sheer unknown of it all. She let out a deep sigh and reviewed the questionnaire that Halston completed. He seemed guarded and hidden behind his responses. Like many of her patients, he didn't seem to have a dire need for therapy, on the surface.

There had to be something that lied beneath his cover-ups and ambiguous answers. After all, he did seek her out. It was her job to uncover the real him. She clasped her navy-blue blouse closer together to hide her generous cleavage as much as possible.

Two knocks ensued at her door.

She quickly swiveled her desk chair around and filed away Halston's questionnaire.

"Yes, please, come in."

"Hello. Hi, I'm Halston."

"Come on in. I have great respect for a prompt man. Please, have a seat. Would you like a bottle of water?"

Sharon rose from her chair to formally greet Halston. She stretched her hand to shake his.

"Oh, sure, thank you. I'll take some," Halston responded.

Sharon immediately got the sense that he was a gentle man, but not a pushover by any means.

"Great. Water has so many healing properties. It's a shame I don't drink more of it. So, before we get started, is there anything you want to share with me? What brought you here?"

"Well, I'd say everything I filled out in the questionnaire pretty much sums it up."

Halston tapped his fingers on his right knee, anticipating Sharon's response.

"Is that right? Well, judging by your answers, I'd say there may be more than meets the eye."

"I mean, nothing much more than anyone else's usual life, I suppose. I've had my share of setbacks and traumas, but I've pushed through them as best as I could," he added nonchalantly.

"As we all do. Listen, this is a safe space. We're here to discuss what ails *you* particularly, not anyone else. Can we start there?"

Sharon suspected Halston may be difficult to penetrate past the surface. However, she was ready and more than equipped for the challenge.

"Ok, I'd say it all started shortly after my wife beat her cancer diagnosis. Things really fell apart after that."

"Wait. So, things got worse and not better between you two after her cancer went into remission? That's something to celebrate; not a feat too many people can claim."

She seemed a bit perplexed but removed her own prejudgments and allowed Halston to continue telling his story.

"Yes, that's right. I know it sounds odd, but that's how it happened. I mean, we had our slight ups and downs like any married couple. Nothing major, I guess. After she recovered, things went downhill. Fast. Within the next few months, a lot of things were in shambles."

Sharon was careful not interject until he gave her a welcoming cue with his body language or verbal permission.

A brief silence filled the room, giving her a green light to proceed.

"Ok, you just said a lot there. Some things obviously happened after your wife's recovery to get you where you are today. Would you say you resent her for getting well?" she asked calmly.

Halston paused for a moment to ponder the question before he answered.

"*Resentment.* I never realized it until now, but I'd say that's part of how I feel."

He paused for another moment, as if he was waiting for Sharon to instruct him on what to say next. The whole process of counseling and therapy was unfamiliar to him. Nonetheless, Halston found that she had a quality which made him feel comfortable with her. Perhaps that's why she was a professional.

"That's a big step to articulate the way you feel. Only if you feel comfortable, let's start wherever you feel most comfortable," Sharon replied cautiously.

Mrs. Pointe, this is from the Mr. I believe it's for you," the waiter smirked. He held a diamond bracelet on the breakfast platter as Halston returned from the restroom.

"What? Oh, my goodness. Halston, I'm going to get you. I am speechless. It's beautiful. Thank you, sir," Kelly smirked at the waiter.

"I don't think she approves of it. Maybe you should try once more," Hector, the waiter, joked with a hearty laugh and thick accent.

Halston carefully lifted the bracelet from the tray and placed it on Kelly's right wrist. Meanwhile, Hector prepared two cups of freshly made guava juice for them to take on their way. Their breakfast was immaculate, complete with scallops, spinach and artichoke omelets, skillet potatoes, fresh strawberries and kiwi, along with orange-pineapple mimosas.

"Babe, now I hope you know I am not going on any excursions wearing this on my wrist. I'm only going to wear it when we go out to eat again or in our villa; that's it," Kelly smiled, as she rotated her wrist, mesmerized by the gleaming radiance that bounced off the surfaces of the diamonds.

"Don't worry, I'll protect you. I won't let anyone get to you or that bracelet," he laughed.

Hector quickly returned with the to-go cups. They were

filled-to-the-brim with the delectable guava juice. Halston left a generous tip for the waiter and walked down the barely cut cement path towards the resort.

"Alright then, maybe I'll keep on it just a little bit longer. Mmmm, how about you and I go sit by the infinity pool and finish off this guava juice while we soak up some sun?" Kelly asked excitedly.

"Even better. How about I go grab the vodka to mix in with the guava juice while we sit outside? I'll run up to the room now and get it."

"See there. I knew I married you for a reason. I love a man with swagger and ingenuity," Kelly replied, with a mischievously sexy grin.

Kelly admired Halston's chiseled physique as she watched him lightly jog back towards their room. Umph. She fantasized about thanking him for the bracelet in other ways he was sure to enjoy.

"Now, excuse me if this comes off too forward. I just don't understand how a man can leave a gorgeous woman like you alone for even one second. He's got to be insane. Your name is?" a nondescript man asked her.

Kelly scanned him up and down in disbelief. She was baffled by his sheer boldness to approach her immediately after Halston walked away.

The man wasn't even the least bit attractive. At least he could have been a momentary flash of eye candy to match his absurd behavior.

"Ah," Kelly uttered, pulling her hand away as the man tried to caress it. "My name is Happily Married. I suggest if you want to keep having a good time here, that you back away before my husband gets back. Got it?"

"Spicy. I like it. No disrespect. He's a lucky man," the guy said, as he threw up his hands and stepped backwards.

Seconds later, Halston made his way around the corner, with the bottle of vodka in hand. He couldn't have synced the timing better to miss what had just transpired.

"Everything alright baby?" he asked, with a concerned look on his face. He read Kelly's uneasy demeanor.

"Oh, yes, I'm fine baby. You don't miss a thing. Just a little unwanted guest. I took care of it though," she assured him.

Halston listened intently, without responding at first. "Point him out," he demanded.

Kelly knew Halston was a quiet storm and quickly deflected the situation.

"You know what? He's insignificant. I'm not about to let him ruin our anniversary. Let's celebrate. My cup has been waiting."

"Alright then, well if you put it that way. Let's keep that smile on your face. I think I spotted him out myself anyway."

Halston poured a generous amount of liquor in her cup and then some in his own. They both walked over to one of the pool cabanas to relax. Their work schedules were so hectic recently, that it felt amazing to reconnect with each other to stop time, even if only for a moment.

"Can you believe it's been five years already? I'm telling you; it seems like yesterday we were still those naïve, starry-eyed kids straight out of grad school," Kelly smiled at her doting husband.

"Naïve? Hmph. Speak for yourself on that one," he laughed.

Kelly pinched the skin right above Halston's knee.

"Abuse!" he exclaimed.

"Oh, I'll show you abuse alright. I think we can have a better paradise of our own back inside the room. We haven't used that jacuzzi on the balcony yet. What do you say we break it in?" Kelly grinned, as she bit the left corner of her bottom lip.

"Well, abuse me all you want then. I agree, let's go."

They quickly grabbed their drinks as they headed back to their room. The fragrant, tropical fresh water smell greeted them when they walked inside. The concrete floors gave the quaint, yet spacious room a cozy echo. Halston walked outside on their balcony to start running the water in the jacuzzi. Their room was on the corner of the resort and hidden from plain sight, which provided the ultimate private getaway. Halston slipped off his swim trunks and took a plentiful gulp of his drink.

"My, my, my. Let me get a move on. I'll be right out baby. You just stay right there and keep looking sexy," Kelly replied, as she walked towards the bathroom.

Kelly unfastened the strings on her lime green bikini top as she smiled at Halston. The sides of her breasts were already peeking from the side of the top.

"I can join you in there instead. We can save the jacuzzi for later."

"No sir. You stay right there, please. I promise I'll be right out."

Meanwhile, Halston inhaled the crisp outside air. Although they had been there for three full days, he wasn't anywhere close to being ready to leave yet. There were so many obligations waiting at home. The escape felt amazing. He felt Kelly's hands reach above him and grip his chest. He breathed in her succulent scent and turned around to face her.

"Guess who? I guess I didn't fool you, did I?" she said. Halston admired her glistening skin and her hardened nipples, as they protruded slightly from her bare, supple breasts. She was scantily clad in only a yellow thong and aqua blue pumps.

"Mmm mmm hmmm. What did I do to deserve this?"

Halston gripped the back of her neck and kissed her deeply.

They exchanged tastes of the liquor on each other's lips as they engulfed one another with each kiss.

"That's exactly the question I ask myself every day. I guess we have something in common. Want a sip?" Kelly asked seductively, as she stepped back and grabbed the complimentary, unopened bottle of wine sitting on the table behind her.

"Can I drink you instead?" Halston requested, with a ravenous hunger in his eyes.

Kelly smiled as she popped the already loosened cork on the bottle of wine and poured some on top of her chest. Halston did not hasten to chase the wine with his tongue, landing on her full breasts. He picked her up and sat on the edge of the hot tub. Kelly instinctively wrapped her legs around his waist, digging her heels into the small of his back to push him in deeper.

Halston moaned loudly as he moved rhythmically and in unison with Kelly. Their motions became one and neither of them even cared that they were making love on the balcony in broad daylight. In fact, it made the feeling even more intense. Kelly scratched her nails from the middle of Halston's back, up to his broad shoulders. She held on as he stood up and kneeled into the jacuzzi. They kissed each other passionately as the sun peered through the trees as if to get a front row seat to their love making.

Kelly reached back into her messy hair bun and pulled out a single razor blade. She slipped it in her right hand, with a loosely clenched fist, as she folded her arms around Halston again.

"Mmm, yes baby, right there," she moaned.

Kelly smiled as she opened the palm of her hand and repositioned the blade between her fingertips. Halston's eyes widened in shock as Kelly felt his grip on her go limp. He held on to the left side of his neck as blood gushed down his chest.

Halston awoke in a cold sweat. His mind was shaken for a bit from such a disturbing dream, but he had to snap out of it quickly. The hospital room was unusually warm, but he didn't complain. He wanted to make sure Kelly was comfortable. He rubbed her head softly as she lay there staring at the ceiling.

Kelly barely got any rest with all the poking and prodding from the nurses. This was not the way either of them envisioned spending their fifth wedding anniversary.

"What if I don't make it? You're not going to find me attractive anymore. I can't take this. Why me?!"

"It's OK baby. I'm here and I'm not going anywhere. I always still want you. We are in this together for life, remember? You're going to beat this cancer. God is going to see us through it," he reassured her.

Halston wiped the tears that were slowly walking down his wife's cheeks, while keeping his own at bay.

April 17th. It was five months to the day when Kelly received the diagnosis that she had breast cancer. It was par for the course for their marriage for the last year and a half. They had trouble getting pregnant, Kelly's aunt passed a week before her birthday and now this. Nonetheless, Halston felt like the storms just made his bond with Kelly stronger. This was just a phase of life that would soon pass.

"I believe you. It's just a little hard to materialize sometimes. I'm not going to sit here sulking and feeling sorry for myself though. It's our anniversary and I'm going to act like it. *Five years*. Can you believe it? I have been in love with you for quite some time, sir," she smiled.

Halston and Kelly dated for three years before getting married. He was two years her senior. The two met shortly before she entered grad school for her MBA. Their lives were hectic then, as Halston was wrapping up his CPA certification at the same time. He proposed to her the day after her graduation. Halston thought she knew it was coming, but she totally shocked.

"I have been in love with you for a long time too, Kelly. It keeps on getting better, no matter what."

The nurse knocked on the door softly, as not to startle Kelly in case she was sleeping. Once Halston acknowledged that it was fine for her to enter the room, she came in with her hands behind her back. Her warm smile was soothing to Halston's soul. Maybe she was coming in with some good news. Then again, he saw the corner of a large square shaped object behind her.

"Don't worry. I'm not coming in to run anymore lab tests. Well, at least not for now. A beautiful little birdie told me there is a great cause for celebration today. Your wife made this for you. We've had it in safe keeping since earlier this week."

The nurse said, turning to reveal a stunning 12x15 inch portrait that Kelly painted for their anniversary.

Halston's breath was taken away. Kelly was a phenomenal artist and she stopped painting a couple of years ago. He never quite understood what made her abandon her paint brushes.

She always replied with a nonchalant, "I'm just not inspired right now. I have to let it happen organically". So, the beautiful portrait that she painted of Halston was even more of a special surprise.

"Wow, um baby. I am speechless. When did you have time to do this? It's amazing. I think I look better on your painting than I do in real life," he laughed.

The nurse quietly slipped out of the room to give them back their privacy.

"I take it that you like it? Goodness, I was so nervous to paint again. Then, I was nervous that you would find out. You have no idea how that smile on your face has lifted my spirits."

Kelly's face beamed with a glowing radiance.

"I have a little surprise for you too," Halston smirked.

He reached into his coat pocket and pulled out a long, black rectangular box. He placed it on her lap to open it. Kelly always loved unwrapping and opening gifts. He especially didn't want to take that joy away from her while she was ill.

Kelly carefully opened the box as she looked in Halston's eyes for some type of hint of expression for its content. She looked down inside the box and gasped. She carefully lifted the platinum necklace out of the box and looked closely at the pendant attached to it. There was a small, handheld fashion mirror with diamonds surrounding the edges of it. Tears started streaming down her face.

"Halston, wow. This is gorgeous. I've been afraid to look in the mirror. I know you've noticed. There's no way it got past you. I've been trying to shake it, but I just don't feel beautiful anymore."

"I know you may not feel like it right now, but you're the most beautiful woman in the world to me. When I saw this necklace, I knew it was the perfect thing to get you. Whenever you're feeling down and I'm not there to remind you how gorgeous you are, just pick up this pendant and look in the mirror," he replied.

Kelly's heart melted as she laid her head to the side of the bed, turning to face Halston.

He leaned into her and kissed her passionately, while he massaged the back of her neck.

Tap. Tap.

Another knock on the door.

The doctor walked slowly into the room, as she offered a sincere smile to Kelly and Halston.

"Good morning. Oh, I know it's been a long night, but I am

almost positive that you were not wearing that beautiful necklace yesterday. That is gorgeous. Mr. Pointe, can my husband go shopping with you? My birthday is coming up next month."

"Thank you, Dr. Bielman. I am totally in love with it and this guy too. Today is our five-year wedding anniversary," Kelly replied, rubbing the side of Halston's forearm.

"Well congratulations, you two! You are such a lovely couple. It's a blessing to still see young and vibrant unity in marriage. We all just need more love, don't you agree?" Dr. Bielman asked rhetorically.

"I would definitely say so, Dr. Bielman. I would be remiss if I didn't let you see what this beautiful artist made for me," Halston replied, proudly showing off his gift from his wife.

"Ah! I love it. You two are just the most adorable couple ever. Plus, you both have great taste in gifts. Speaking of gifts, I do have a bit of good news to share. I'm sorry it's not as aesthetically appealing, but I think it will evoke some warm feelings just the same."

Dr. Bielman smiled as she handed over copies of the latest lab results to Kelly and Halston.

They both looked at the charts and photos with a cautiously optimistic expression. Neither one of them knew exactly what everything meant, but they could tell from the context of Dr. Bielman's presentation of it, that it had to be something worth celebrating.

"Ok, I think this is good news, but I don't want to get my hopes up," Kelly smiled, with tears forming at the corners of her eyes.

"You're exactly right. It's excellent news. These results confirm that your white blood cell count has virtually returned to normal. The cancer cells are completely gone. We'll be able to get you out of here by this afternoon," she gleamed.

"Oh, are you serious? This is the best news I've heard all year," Halston cried with joy.

"Yes, it definitely made me ecstatic to share it with you as well. We were able to slow down the growth since we caught it early. You came in just in time for us to be able to stop the cancer cells from multiplying. Everything worked out and what better day to learn about it than on your anniversary?"

"Do I still need to monitor it? What do I do now?" Kelly asked.

Although she was excited to receive her new diagnosis, she was still slightly pessimistic about the cancer returning.

"You live. Go on and do all the things you loved doing, just as before. I would even throw in some new hobbies if I were you. We will schedule some routine checkups. You're a healthy woman, so I would say just continue that, stay active and keep positive thoughts," Dr. Bielman reassured her.

"Thank goodness. I can deal with that. Forgive me if I seem doubtful. I just….it's just hard to believe that I won't have to deal with cancer anymore. Thank you for all your help, Dr. Bielman," Kelly responded.

"Yes, thank you for everything. We are both forever grateful for everything you've done to heal my wife," Halston added with immense appreciation.

"It's my pleasure to help. Kelly, you're a fighter and you've pulled through this. How about you both order some breakfast? I know you've got to be starving by now, especially with all the excitement. I'll prepare your discharge papers. You can keep the results I just shared with you. Those are your copies."

Halston leaned over and held Kelly's head close to his chest as Dr. Bielman left the room. He cried with tears of joy that his wife's cancer was gone. Although he was willing to be strong for her for however long he needed to be, he was relieved that this storm in their life was over.

"Thank you for loving me, baby. A lot of men would have given up and tapped out on their wives going through something like this. Sometimes I feel like you love me more than I deserve," Kelly replied solemnly.

She seemed dazed and unsettled about her new reality that she was cancer free. Perhaps her new diagnosis hadn't fully gelled into her psyche just yet.

"I'm never giving up on you. I'm here for the long haul. I know that you would do the same for me too. We're going to get through life together, moment by moment, just like we always have," he assured her.

"You're right. We sure are and there's no one I'd rather spend those moments with than you, Halston."

"I guess we should order some food. I know it's been a while since you've eaten. How is your appetite?"

"I am hungry, surprisingly."

"Alright then. Your wish is my command. How about we get something here and then I'll take you out to dinner later this evening?"

"Really? Oh wow, I would um….I'd really love that. It's nothing against you. You've been perfect. It's just that it's been a little while since I've felt glamorous, special even," Kelly replied, with water forming at the corners of her eyes.

Halston placed their orders for breakfast which included an omelet, with grits on the side for Kelly and a bowl of oatmeal with bacon on the side for him. Kelly smiled and shook her head at his choice of bacon. She had been trying to get Halston to stop eating bacon for a while, but it was useless. He was a man that wouldn't be swayed against his beliefs easily. She smiled and rubbed his hand. She could care less now about a couple of slices of bacon on his plate. Nothing could bring down the natural high she was feeling.

Kelly's face glowed with joy as she and Halston crossed the threshold of Silver Spoon. They both loved the food there, but it was Kelly's absolute favorite restaurant. Halston surprised her with an evening reservation. Although she knew they were going to dinner, she greeted the night with no expectations or guesses for their plans. She wore a stunning, deep royal blue dress with purple (her favorite color) Louboutin stilettos and accessories to match. Halston sported a deep purple, button-down shirt, gray slacks, and black Cole Haan boots.

Kelly even managed to carve out enough time to go to the salon before dinner to get a new haircut. It was an auburn asymmetrical bob and she was in love with it. Thankfully, she didn't lose much of her hair from the chemo treatments. Nonetheless, she did have more breakage on the left side than the right and decided the asymmetrical cut would be best. Halston complimented her beauty several times on their way to dinner. She could see that spark in his eyes, which in turn made her soul illuminate.

"I hear tonight is a special occasion. Happy anniversary to you both," the waiter ushered them to their seats.

"Thank you so much. We love this place. Feels nice to be back. It's been a while," Kelly replied, as she locked her arm inside of Halston's.

"We are elated to have you back. Excuse my manners. My name is Martin and I look forward to providing the ultimate dining experience for you both tonight," he exclaimed.

"Thank you, Martin," Halston responded.

"You're very welcome. Can I get you started with something to drink while you peruse the menu this evening? We do have a wonderful new cabernet that has a hint of chocolate, with a woodsy finish. I highly recommend it," Martin offered.

"Nice. Yes, we'll take two glasses of that," Halston confirmed.

"Yes, you had us both at chocolate," Kelly chimed in.

"Awesome, you won't regret it. I'll grab two waters for you, the wine and some fresh bread. Take your time looking over the menu."

"Oh my God. Let me get myself together. I can't mess up my makeup."

"I take it this is a good surprise?"

Halston flashed a wide-mouthed grin in excitement.

"You better believe it," she laughed.

Martin quickly returned to their table with their wine, toasted garlic bread, and water.

Kelly wondered how the wine would impact her since she hadn't tasted any alcohol in a long time. Nonetheless, she was ready to take her chances. She replayed Dr. Bielman's words in her head.

You live.

"Alright, if you're ready, I can take your main course order or I can come back in a few minutes if you need a little extra time to decide," Martin said.

"I think we're ready," Halston replied.

Their favorite dishes rotated between three menu items they typically ordered.

"Sounds great. In that case, what can I get started for you?" Martin offered.

"I'll have the prawns in lemon butter sauce, with the Greek salad," Kelly said.

"Alright, prawns in garlic sauce, with the Greek salad. That's a wonderful choice. How about you, sir?" the waiter asked.

"I'll have the flat iron steak with mashed potatoes and asparagus," Halston replied.

"Excellent. I'll get these orders in and top of your wine in the meantime," the waiter responded.

"Cheers to five years down and a lifetime to go."

Kelly raised her glass to toast Halston. She felt liberated to sit in a restaurant, enjoying her husband's company instead of worrying about her next cancer treatment. Kelly softly exhaled a deep sigh of relief.

"You've got that right! There's no one else I want to spend the rest of my life with," he replied.

"Mmmm, oh no. I can't believe it. I hope she does not look over here," Kelly pleaded solemnly.

"Huh? Who are you talking about babe?" Halston asked, eager to turn around.

"Don't look now, but it's Amber," she said, as she lowered her eyes to the table to avoid making any remote semblance of eye contact.

"Well, what do we have here? A romantic evening for two! This is adorable. Kelly, you look stunning. I take it that everything with your health is all worked out now, huh?" Amber asked, with a daubed smile.

Kelly barely looked down to take a sip of her water and there she was. Amber pranced her Bambi-like legs across the room in stealth mode. They didn't even hear her coming.

"Hi Amber. Thank you. Halston and I are just enjoying some quality time together for our anniversary. I'm doing well now and look forward to being back in the office next week."

Kelly quickly shifted her attention back to Halston. Her body language instructed Amber to leave them alone. Kelly knew that Amber would be the type to tell everyone at work tomorrow that she saw her out at a restaurant. That was the last thing she needed. She planned on telling her boss that she was cancer free and would be back at work next week. She just wanted to savor the moment without thinking ahead.

Leave it to Amber to suck all the oxygen out of the room....and anything else she can get her lips around.

"Well, I didn't mean to intrude. I just saw you two lovebirds over here and had to say hello," she said, as she gently rubbed the top of Halston's left shoulder. Happy Anniversary! I'll get back to my girls, but see you soon Kelly," Amber replied.

"Thanks, Amber. Enjoy yourself. See you soon," Kelly replied. Her smile forcibly stretched across her face like outdated wallpaper from 1996.

"Well, that was interesting," Halston said sarcastically, as he tried to make light of the situation. He knew Kelly was highly irritated by Amber.

"That's one way to put it. Goodness, I'm glad she's gone now. You know what? I'm not going to let her ruin our beautiful evening. It's our anniversary and we are still in celebratory mode," she smiled, raising her glass to toast with Halston.

Halston was a pessimistic man by nature. He tended to always think the worst so that he could be prepared for any type of situation life threw at him. However, the last few months proved to throw some curve balls that even he couldn't have predicted. He wanted to pour the moment inside of their half empty wine bottle and seal it with the cork.

"It sure is and I'm the luckiest man in the world," he replied, as the waiter came to the table with their entrees.

"We have the prawns in lemon butter sauce for the beautiful lady and the flat iron steak for the gentleman. Is there anything else I can bring to your table to enhance your dining experience this evening?" the waiter asked.

Halston paused for a moment to defer to Kelly in case she wanted to add anything else to her meal. "Everything looks great. I think we're fine," Kelly replied.

The waiter nodded at them both and gave a special glance to Halston before he walked away from the table.

Kelly glanced down and saw her phone lighting up inside of her purse. She purposely placed it on silent to be fully present in the moment.

"Mmmm, I could get used to this," Kelly sighed, savoring every morsel of her first bite.

"I'm with you on that, baby. This is delicious. The best part is seeing that beautiful smile on your face," he grinned.

"How do you do it?"

"What's that babe?"

"Always know the right things to say. You truly have a way with words."

"Well, I aim to please and I always want to keep that sparkle in your eyes. So, believe me that the pleasure is mine."

"As do I. I'm so blessed to have you. Babe, you want to know something else? This food is so delicious and much better than the hospital food. My goodness, my taste buds have never been happier."

That was the exact reaction Halston wanted. He knew it had been difficult the last few months. As a result, he vowed to do everything in his power to make her feel special again. Tonight, he saw a glimpse of the woman he knew before she became ill. They conversed about all the times and funny memories from their courtship as they finished the last of their decadent meals.

Martin returned to the table to clear their plates and top off their drinks again.

"I hope you both enjoyed the meal tonight. Will we be having dessert as well?" Martin inquired.

Halston glanced over at Kelly and her expression indicated she was likely too stuffed for dessert. After their long history together, they were able to read each other's facial cues without speaking.

"You know, I think we may pass on it tonight. We are both stuffed but thank you for asking. The wine was a great choice too, by the way," Halston replied.

"Ok, I totally understand. I'm so glad to hear you enjoyed the wine. I thought you would. I'll get these plates out of your way and I'll be back shortly with your check," Martin stated.

"Thank you," Halston answered. "That was so delicious. I almost forgot how great this place is."

"Goodness. Who are you telling? Yes, amazing food. Even better company. A night so great, even Amber could not mess it up," Kelly laughed.

Martin returned a few minutes later with two Silver Spoon signature mint chocolates and the check in-hand. "Oh, there's one more thing for you," he grinned mischievously.

A second waiter crept behind Kelly's chair, holding a generous slice of cheesecake with a sparkling, heart-shaped candle on top. "Happy Anniversary!" both waiters exclaimed as the dessert was placed on the table.

"Your husband let us in on a little secret that cheesecake is your favorite dessert. This is our new, Dutch Apple Crumb Cheesecake that we recently added to our menu. It's on the house to help you both celebrate this evening," Martin said.

Kelly could no longer keep her composure. Cheesecake was indeed her favorite dessert and Dutch Apple Crumb pie was Halston's. The beautiful, sparkling dessert in front of her symbolized the perfect union they shared and another sign of hope that life was finally looking up.

"You are going to pay for this mister," she laughed, as she reached inside her purse to grab a tissue for her watering eyes.

"Who me?" Halston laughed.

They blew out the candle together and silently made the same wish: that their dark days were over, and sunshine was on the horizon.

CHAPTER 4

The next few days flew by. It was Tuesday, April 23rd, just a few days after their anniversary and Halston's first day back at work since the previous Tuesday. He laid in the bed and glanced at the time on his phone – 5:58 am. His alarm would sound in the next couple of minutes. Kelly was still sleeping soundly, so he decided to proactively cancel his alarm instead. He gently ran his hand across her shoulder in amazement. Her presence in the bed beside him still felt like a dream after she was in the hospital for so long.

Work had been a beast lately, but he was making it through the best way he knew how. He couldn't afford to have a pity party for himself. He feverishly looked for new work in the meantime. His current company was becoming more toxic lately and he knew his days there were numbered. Kelly always urged him to start his own practice since he was such a sharp CPA. Although it was a nice dream, it wasn't anything he could focus on right now.

"Aw, is it time for you to go already?" Kelly moaned.

"I'm sorry babe. Believe me, there is nothing more that I would enjoy than to stay here with you. I'm leaving an hour early though. I told them I'm not working long hours anymore for a while," Halston replied.

"I know, baby. Well, I think you are more than deserving of that.

It's about time to reclaim some of the time you've put in. Good for you," she said, still half-asleep.

"They have definitely gotten more than they deserve. I'm not letting anything take away my focus form you again. Nothing. I'm going to shower and then make a smoothie for breakfast. Do you want one too?" Halston asked.

"Mmmm, that sounds tempting but I'm ok. Thank you, baby. Wait. A smoothie and no bacon? Someone is turning over a new leaf," she smiled, as she rolled on her side in the bed.

"You've got jokes; I see. Yes, contrary to popular belief, I'm trying to do better. I like smoothies sometimes," he rebutted with a hearty laugh.

"I like it. Don't worry about dinner tonight. I feel like cooking. I'll make sure it's something you like."

"Thank you, babe. You are an excellent cook, so I know whatever it is, it's going to be great."

He finished his morning routine, minus his usual workout, made his smoothie and kissed Kelly on the forehead before he left for work. The drive was just long enough for him to finish *The Four Agreements* on Audible during his commute to work. The positive reinforcements that the book provided helped him get in the game mentally for the day. The 30-minute trek seemed to fly by as he pulled into the parking garage at work.

Halston pushed the button to turn off the ignition and let out a slow, deep breath before he exited his car. He was promised a promotion over six months ago, but he kept getting the run around and excuses as to why it hadn't been granted yet. Each day afterward was another chip away at his ego. He knew he was selling himself short by staying there, but he wasn't able to just pack up and leave.

At least I missed that lame company meeting yesterday, he thought as he pressed the elevator button to go up to the fourth floor. Two other men he didn't recognize were already on the elevator. The time was just after 7:30am, about 15 minutes earlier than he usually arrived. He noticed they were going to the fourth floor as well.

"Good morning," one of the men initiated.

"Hello. Good morning, gents," Halston replied to both men.

Both men nodded cordially as the elevator dinged for their stop. All three men spilled out of the elevator at their collective destination. Halston exited first and marched towards the double doors for Axl Corp. He noticed one of the men from the elevator trailed closely behind him.

"Excuse me, sir. I'm here for an interview with Mr. Bosniac. I'm a bit early but is his office through those double doors?" he inquired.

"Oh yes, it is. He's my boss. I'll let him know you're here early," Halston replied.

He kept a tight poker face, despite his surprise. Although he was only out of the office for roughly a week, he didn't hear about any new openings in the department. He and Mr. Bosniac weren't exactly best friends though, so it wasn't totally far-fetched.

"Ok, thank you. I really appreciate it."

Most people didn't get into the office until 8:00am, so Halston didn't expect to see many people there besides Mr. Bosniac. You could always count on him to be the first person in the building, nearly beating the janitors to turn the lights on.

"Ooh, look who's back and quite dapper might I add," Julia greeted him.

Julia was also one of the few that arrived before 8:00 am. She was a fast-rising employee in the department who started as an intern and had already been promoted twice in one year. Although she was punctual, that was about the only professional skill she possessed. All bust and no brains, at least not the kind needed for her job description. She also relentlessly flirted with Halston, despite his incessant unreturned advances.

"Thank you, Julia. Good morning. It's good to be back," he replied with all the professionalism he could muster.

"Mmmm, my, yes, it is. How is the wife? If she all better now?" she asked, with a slight pout of her bottom lip. The plunging neckline on her blouse was apropos for her usual attire.

"Yes, she's much better now. Thank you for asking. Well, it's Tuesday. I'm a day behind to the week, so I better get to it."

"I understand. Well, there's a piping hot, fresh cup of coffee in the breakroom if you're interested, once you get settled," she replied with a less sexually-charged tone.

"Nice, thank you Julia. I will definitely help myself to a cup here soon," he smiled curtly. His phone buzzed in his pocket as he walked towards his office.

Mr. Bosniac stepped out of the breakroom, with a steeping cup of coffee in his hand.

"There he is. Halston! Good to have you back, sport. It's going to be crunch time here on a few initiatives this week. Susan just sent out the minutes from yesterday's meeting. You should look it over before you start your day. Your team's numbers improved from Q1, but we've got a big Q2 push we need to meet," he ranted.

"I'm on it, Jerry. I read the email this morning before I got in. It's great to be back. Oh, I didn't catch his name, but your interviewee is outside in the lobby," he responded.

"Great! He's early. I like it. Thanks Hal," Mr. Bosniac replied in a cheerful tone.

Halston hated when his boss called him 'Hal'. The tone always seemed sarcastic, and it almost always meant one of two things: he was lying or being condescending. In that moment, he felt it was a mixture of the two.

He settled in his office and opened the blinds to let in some natural sunlight. Halston checked his phone and saw an unread message from Kelly:

You've got this! This is just a stepping-stone. I love you. See you tonight.

He briefly forgot about the worries of the day and texted her back before booting up his laptop. She was the only reason why he kept putting up with the foolery that Axl Corp had to offer.

CHAPTER 5

Kelly laid in bed until just after 8:30 am. She had to get back to work soon, but it felt nice to sleep in a bit today. She searched online for a beginner's Pilates video from one of her favorite YouTube personalities. Her energy was higher than normal, so she decided to try a light workout.

She felt liberated and triumphant for the first 15 minutes of the workout. She almost felt like her normal self again before cancer. Suddenly, Kelly felt a wave of fatigue wash over her. Her energy waned as she tried to push through the next segment of the workout video. She couldn't do it.

The video instructor chanted, "You can do it. You can do it. Don't stop." However, Kelly couldn't do it. Her defeat was more than just mind over matter. Tears trickled down her cheeks and behind her ears as she lay on the floor. The video played while she lay listless on the ground with her palms faced upward. She sighed deeply and rolled over on her side.

Kelly stopped the video and opted for something to lift her spirits. She scrolled through other YouTube videos and landed on Pharrell Williams's "Happy". She felt trounced, depleted, unattractive; anything but happy at that moment. The phone rang as she struggled to dance her way through the physical pain and mental anguish.

Her mother.

She paused before answering the phone on the fifth ring. Talking to her mother was like a box of chocolates, minus the nostalgic *Forest Gump* feeling; 'you never knew what you were going to get'.

"Hey, Mom. How are you?"

"Aw, I'm doing great baby. The question is how are you? How are you feeling?"

"I'm actually feeling good today. I just finished doing a Pilates video at home and about to cook breakfast in a bit."

Kelly tried to muster up an extra pep in her voice to mask how she truly felt.

"Look at you. That is awesome. Your father and I knew you would bounce back. Just be careful not to overexert yourself, baby."

"Oh no, Mom. I'm taking it easy as much as I can. After I cook breakfast, that will likely be the extent of my activity today until dinner tonight when Halston gets home."

"Hmph. Ok, I know this is unsolicited two cents, but I can't keep quiet. Baby, Halston couldn't cook you breakfast this morning before he left for work? I know he's working again now but you're still recovering. Shouldn't he be the one cooking dinner tonight?"

"Mom, it actually makes me feel better to try to move around and cook. I'm going back to work soon anyway. Plus, Halston asked if I wanted a smoothie this morning. I told him no."

Kelly tried her best to keep a respectful tone, despite her growing irritation.

"Ok, you know I guess it's just a generational thing. Your father just tried to sign us up for some pyramid money exchange thing. It seems legit. You know I told you last week that your Aunt Shannon did it and she tripled her investment. It's about the hustle though. You know? I don't always agree with the financial decisions your father makes for us, but he's a hustler. I'll give him that," her mother ranted.

"Mom, excuse me for asking but what exactly are you trying to imply?"

A stronger tinge of agitation brewed in Kelly's tone.

"Look, Halston is a nice guy but nice doesn't pay the bills. I'm just looking out for you, that's all. What happened to that big pro-motion he was trying to get months ago?"

"They've been working on it, but he's actually looking to start at another firm in the meantime. His current job has great benefits though, even better than mine," Kelly rebutted.

"That's what I'm talking about. What happens if he gets a job and has to start less at whatever his salary is now?" her mother continued.

"Mom, please stop. Halston makes good money, we're fine. He's supportive and he always provides for us. Always."

"I hear you. I understand. Your father and I just want the best for you. That's all."

Deep down, Kelly was nervous about all the doctor's bills that had been racked up in the last few months. They were fine for now, but they couldn't afford any other mishaps. As brass as her mom's delivery was, Kelly understood where she was coming from.

"Thank you. I love you both and I know you just care about me," Kelly softened.

"Good. Well enough of my lectures. You're a grown woman and your father and I know you have to follow your own path. Speaking of him, I'm thinking of planning something big for his 60th birth-day. If you don't mind, I'll email some ideas I have to you. You've always been a wiz at the creative stuff; much more than I am," her mother stated.

"I'm sure whatever you have is amazing. I look forward to seeing the ideas," Kelly replied with a gleeful tone.

"I appreciate that vote of confidence. We still have a month or so before all that, so it's no rush. I just want to start a little early."

"I understand. The big 6-0. We have to make it memorable for Daddy."

"I'm sure he'll be thrilled. I'll let you get back to your day and relax. Let us know if you need anything. I love you."

"I love you too, Mom. Thanks for everything. I'll talk to you later."

She placed the phone on the counter and sat on the couch. Her fatigue started to wear off but she didn't want to push herself too far. Kelly laid across the couch and watched an old episode of *Property Brothers* on HGTV. She barely made it through the beginning of the show before she drifted off to sleep.

:06 pm. Halston looked at his phone and back at his computer screen. He placed an order for pickup at Pei Wei for lunch. It was always his go-to meal whenever he couldn't decide what to eat for lunch. He wasn't too fond of the cafeteria's food downstairs, unless it was breakfast. Halston submitted his last report of the afternoon through the portal and made a short to-do list for the remainder of the day.

He stepped outside of his office and noticed Mr. Bosniac's door was closed. Halston thought it was odd, considering his boss typically talked loudly on the phone with his door wide open. He didn't care enough to try to figure out why Mr. Bosniac was suddenly so secretive.

The elevator took forever to reach his floor. His stomach growled as he anxiously waited to descend to the lobby. He contemplated taking the stairs instead, but the elevator opened just before he stepped away.

"We meet again."

The young man he ran into in the morning was walking towards the front entrance of the building when Halston exited the elevator.

"Ah, yes. You had the interview with Mr. Bosniac. I didn't catch your name. I'm Halston," he replied.

Halston wasn't in the mood for small talk but he avoided being rude.

"Nice to meet you, Halston. My name is James. A bit of a late lunch?"

"I guess you could say that. The day just got away from me. So, what position did you interview for today?"

"It's supposed to be a bit of a hybrid role from my understanding. A mix of an account manager role and a team manager," James answered.

Halston paused for a moment. He sensed James held back some pertinent details about the interview.

"Nice, well it's a little late for you still to be hanging around. Sounds like you nailed it."

"Thank you, Halston. I sure hope so. Well, I don't want to hold you up from your lunch. It was nice talking to you and thanks for the vote of confidence."

"You're welcome. It was great talking to you too. Best of luck to you, man."

James's handshake, a simple action Halston used to judge every man, was flimsy. Their interaction only cemented Halston's thoughts of James's seemingly sketchy attitude. He didn't understand why James still loitered in the building well after his interview ended. Nevertheless, he decided not to let the thought consume the rest of his afternoon.

Halston arrived at Pei Wei in less than 10 minutes. Thankfully, the waiter placed his order on the counter as soon as he entered the restaurant.

"Hello, sir. Coming in for a pickup order?" the chipper waiter asked.

The waiter had a barely-there goatee and didn't look a day over 18 years old.

"Yes, a pickup for Halston. I had the Kung Pao Chicken, extra spicy, and two crab wontons," Halston answered.

"Perfect timing, Halston. We just finished your order. Here you are. Have a great day."

"Thank you. Same to you."

Halston returned to the office and decided to eat in the break-room for a change. He didn't want to seem so antisocial and remain locked in his office all day.

Julia sauntered in the breakroom before he took the first bite of his food. She spoke to him and looked surprised as if she didn't know he was already there.

The room was brightly lit and newly remodeled. The dining area was spacious, with blue and green accented furniture that complimented the company's brand colors. Halston sat at the table on the far right, underneath the TV and opposite of the microwave. CNN alerts played softly in the background.

"Well, hello mister. A late lunch for you too, huh?" she asked. Her exaggerated yawn and stretch purposely exposed her midriff.

"Yeah, I guess it is a little late for lunch," Halston smiled. He figured there was no harm in small talk with Julia.

"Mmmm, Pei Wei. One of my faves. You have good taste," Julia added.

"Thank you. I must admit, it tastes even better today. I haven't had it in a while," he replied.

Julia removed her glass container from the microwave and proceeded to sit directly across from Halston.

Great.

Two empty tables were available, but of course she chose to sit with him. He couldn't help but see her full breasts peeking out of the top of her blouse every time he took a bite of his food.

"My lunch is much less delectable. I have leftover lasagna," she gleamed.

"Nice. Well, it smells and looks great. Plus, it's probably healthier than this," he exclaimed.

Thankfully, he was almost done with his lunch.

"Touché. It will have to do until dinner tonight. I'm so glad Kelly is recovering well. We were really concerned," she added with a tone of sincerity.

"Thank you. I really am too. She is back on her feet and feeling like herself again. Brighter days are ahead and we're both grateful," he responded.

"Amen to that. That's such a blessing," Julia chimed in.

Her lips pouted as she licked the remnants of tomato sauce from the left corner of her mouth. She seductively squirmed in her seat to make her breasts more pronounced as she leaned over the table. Her body language suggested that she wanted to be next on his plate to devour.

"Yes, certainly. Well, I have a few more things to knock off my to-do list before the end of the day. I should get going but it was nice catching up with you," Halston exclaimed.

He attempted to tow the line of cordiality without offering any flirtatious invites.

Julia got the point but pretended like she didn't.

"Ah, gone so soon? Alright, I guess duty calls. I'm sure I'll see you around before we get out of here this evening," she sighed.

"Yeah, sounds good. Enjoy the rest of your lunch," Halston responded with a curt nod and a crisp about-face as he exited the breakroom.

He heard the remains of a discussion in Mr. Bosniac's office as he walked past the closed door.

"No doubt. He's a fine candidate, for sure. We'll see how it all pans out, but I think he's the guy."

Was he talking about James?

Something about Mr. Bosniac's tone made the hairs raise on the back of his neck. Nevertheless, he had to finish up his bookkeeping for two of his largest clients. He was technically a couple of days ahead but he didn't want any negative thoughts to interfere with his mojo. Halston closed his office door and firmly plugged his air pods in his ears. If he wrapped up his work by 4:30 pm, he could beat the rush hour traffic going home.

Ugh. He checked his MacBook and noticed a missed voicemail from his Dialpad call app. The voicemail came from Monnie, his most difficult client. He was willing to bet money that her message was abrasive and filled with complaints; her usual M.O. Surprisingly, she called to say she was glad he was back in the office. She went on to say that she felt like the account was in good hands again. Halston was shocked. He smiled as he played the message back once more before he resumed his work.

Halston was a pessimist by nature, at least by the account of other people. He considered himself a realist. Either way, he was elated about the positive news and chose to revel in that moment. The tables seemed to finally turn for him.

CHAPTER 7

Swoosh.

Devin hit another bucket. It must have been sheer luck because he wasn't that great of a basketball player. Halston and Omar weren't either, but Devin was on fire.

"Halston, do you see this?" Omar questioned.

"I do, and I can't believe the miracle I'm witnessing," Halston laughed.

"Both of you can shove it. Respect the skills. Respect the name," Devin replied, with a playful arrogance, as he wiped the minimal sweat from his brow.

"This dude has got to be dreaming," Halston rebutted.

"No doubt and we're stuck in this nightmare. Fellas, that's about a wrap for me. I've gotta get fresh for my date tonight. No disrespect to you two married men. I'm newly single and ready to mingle," Omar added.

"Ah, somebody is ready to live his second life. I'm not mad at you man. Go get it. That's a wrap for me too. I should get going to see about Kelly," Halston panted, slightly out of breath.

"Alright, let's wrap up then. Same time, next Tuesday?" Devin questioned.

"Works for me," Halston said.

"Yep, me too," Omar answered.

"Halston, I'm so glad Kelly is back on her feet now. Lynelle and I were praying for her. She's a fighter. The guy by her side isn't half bad either," Devin said.

"Yeah, man. Seriously, it is great that she's feeling like herself again. I knew she would beat it," Omar added.

"Thanks, fellas. I'm so glad to have her back too. I lost my faith there for a moment, but things have really been looking up," Halston admitted.

"No doubt. Hey, Lynelle and I are thinking about doing another Halloween party this year. The best costume wins $200. Halston, you and Kelly should come. Omar, come too and feel free to bring your flavor of the month. I'll be surprised if this one survives another three dates," Devin snickered.

"Don't be upset because you're unable to do what I do. I'll let you live vicariously through me," Omar taunted.

"Whatever, man. Let me get out of here. The Halloween party sounds good, Devin. I'll tell Kelly about it tonight. You know she loves stuff like that," Halston said.

"Yeah, it's going to be a big one. Lynelle really wants to go all out this year," Devin replied.

The men prepared to leave the basketball court and go their separate ways. Halston checked a few work messages from his phone on his way out. Just as he was about to get in his car, he noticed a familiar face. James, the man Mr. Bosniac interviewed.

James recognized him too and moved towards him. "Halston, right?" he inquired with an outstretched hand.

"Hey, man. I'm sorry, I'm horrible with names but I remember the face. You had the interview at my job," Halston answered.

He offered a firm handshake but purposely pretended he didn't remember James's name. He remembered. He just didn't want James to overestimate his importance.

"Yes, it's James. I totally understand. Good to see you. I take it you just finished a game?"

"That's right. James. Good to see you again too. Yeah, I meet up with a couple of my friends here to play once a week."

"Nice. I've never been much of a basketball player. My brother has always been better at it than me. I love running and I usually go on the track just behind the court. Helps me gather my thoughts and run off the day so to speak."

"Yeah, man. I hear that. Nothing like a good run to free the mind. Have you heard anything back about the position?"

"I did. I heard back from Mr. Bosniac on my way here. He said he has to interview a couple more people, but he claimed that I'm a strong contender."

"That's definitely a good sign. I'd say congratulations are almost in order."

"Well, I hope so. Thank you. I appreciate the vote of confidence. I won't keep you. I know you're on your way home."

"Yeah, I should get going and home to the wife. Have a good run man. I'm sure I'll see you around," Halston assured James.

Halston had a funny suspicion about James. He felt like he was hiding something, but he couldn't quite put his finger on it. Nonetheless, he decided to not let those thoughts ruin his evening. He checked his phone and saw that he had a missed text message from Kelly.

Hey babe, do you mind picking up some oregano oil on your way home?

Kelly was really into holistic remedies lately. She swore by the immune support benefits of oregano oil.

Halston was about to text her back at the red light, but he decided to call her instead.

"Hey babe. I wasn't expecting to hear from you so soon."

"Hey baby. How are you? I would have actually been on the road sooner, but I ran into that guy James that interviewed at my job a while back."

"No worries. I knew you were with the guys. I look forward to seeing you when you get home. That's cool you ran into the guy from the interview. What's his story? Didn't you say the position he applied for was something you hadn't heard of before?"

"Yeah, I can't quite figure him out yet. He seems ok. I ran into him as I was leaving the court. He came up there to get a run in on the track."

"Hmmm, I guess time will tell. Well, I started the vegetables for the stir fry. I can just never make the chicken like you do, so I left that part for you. Thanks for picking up the oregano oil too."

"Of course. You're welcome, baby. You are a great cook, but I appreciate that vote of confidence. I hope you're getting a chance to relax now."

Although she was pretty much back to normal since successfully completing her chemo treatment, he didn't want her to overexert herself. However, it was to no avail. Kelly was hardly a woman to rest on her laurels.

"I am, in a way. I started on a new painting a little while ago. I'm not even sure where I'm going with it; just enjoying the process in the meantime. That new Shonda Rhimes show is on too, so I feel good," Kelly exclaimed.

"Look at you. I'm so glad you're getting back to what you love. I can't wait to see the painting. I know how much you love Shonda Rhimes, so I'll let you get back to the show. I should be home in about 20 minutes. See you soon, babe.".

"Ok, babe. Sounds perfect. See you in a bit," Kelly replied.

Halston pulled into Trader Joe's to grab the oregano oil for Kelly. They both loved the grocery chain for its cleanliness, ease of getting through the store, and high-quality products. He suddenly had a strong craving for their miniature-sized oatmeal cookies as he walked through the double-doors. He stopped to grab a bouquet of flowers for Kelly too. He wanted to give her a just because gift to make her smile.

Halston picked up the oregano oil, grabbed the cookies, a pack of mints and the flowers, as he headed towards the first open register.

"Good evening," the cashier greeted him.

The woman had stringy red hair that looked like it had been dyed one too many times. Her stature was petite, as she stood just over five feet tall.

"Hello. How are you?" Halston replied, with a genuine smile.

"Have you ever been triggered to do something you know you

shouldn't do, yet you feel compelled to do it anyway?"

Silence.

Halston didn't quite know how to respond. He mustered a nervous smirk to ease the tense atmosphere in the air.

"I know. I should talk myself out of it. Don't mind me. Life gets even the best of sometimes, right? Your total is $29.28," the cashier stated.

Her tone quickly shifted to a more chipper, slightly aloof demeanor. Perhaps she sensed she made Halston uncomfortable and tried her best to lighten the mood.

"Alright, and yes. Life does have a way of triggering us at times. Just don't do anything I wouldn't do."

Halston flashed a mischievous grin back at the cashier. He could see the wall of shame she built quickly crumbling in her gaze.

"Well, I will make sure I do just that. Thank you. You have yourself a great night, sir. See you soon."

"Thank you. You have a great night too. Take care."

Halston chalked up his encounter to an overworked woman who likely needed some rest. Unbeknownst to him, he would soon understand her sentiments deeper than he realized. He opened the oatmeal cookie container to grab two cookies once he was inside the car. The empty, calming sound of his own thoughts rode with him the rest of the way home.

h, yeah. You are so silly. Well, I hear my handsome suitor walking through the door now. Let me go, but I'll talk to you later," Kelly giggled.

Halston's brows furrowed as he closed the kitchen door through the garage. He was a bit perplexed that Kelly rushed off the phone so quickly. She typically talked to all her friends in front of him; even at times when he wished she wouldn't.

"Hey babe. You didn't have to get off the phone on my account. How are you?"

"Oh, no. You're more important. Besides, that was just Rita. You know she's always cracking jokes," Kelly laughed, as she stood up to greet her husband with outstretched arms.

"Mmmm, I see. She is a hoot. I'm glad to be home to see you. Let me see what you've been working on over here. Is it ok?"

"Ah, wait. Are those flowers for me?"

"Ooh, my bad. I'm afraid they are for my mistress," he laughed.

Halston kissed her deeply and gripped her supple ass. He knew she liked when he randomly groped her. Halston also noticed Kelly was blocking an easel that she started painting on behind her.

He respected the privacy of her art process. It was a world he didn't quite understand, but it was part of his attraction to Kelly. Halston loved her free, creative spirit; a great compliment to his more rigid mindset.

"Whatever man. These are beautiful. Let me put them in water. Oh, and of course, I'd love for you to see what I painted," Kelly beamed.

She playfully blocked the mid-sized canvas before she fully revealed it to Halston. Although she knew he adored her artwork, she was nervous each time she showed him.

"Ta-da! Here it is. Give your honest opinion. What do you think?" Kelly pleaded.

Her need for acceptance in that moment was evident by the sparkle in her eyes. Even her tone turned a bit childlike.

Halston gasped.

Silence.

The painting was a male and female hand intertwined, amidst a backdrop of a colorful sunset, complete with rich hues of purple, yellow, orange, blue and red. The hands in the painting seemed to illuminate and inspire the bold sunset behind them.

"I am absolutely speechless."

"I need to add a few more color strokes here and there and define the hands more clearly. I'm not finished yet," Kelly replied, noticeably deflated.

"It doesn't need a single extra stroke. It's beautiful," he assured her.

"Really? You think so? Thank you, baby," Kelly grinned.

"I know so. You are so talented. Imagine me trying to paint this. It would be twigs for hands with just a mess of colors behind it; a complete disaster," he laughed.

"Silly. Well, thank you. Let me take these bags from you. I see somebody can't stay away from those oatmeal cookies. They are irresistible," Kelly said, as she reached inside the plastic container to grab a few of the miniature cookies herself before she placed the bags on the counter.

"Irresistible, just like you. Let me get this sweat off and how about I have some dessert before dinner?"

He looked at his wife like a salacious devourer.

"You never have to ask me for dessert. It'll be hot and ready for you," she smirked, with a seductive glimmer in her eyes.

"Well, you hold that heat then. I'll be right back."

He hurriedly removed his workout clothes and turned on the shower. His sex drive had been exceptionally high since Kelly's health was back to 100 percent. He felt like he needed to make up for all the lost time. Honestly, he didn't need an excuse. He viewed Kelly as a fine wine that continued to get sweeter with time.

Meanwhile, Kelly flipped her phone over on its screen and began to undress as soon as she heard Halston start the water for his shower. She could tell he was a little jealous when he walked in and heard her get off the phone so quickly. She wanted to prove to him that he had no need to worry. Deep down, Kelly liked when he showed signs of possessiveness. Early on in their relationship, she questioned his desire for her because he seemed so nonchalant. Over time, she learned that was just his way.

The woodsy vanilla aroma of Halston's bath soap intoxicated her sense, as Kelly entered their bedroom. The warm humidity floating in the air from the shower's steam was no match for the moisture at the meeting of her thighs. Her spine tingled as she quietly stepped in the shower behind Halston and squeezed his chiseled chest.

He turned around to face her and kissed her lips passionately, as he groped her backside. He slid his left hand around to the front of her thighs, traced his fingertips up towards her navel and back down – right outside of her ocean of love. Halston felt her shiver as he sucked on her bottom lip. He inserted two fingers slowly inside of her. He moved his fingers in and out in a rhythmic motion while she gripped the shaft of his penis.

Kelly felt his knees buckle as she tightened her grip on his erect member. She loved the way he kissed her lips like it was his last supper. Her spine tingled as he knelt in the shower to kiss the lips below her waist. He lapped his tongue generously around the outer walls before he hit the bullseye with powerful, penetrating thrusts. She let out a shriek of pleasure as he varied the tempo between delayed and quick strokes of his tongue. There was no sense of time in her head, but he had to have been tasting her juices for over five minutes straight.

"I can't....feel. My legs. YES! Don't stop....I love you. I love you. I love you," she screamed.

Kelly inhaled so deeply that her back started to cave in. Each time she exhaled, Halston licked her more forcefully – which took her breath away again. Never had she enjoyed a struggle to breathe so much. She almost had to pry his mouth away from her to return the favor. Although she enjoyed the way his lips, tongue, and after-five shadow scratched against her thighs, she desperately wanted to taste him. If for nothing else, she had to at least attempt to match the way he made her feel.

She brought his face up to hers and kissed him deeply, while she sucked his tongue. Kelly opened the shower door, as she stepped out first. She reached back to grab him by his large penis and lead him to the bedroom. Right before they got to the bed, she turned to face him and lowered herself to kiss his throbbing member. She worshipped it gently at first, before she sucked harder and faster.

Halston moaned loudly as Kelly engulfed all of him. He felt her tongue lap wildly around his penis. His thighs tingled as she grazed her fingernails up and down his legs, all the while keeping him firmly planted in her mouth. He couldn't take it anymore and abruptly removed himself from her jaws of life. As good as the feeling was, he couldn't stand another second without being inside her.

He picked her up with a swift surge of forcefulness, as she instinctively wrapped her legs around his waist. He thrusted inside of her, slowly at first. Their lips locked for dear life. Halston's hips moved in double-time with each dueling battle of their tongues. He placed her gently on the bed as Kelly dug her nails into the broadest part of his back. Her toes became his feast as her legs rested on his shoulders, while still inside of her.

"Damn. Shit. What are you doing to me? Yes. Please. Don't. Stop," Kelly mumbled.

"Never," he promised, as he kissed his way up from the bottom of her left calf to the back of her knee cap.

Halston rested her legs on the bed as he continued to thrust inside of her with a fierce urgency, military style.

Kelly allowed him to penetrate her in that position for a little while longer, until she flipped him over and took control on top. She saw the surprise and fire in his eyes. Neither one of them were able to last long when she was on top. She grinded her hips back and forth before gyrating in full circles. Kelly relished in each throbbing sensation that matched her movements on top of him.

"I feel you getting wetter. It's so tight."

"All for you, baby. It's yours. All yours."

They both moved in a steady rhythm in unison until they couldn't take it anymore. Halston exploded like a rocket inside of Kelly. She overflowed simultaneously, all over his lap.

"Ah. Yes, I didn't know how much I needed that," Kelly exhaled.

Her body went limp as she collapsed onto Halston's chest.

"You can say that again, baby," Halston agreed.

They both laid there in the afterglow of their intense lovemaking until they fell asleep. Dinner would have to wait. Besides, they were both already full of each other.

CHAPTER 9

"Rise and shine, beautiful."

Halston tapped Kelly lightly on her shoulder to wake her up for breakfast. He was typically out the door for work by now, but he wanted to surprise her. Plus, he wanted to show her how much he enjoyed last night.

As the dew collected on the windows outside of their bedroom, he had an extra boost going into the last day of the work week.

"Ah, baby. What is this? I thought I smelled waffles and I assumed I was dreaming. You are the absolute best," Kelly beamed.

"Of course, you deserve it, baby. I made these with your special protein powder, the vegan sausage patties and I cut up some strawberries for you too."

"Goodness. What did I do to deserve you? That's the real question. Thank you. This will help me ease into this presentation I have to do this afternoon for the new client. Well, that and the amazing orgasms you gave me last night," she flashed a seductive smile back at him.

"You deserve the world, baby. There's more fruit if you want more. I went ahead and made the chicken to go with the stir fry too. I'm about to get out of here for work. I know you're going to knock that presentation out of the park. I'll call you later to check on you," he promised.

"I really appreciate you. Thank you. I love you. Be safe on your way in to work."

"I love you too….so much. Be safe too. I'll see you tonight." He leaned forward to kiss her on her forehead.

Halston started his commute to work, even ahead of his normal time. He felt invincible and energized; ready to take on the world.

He decided to listen to one of his favorite new podcasts, *What Triggers Us Makes Us Stronger.* Devin put him on to the show and he was hooked ever since the first episode. They were only four episodes in, so he didn't have much to catch up on. The show covered controversial ideals and topics on everything from race, corporate America, finances and relationships.

Today's episode, "If You Cheat On Me…", discussed past relationship escapades of the two male hosts and their prior conquests and failures. Thank goodness, he didn't have any experience in that department with Kelly. Nonetheless, the banter on the podcast was quite entertaining and served its purpose for giving him the mental break he needed before arriving at work.

One of the hosts, Levi, spoke about how he once hid in the dumpster of a back alley to spy on a lady that broke up with him. Halston laughed out loud like he had a car full of passengers riding with him. He pulled into the parking garage at work, with eight minutes left on the podcast episode. He looked at the clock and noticed he arrived 15 minutes ahead of schedule, so he sat in the car and finished the episode.

Halston straightened his navy-blue blazer, with brown elbow patches, from Banana Republic. His jeans were from there too, with a pair of brown Kenneth Cole boots that perfectly matched the brown elbow patches on his blazer. Although Fridays were casual in the office, he liked to dress a notch above jeans and a simple polo.

Even mother nature seemed to celebrate his glorious mood. The birds chirped loudly, the skies were crystal-clear blue, and a light breeze ensured the temperature was just right. He ascended the stairs to get to the lobby and subsequently the elevators.

Halston rode the elevator alone, not an unusual occurrence at this time of morning on a Friday. Most people that worked in the building did not stroll in until closer to 9:00 am at the end of the week. Oh, but of course, Julia was already at her desk when he entered the double doors of the office.

An eerie, thick silence filled the air when Halston arrived. He initially chalked it up to that Friday feeling of already being mentally absent from the building by the time you arrive. However, Julia confirmed the shift in the atmosphere.

"Oh, hey, Halston. Good morning. How are you?" she stated.

Her greeting was friendly, yet curt. Chipper, but void of any flirtation; highly unlike Julia.

"Hey, Julia. Happy Friday. I'm doing well and yourself?" Halston replied.

He tried to hide his surprise, but he guessed he didn't play it off too well.

"I'm great. No such thing as a bad Friday, right?"

"Is everything ok, Julia? You look a tad bit flushed if you don't me saying so."

"Yeah, I'm fine. There's just something I need to tell you. You probably want to put your things down first. I can come to your office and speak with you."

Julia cleared her throat and looked as if she swallowed shards of glass.

"Ok, let me put my things down. I'll be ready in five minutes."

What the hell did she want to talk to him about?

Halston had no idea what Julia was up to, but he knew had to be unpleasant news. He walked to the break room to place his lunch in the refrigerator. Suddenly, his bright and positive mood turned into a dismal forcefield of nature. He walked past Julia again and exhaled deeply as he walked into his office. Mr. Bosniac's door was closed, and a few other people started to trickle in the suite.

Halston acknowledged Julia, as she walked through the door. He had just finished perusing his email inbox. There were a few unread messages, but nothing alarming at first glance.

"Hey, um….do you mind if I close your door for a second?"

"Sure, be my guest. Go ahead. Have a seat."

Under most circumstances, Halston wouldn't be caught alone with Julia in his office, especially with his door closed. However, these weren't normal circumstances.

"Thanks. Look, I don't really know how to say this but Mr. Bosniac is planning on letting you go," she spilled.

"Wait. What? Are you serious? Did he tell you?" he asked.

His forehead wrinkled with confusion at the news Julia just uttered.

"Not exactly. I was here earlier than normal. I'm leaving early for a doctor's appointment this afternoon. I accidentally overheard him talking on the phone about your position. I just wanted to let you know. I couldn't sit there and hold that in."

"Wow. Well, thank you. I'm a bit at a loss for words. I guess he'll start the hiring process soon. I'd love to hear what grounds this bullshit is based on."

He paused and stared at the wall, above Julia's head.

Julia shifted uncomfortably in her seat.

"I'm sorry. That was inappropriate," he muttered.

"Don't quote me on this, but I have a hunch who it might be," she spoke softly.

Then it hit him. How could he not have seen it coming?

"Don't tell me it's that hotshot kid, James?" he questioned.

His inquiry was more of a declaration.

"Yeah, I think so. If it means anything to you, I saw his resume and he doesn't have nearly as much experience as you do. I don't know what he could be smoking to put that guy over you."

"I don't get it either, but this corporate world is not fair to say the least."

An awkward silence filled the office. Halston glanced at his laptop. Seven emails had arrived in his inbox since Julia entered. None of them were from Mr. Bosniac.

"Thank you, Julia. Seriously, I appreciate you telling me about this news."

"Of course. You're welcome. There's no way I could sit here without saying anything to you."

"That's very kind of you. Well, I guess I should get the day started for however long I have left, right?" Halston laughed sarcastically.

"You have already done so much for this company. You do what feels right. Let me know if you need anything."

Her blouse rode up just enough for Halston to see the top of her black lace panties as she rose from her seat.

Halston quickly looked away. The last thing he needed was a sexual harassment suit on top of getting fired. Although he didn't think Julia would do something like that, he also wanted to avoid giving her any wrong ideas.

"I will. Thanks Julia," Halston replied in a professional tone.

Julia closed the office door behind her as she walked out.

Halston buried his face in his hands and resisted the urge to scream.

Was it even worth him finishing out the workday?

Should he just say an emergency came up and leave to start looking for a new job?

When was Mr. Bosniac going to tell him?

Halston snapped out of his moment of anger and looked at his phone. He noticed he had a missed text from Kelly. She sent him a stunning selfie from the driver's seat of her car. Her face radiated with magnificence. Her maroon blazer complimented her shoulder-length auburn-highlighted bob perfectly. Seeing her beautiful face temporarily boosted his spirits.

Guess who's ready to knock 'em dead today for this presentation? Thank you for extra the glow this morning.

Halston smiled and relished in the flashbacks that quickly flooded his mind.

"Whew, what a day," he exhaled aloud.

Now wasn't the time to burst her bubble and break the news that he was soon-to-be fired from his job. After all, he hadn't even officially received the news from Mr. Bosniac. It could all be a fluke. Nevertheless, he had to find a new stream of income, quickly.

Of course you will, because you're freaking awesome.....not to mention gorgeous. You've still got me floating on cloud 9 over here too.

Bing.

The instant message alert sounded on his laptop. Of course, it was Mr. Bosniac.

Happy Friday, Halston. Could you come to my office when you have a sec?

Bastard. Fuck you and your sec.

Sure, I'll be there in five minutes.

Halston chose the latter response to his boss instead.

He didn't feel the need to return any niceties at this point. Plus, their relationship was never filled with them anyway. Halston took several deep breaths as he glared at the seven unread messages in his inbox. He couldn't focus on getting any work done until he had his discussion with Mr. Bosniac.

The office was nearly full now. The space was fairly small with eleven people at one time when everyone was there. Julia gave him a reassuring, firm smile as he walked past her to Mr. Bosniac's office.

Halston knocked on Mr. Bosniac's office door. The wait time for his response seemed like an eternity.

"Come on in," Mr. Bosniac yelled from the inside.

The loudness of his voice seemed to mock the situation further. Nonetheless, Halston kept his cool and calmly entered the office.

"Hello, Mr. Bosniac. How are you?"

"Just peachy, man. Go ahead and close the door behind you."

"Glad to hear."

Halston took the liberty to have a seat in front of Mr. Bosniac's desk, without waiting for an invitation.

"Well, there's no easy way to say this but to get straight to it. I'm sure you heard that I've been interviewing for a few new roles within the company. We have a couple of promising new hires coming. However, there's a guy named James that I believe you've met. We need to make some budget cuts and you've been a great partner with us for the last nine years; exceptional work. We're going bring James on board but he will be taking over your role, along with some added responsibilities."

An awkward pause filled engulfed the short distance between

Halston and Mr. Bosniac.

"With that said, unfortunately, we simply don't have room for you here anymore. Don't worry, you will be rewarded with a very handsome severance package," Mr. Bosniac continued.

"Hmm, I see. Well, looks like I didn't have much of a say in all of this. So, I guess I will finish out my time and move on to the next phase of my life," Halston replied.

He quickly envisioned himself grabbing Mr. Bosniac by his navy-blue cotton collar and slamming him down to the ground from his gaudy, executive chair. Then, he thought about stomping his face in with his boots until Mr. Bosniac pleaded for mercy. Alas, it was just a fantasy. He had to stay calm to avoid an even bigger issue if he lost his temper.

"You have given so much to this company. I would have done more if I could. Everything was out of my hands. I hope you understand," Mr. Bosniac replied with a plastered smirk.

His facial expression said, "This is just corporate bullshit that people in my tax bracket have to say when we fire people."

"No need for the explanation. I'm sure you tried your very best. You always have," Halston replied.

Maybe that last subliminal dig was a bit much. Fuck it. This would just free up his time and energy to get out this hell hole. Besides, he wanted to leave the job for years but could never find the right time. Love it or hate it, that time had come.

"Great. I'm glad there's no hard feelings. I have a 9:30am meeting I have to prep for, but if there's nothing else you need from me, I'll let you get back to your day," Mr. Bosniac replied, with his torso already position towards his laptop.

I'll let you get back to your day. Nope, thanks for letting me get back to living. You fucking bastard..

He nodded and looked Mr. Bosniac squarely in his eyes before he rose from the chair and walked out of his office without closing the door behind him.

elly's tears flooded all over her blouse. Just when she thought she had reached a new high, here she was again riding on a new plateau. The words from her mother on the other end of the phone were gibberish at best. She couldn't make much sense of what she said. At that moment, she honestly couldn't care less.

"Kelly? Baby? Is everything ok? What's going on?"

She sensed she was being tuned out but now she was genuinely concerned about her daughter's well-being.

"Ah, yes! Forgive me, mom. Everything is in place. Don't you worry. What was the last part you said?"

Kelly missed the last several minutes of her mother's rant. Nonetheless, she was the mastermind behind her father's 60th birthday party. So, she didn't feel an urgent need to listen to her mom rehash the details she either previously relayed or would end up executing herself.

"Umh hmmm. I knew you were distracted. I know you're working hard. Go ahead and spill it. What has you so emotional?" her mother probed.

"Halston. He just....whew. He really gave me a nice surprise today. I had a big presentation and he –," Kelly relayed.

Her sentence was abruptly cut off before she could tell her

mother about the beautiful edible arrangement he sent to her office.

"Oooh, look at that. That is so nice baby. Your father used to do little nice things for me from time to time. I can only say hold on. Once you've been married as long as we have, you'll be lucky if you still get a hug and a smile. I'm sorry, I digress. Back to business…" her mother continued.

"Thank you, Mom. Back to Daddy's party. It's coming up in less than two weeks. I think we've got everything ready. The venue is secured, the caterer, party favors and the video montage should be finalized this week," Kelly rattled off the details to pacify her mother.

Thanks to her mother, her post-presentation high deflated quicker than a popped balloon.

"I don't know what I'd do without you, baby. I tried to get your brother to help, but you know how that is. I cannot thank you enough for everything you've done. I know you're at work though, so I'll let you get back to your day. Tell that handsome son-in-law of mine I said hello."

"Yeah, Melvin is a special case for sure. I'll see if I can talk some sense into him. I'll pass the message along to Halston too."

Kelly hung up the phone and plucked a pineapple from her edible arrangement. The sweet fragrance smelled like honey dipped lavender and tangerines. It was simply heavenly. She felt so blessed to have a loving husband like Halston. Plus, it didn't hurt that she kicked ass on the presentation too. She had a lot riding on it, including a promotion that she had been promised since before she went on medical leave. Today felt like the ultimate comeback.

Tap. Tap. Tap.

The knock on her door startled her out of her daydream.

"Ah yes, come on in," Kelly answered.

The downside of her cozy office was she could only see when people walked up to her door from the right side, due to the slim window. However, if the person approached the door from the left side, she had no way to know who they were.

It was her co-worker, Melina. She played an instrumental part in making sure all of her work got done while she was on medical leave and she even offered some critical nuggets to today's presentation. Kelly didn't consider too many work people as friends, especially women. Melina was different.

"Melina, girl come in here. I didn't know who that was out there," Kelly beamed.

"I just had to come by and tell you in person how great of a job you did on that presentation. You blew that thing out of the water. The clients are already singing your praises and it hasn't even been two hours. I think you've got this one in the bag."

"Are you serious? Wow, that is great news. I couldn't have done any of this without you. You really pulled through for me. As a matter of fact, have you eaten lunch yet? I am starving."

"Yes! Ooh, great minds think alike. I came to grab you in hopes that you hadn't eaten lunch yet. I know you're all healthy and shit. I'm trying to do better too and get fine like you. How about we try that new vegan spot on Cherub Street?"

"You are already working it. I could never fill out that dress like you. Come on, let's go. I just need to run by the ladies' room. Want to meet by the elevator in five minutes?"

"I'll be there. Let me go get my purse. See you in a bit. I see that beautiful arrangement too. I think I've asked you this already, but does your hubby have a brother? Cousin? Hell, a young uncle?" she pleaded.

"You are crazy, girl. Stop it. I do love him something serious. He's good to me. Better than I deserve," Kelly exhaled.

Melina sauntered back to her office to grab her purse. Much like Kelly, she didn't get along with many women. She was ecstatic that Kelly beat her cancer. Selfishly, she was glad Kelly was back at work too. Covering her accounts was no small feat, even if it did give her greater visibility within the company.

Melina answered an email on her phone while she waited for Kelly to exit the bathroom by the elevator.

"Ok, I'm ready. I'm so hungry. Girl, I was trying to stop my stomach from growling during that meeting."

"Even if it did, I probably wouldn't heard it over mine."

"Too funny. Let me tell you. This restaurant has good reviews, but don't blame it on me if you think it's nasty."

"Oh no. Don't back down now. This is all on you, sister."

"I'm just giving you a hard time. I'll drive."

Both of the ladies glided out of the elevator into the parking garage.

"I trust you. I'm just giving you a hard time. It's so good to have you back. You are such a fighter. I'm just proud to know you."

"Thank you. I really appreciate that. It hasn't been easy, but God and my family pulled me through. I'm just so grateful to be on the other side."

The thumping bass from her speakers blared loudly in the car. The sound startled her. She forgot that she played her ratchet play-list on her way to work to amp her up for the meeting, after her morning prayer.

"Ooh, don't turn it down on my account. Blessed and bougie, I see. I'm here for it," Melina chuckled.

"I see that," Kelly laughed, as she watched her friend do her best chair dance boogie at the red light. "Seriously, thank you for holding everything down while I was out. I know you have your own accounts and work to tend to. You know I don't fool with those other women in that office; much less any women, period."

"You can say that again. Those jealous wenches are like crabs in a bucket. You know I'm here for you. Anytime. I'm only glad you're ok and back to your sassy, beautiful self."

"We are almost there. Excuse my stomach if you hear it rumbling," Kelly warned.

"Alright, you usually don't steer me wrong. My stomach is rumbling too and I'm trusting you that this vegan place won't let me down," Melina sarcastically cautioned.

"Ooh, wait. I almost missed the turn. This street gets me every time. Here it is."

Kelly swerved into the parking lot and got a parking space on the side of the building. Although it was past the typical lunch-hour crowd, they had quite a few customers. The beige colored building was trimmed in a dark brown, which gave it a rustic, cozy feel.

"Well, I'll say. The Savory Spot. Umph. Here we go, girl," Melina teased.

"Trust me, you are going to love it. Who knows, this might just turn you out and pop your vegan cherry."

"It's a sad day when I have to look to food for sexual pleasure. Don't remind me. No cherries have been popped here for quite some time."

"Girl, come on. Let's get in here."

The two ladies waited to be seated for only a couple of minutes, before a bubbly young waitress ushered them to their seats.

"Is there anything I can start you ladies off with to drink?"

Her name tag read Tonya in all capital, gold letters on top of a black background.

"Sure, I'll actually have a water with easy ice and lemons, please," Kelly replied.

"Ok, you got it. How about you, mam?"

Tonya directed her gaze towards Melina to decide on her beverage.

"Umm, let's see. I'm a first-timer here. Some of these juices look good. I'm going to be brave and try the cactus guava kiwi juice. If I don't like it, blame her," Melina replied as she playfully pointed towards Kelly.

"Let me tell you, that's one of our most popular drinks. So, I think your friend is safe. I'll have your drinks right out and give you a moment to look over the menu."

"Ooh, I know you can appreciate some good spaghetti. They have some awesome spaghetti and meatballs. They're made with beets. I know, it sounds weird. It's so good though," Kelly promised.

"Funny thing is I was eyeing that. I must say, they have some appetizing options on this menu. Umph, and another delectable option just walked through the door. Don't look now, but I'll let you know when you can turn around to get a peek at him."

Melina focused in the unknown man's direction like he was a thick, juicy steak in the middle of the Serengeti, surrounded by a pack of lions. Her stare implied she was the lioness waiting to pounce on him any moment.

"Really now? Ok, let me know when the coast is clear," Kelly responded in a cool, unbothered tone.

This was a regular occurrence whenever she went anywhere with Melina. It was one of the things she really missed about her when she was ill.

"You can turn now and look. Check him out. Don't be too obvious."

Kelly shooed her away with her hand as she positioned her body slightly to get a view of the gentleman behind her.

"Ha! It really is a small world. You're talking about the guy on our left, correct?"

"Yeah, definitely not his friend. I mean, he looks ok but he's not really my type. Wait, do you know him? You better introduce me if you do."

"Not so fast, hot momma. That's Devin. He's one of Halston's best friends. There's just one problem: he's happily married."

Kelly tried her best to let Melina down gently. Nevertheless, she saw the disappointment spread across her friend's face.

"Ugh, well does he have a brother? Damn, all of the good ones are always taken. Hopefully, they sit close to us so I can at least get a closer look at him."

Meanwhile, the waitress made her way back with their drinks, balanced on a circular, wooden tray.

"Alright, ladies. Here are you drinks. Have we made our lunch selections for today?"

"Yes, I think we're ready. I'll have the Better-Than-Your-Average Nachos and a small cucumber and tomato salad."

"Oooh, the nachos are one of my favorite things on the menu. Great choice. How about for you? I know it's your first time, so I can answer any questions you may have about the menu or the ingredients."

"Thank you so much. Believe it or not, I think I've settled on something. I'll try the Spaghetti and Beetballs. Is it ok if I have it with green beans, instead of the asparagus spears?"

"Of course, you can. So, I have the Better-Than-Your-Average Nachos, with a small cucumber and tomato salad and the Spaghetti and Beetballs, with a sub of green beans instead of asparagus. I'll have that out for you ladies shortly. Is there anything else I can get you in the meantime?"

"I think that's it for me," Kelly replied.

"I'm fine too. Thank you, Tonya," Melina chimed in.

Kelly noticed that Devin and his friend were seated diagonally across from Melina and herself.

"Ahem. Are you go to make an introduction?"

"Hold your horses, mam. I'll walk over to him and say hello," Kelly laughed.

"Hold on, that's my best friend's wife. What a small world," Devin said as he recognized Kelly.

"Devin? I thought that was you, but I wasn't sure. This is quite a surprise, I must admit. I didn't really take you to be the vegan type."

"Yeah, you know me well. My co-worker Al said this would be a good spot to try. I let him pull my arm in coming here. I told him it's all his fault if the food isn't good," Devin admitted.

"Oh, geez. You sound like my friend. She said the same thing. Devin, this is my co-worker and friend, Melina. Melina, this is Devin, Halston's best friend and a close friend of mine as well. Nice to meet you too, Al," Kelly gestured in Al's direction.

"Thank you, it's a pleasure to meet you. Somebody has to keep him in line, right?" Al joked.

"Amen to that," Kelly laughed.

"Hello Devin, it's a pleasure to meet you," Melina replied.

She totally disregarded Al's presence. Although she knew she didn't stand a chance with Devin, she wanted to make it known that she was attracted to him.

"Thank you. The pleasure is all mine."

Devin extended his hand to give Melina a firm handshake.

"Well, I don't want to interrupt your lunch but I'm really glad we ran into each other. I'll have to tell Halston I saw you today. Have a good one," Kelly said.

"Yes, nice to meet you both," Al replied.

Melina noticed Al looking her up and down, but she wasn't the slightest bit interested. Her eyes were locked on Devin. Too bad he was taken. Most of the good guys were.

"Oh, wait. Melina, if you're not doing anything on Halloween, you should join us for our annual Halloween party. My wife and I do a big bash every year. Plus, Halloween falls on a Saturday this year," Devin suggested.

"Ooh, I absolutely love a good costume party. Sure, I would love to come. I don't want to intrude though if your wife has already finalized the guest list," Melina replied bashfully.

Although she was extremely attracted to Devin, she didn't want to cause any dissention with his wife.

"No intrusion at all. The more the merrier. My wife and I always invite extra people leading up to the night of the party. It'll be fun. Kelly and Halston will be there. Al will be there too."

"Ok, well it's settled then. I'm looking forward to it. Thank you for the invite."

"You're welcome. There's a prize for best dressed male, female and best couple. Not like I think you'd dress anything less than impressive."

"Girl, I'm telling you. You are going to love it. Their parties are the highlight of the Halloween season. You know I'm not even usually into all of that stuff," Kelly chimed in.

By now, Tonya had exited the kitchen and was making her way towards them, with the drinks for Devin and Al, along with the entrees for Kelly and Melina.

"Awesome. I love a good competition. Sounds great," Melina smiled.

Both ladies made their way back to their seats. Melina cleared her throat and playfully widened her eyes at Kelly, as they both sat down to enjoy their lunch.

"Perfect timing. Looks like someone was having a bit of a reunion. It truly is a small world, isn't it?" Tonya asked.

Kelly could tell she was prying in a subtle way, but it didn't bother her.

"Yes, it's a big coincidence we even ran into him," Kelly replied.

"Oh my God. This looks delicious. Looks like I might have to eat my words, girl. Vegan isn't so bad after all. Thanks Tonya. This drink is delicious too," Melina said.

"You're very welcome. Would you like a refill on your drink?" Tonya asked.

"I think I'm fine for now, but can I have a glass of water with some ice and lemons?" Melina asked.

"Certainly. I'll get that for you now and I'll top off your water too," Tonya replied, as she gestured towards Kelly.

"Ooh yes, I'll have to settle for some cold water since I can't get Mr. Devin to top off this heat over here," Melina laughed, after Tonya walked away.

"You are such a mess. I can't take you anywhere," Kelly snickered.

"That's ok. That's why you love me," Melina rebutted.

CHAPTER 11

Only a couple of weeks remained until Kelly's father's big birthday party. Although Kelly was excited about the celebration, she was also eager to have the moment behind her. Plus, she didn't feel like herself lately. She was lethargic and easily exhausted.

She chalked it up to an adjustment to her new medication and thought she possibly was over-exerted. After all, between work and trying to plan her father's party, she felt like her wheels were steadily spinning.

"Babe, I have an honest question. Do my eyes look puffy? I feel so tired lately."

"Not at all, baby. You look beautiful. I don't see any puffiness. I have noticed you've mentioned being more tired lately. Anything I can help with or take off your plate?" Halston asked.

He had just over three weeks left before his last day at work. He still hadn't told Kelly the news yet. Mr. Bosniac decided to keep him on as long as possible to help James get up to speed. Such corporate bullshit. Despite his seething anger about his job situation, he never felt like it was the right time to bring up his pending job situation to Kelly. This wasn't an opportune time either.

"Do you want to call my mother back for me?" Kelly laughed.

"Uh oh, is it that bad?"

"Yes, she wants to be the boss and order me around. Hey, I don't mind it if I can sit back and really let her call the shots. I don't have a problem just showing up. Lord knows, that's all Melvin is doing. She says one thing but then meaning another and I end up executing it all. I'm sorry. You don't need to hear all of this. Let me put on my big girl panties and give her a call back," Kelly sighed.

"Ok, babe. Well, if you need someone to help you get out of your panties when you get finished, I'm your guy," he replied, as he bit the left corner of his mouth.

"Get on now. You are such a bad boy. Let me make this call quick though, so I can take you up on that," she replied, as she grazed her fingernails in his beard.

Halston sighed deeply as Kelly walked into the other room to call her mother. He wondered if she had a hunch that something had gone wrong with his job. Although she didn't act differently, he suspected her woman's intuition gave her a hunch that there was trouble in paradise.

He realized she was already under a lot of stress from planning her father's party. Plus, if the word got back to them that he lost his job, that would surely create even more tension between her parents and him. They were always polite, accepting, and even grinned ear-to-ear at him and Kelly's wedding. Deep down, Halston felt like they merely tolerated him.

Perhaps it was residual from his family upbringing as well. He overcame a rocky relationship with his mother after his father passed away. Halston was and only child; everything fell on him. His mother always expected him to be her savior and rescue her from her hardships.

She drank heavily in her teenage years and pushed away any real connection she could have had with her only child. When she passed a couple of years before Halston started dating Kelly, he was sad but not heartbroken. He couldn't feel something for her that didn't exist. Maybe that's why his sense of familial norms was somewhat warped.

His daydream was broken by hurling sounds coming from the

bedroom. He realized it was Kelly and quickly ran into the room. Through her cancer treatments, he became increasingly astute to any irregularities in Kelly's health. He prayed silently that it was just something mild.

"Hey babe. You don't sound too good in there. Is everything alright?"

"Um, yeah. I think so. No. I had a wave of nausea hit me suddenly. I didn't even call my mom yet. I could feel it coming on," she confessed.

"Let me make you some of that chamomile tea you love. That should help settle your stomach. I'll grab you some Alka Seltzer too," he replied, in a hurried, yet composed tone.

"Thanks, babe. I know this really kills the mood. Shit, I hate throwing up."

"Don't worry about that. You just concentrate on feeling better."

Halston hurried to the kitchen to prepare some tea. While the water heated, he dropped an Alka Seltzer tablet in a glass of room temperature water. He knocked on the door first to hand her the medicine.

"Ugh, I guess I have to let you in. This is the ugly part of marriage. Seeing each other like this. Don't look. I'll just grab the glass."

"Come on now. I'm here for the long haul. It's going to take more than a little vomit to scare me away."

"Mmmm, thank you. I think my stomach is starting to settle now. This helps."

Kelly cautiously continued to sip on the rim of the small glass.

"Good, I'm glad baby. The tea will be ready too in a few minutes."

"Ah, thank you," Kelly slurred her speech.

She laid on the bathroom floor next to the toilet. The cold tile soothed her stomach. As she heard Halston's footsteps coming towards her, her mind began to wander. Her period was late, but only by a week.

Oh my God. That explains those strange cravings.

Some foods tasted abnormal to her and she noticed her mood changed more frequently. She tried to brush it off. She and Halston were in a good space to have a baby. Her health was better. They were both financially stable and progressive in their careers.

She decided she would go get a pregnancy test tomorrow. At that moment, she only wanted to focus on getting well.

"I don't think the bathroom floor is the best place for you to take a nap. Here you go. You'll feel better once you drink this."

"Mmmm, I guess you're right. There's a bright side to this. I didn't have to listen to my mom nag about the birthday party after all. I'll just text her and say I'm not feeling well," Kelly chuckled, as she mustered up all of her energy to pick herself up from the floor with her tea in hand.

"Whoa. Easy now. I'm here to help."

Halston wrapped his arm around her waist as he single-handedly pulled her on his right side. He pulled back the bed sheet and placed her tea on the nightstand.

"Ah, thank you. I promise I am going to make it up to you."

"No need to make up anything to me, baby."

Kelly's phone rang as soon as Halston laid down next to her on the bed. The vibration knocked against her tea cup and rattled the spoon inside.

"Well, look who it is."

Kelly flashed the screen of her phone to Halston. It was her mother. She rolled her eyes and sighed as she picked up the phone.

Halston waved his hand to gesture for her to let it go to voicemail, but to no avail.

"Hey. Hello Mom. How are you?"

She tried to lay her sluggish voice on thick to give her mom a hint that she didn't feel well. It didn't work.

"How are you, baby girl? Have I told you how much I appreciate you for everything you're doing with this party? I went through my list today and I think we're all set. How's that handsome Halston? You should get some quality time in with him."

Kelly pulled the phone away from her ear and looked at the screen. She could hardly believe that her mother was being so accommodating.

"Aww, thank you, Mom. I'm so glad to hear that. I think Daddy is going to be so excited. I can't believe it's just nine days away. Halston is right here next to me. I haven't been feeling too well."

"I'm sure he's taking great care of you. What's wrong exactly?"

"Oh, I just had a little nausea. I think I'm on the downside of it now. Hopefully, at least. Halston made some tea for me. That helped settled my stomach."

"Ok, that's good to hear. Can you believe your brother said he would pick up the balloons for your dad's party? I was shocked. I'll have some on standby just in case he forgets or doesn't get them. That's enough of me talking. I want you to get some rest. Let me know when you start feeling better."

"Ok, mom. Thank you. I will do that. I love you."

"I love you too, honey. Feel better."

Kelly placed the phone back on the nightstand and double-checked to make sure she hung up the line.

"Well, it must be a new day," Kelly laughed, as she rolled towards Halston and placed her head on his chest.

"Sounds like your mother was in a really good mood. Were you able to get a reprieve from helping her with your dad's party?"

"Well, not exactly. I got something even better. She acknowledged that I was tired and didn't make it about her. I don't know how long that's going to last, but I'll take it."

Only three days remained before Halston's father-in-law's party. He had just under two weeks before his last day at work. He decided he would tell Kelly that he lost his job that evening. Time was drawing near, and he could not hold out any longer. In the meantime, he dreaded every minute of teaching James his role.

Although he didn't have anything against James, he was more than done with fulfilling any of the duties that Mr. Bosniac instructed of him. Thankfully, James had a dentist appointment that day which gave him an out from having to ask him if he had lunch plans.

Halston walked in the breakroom and decided to eat his lunch slightly earlier than usual. He ran into Kyle, one of the managers from a different department. Kyle was a sharp dresser, tall, poised and one of the 'good 'ole boys' that corporate America adored.

"Hey there, Halston. Long time no see. It's a shame this place creates such silos. I've been so headfirst into my work; I feel like I haven't seen a few people in the office lately."

"Hey, Kyle. No worries, man. I totally understand how it goes. I've been trying to wrap up the last of everything here in the last couple of weeks."

He didn't think Kyle was being insensitive. However, true to the corporate rigmarole, he seemed to have forgotten about the announcement of Halston's soon-to-be departure from the company.

"If you don't mind me saying this, Bosniac and this whole company are going to suffer in your absence. I heard about that new hot-shot kid, James. Let me tell you, I've seen a lot of people in and out of this company. I don't think he can fill your shoes."

"Well, I appreciate the vote of confidence. Thank you, Kyle."

Halston masked his true sentiment towards Kyle's statement. Kyle wasn't the type of guy to pass out undeserving compliments. Too bad Mr. Bosniac didn't see it that way. Halston told himself he didn't have much longer to suffocate in such a bullshit environment.

"Well, hey there gentlemen. Halston, I'd say you likely have more training to do with James. Is that right?" Mr. Bosniac sneered.

His arrogant demeanor challenged Halston to disobey his warning.

"I'll get to him shortly. He went to lunch, that thing we all take," he replied.

Halston returned an arrogant tone, with a haughtiness that topped his boss's.

"I suppose," Mr. Bosniac replied dryly.

"Well, it's getting a bit stuffy in here. Let me get back to my desk. You keep your head up, Halston," Kyle interjected.

Kyle gave Halston an approving smirk as he exited the breakroom.

"Thanks, Kyle. You take care."

Halston was beyond sick of Mr. Bosniac's condescending tone. He already knew he wouldn't dare ask him for a recommendation. His worked spoke for itself and he didn't need Mr. Bosniac to validate him. A part of him wanted Mr. Bosniac to make another slick comment so he could completely lose his cool.

Wait a minute. You still must survive after this and provide for home.

"Well, what's for lunch?" Mr. Bosniac inquired.

Now he wanted to make small talk. Halston curtly answered without giving an ounce of enthusiasm or deflection in his voice.

"Left over stir fry that I made earlier this week."

"Nice, I'm going to meet a client at Grand Lux. I'll see you in a bit when I get back. Keep up the fine work you're doing with James."

Julia meandered in the breakroom just as Mr. Bosniac was about to leave. Halston was never so excited to see her. She helped break the awkward silence in the room.

"Good afternoon, gentlemen."

Julia's greeting was clearly directed more at Halston than Mr. Bosniac.

"Hey, Julia. How's it going?" Mr. Bosniac replied.

He gave her a slightly flirty twinkle in his eye.

Julia quickly shifted her gaze away from him. There was only one man in the office that was worth her 'no mixing business and pleasure' rule.

"What's going on, Julia?" Halston responded.

"I am well. I can't complain and I'll be even better as soon as I eat my lunch. I'm starving," she admitted.

"Sounds great. I'm meeting a client for lunch at Grand Lux. You're welcome to tag along if you'd like," Mr. Bosniac propositioned.

"Ah, well thank you so much for the gracious offer. I have to pass this time; so much work to wrap up before I leave today."

Julia cut her gaze over to Halston with an expression that said, *what the heck is going on?*

"Suit yourself. I understand how it is when duty calls. That's why you're one of our brightest team members."

"Thank you. I appreciate that."

Julia waited until Mr. Bosniac was out of her eyesight before she moved towards the breakroom table to sit next to Halston. She exhaled in agitation as she pulled out her crackers and opened the lid on her chicken salad. The strong scent of fresh onions wafted in the room.

"Rough day?"

"Not so much, but I am glad his ass is gone. I never understood how you tolerated him as a boss. Thank God for change. We will miss you around here, but leaving this place is a blessing in disguise."

"Tell me about it. I'm ready for the new beginning. I'll miss you and a few of the others, not him."

Halston locked eyes with Julia for a moment. In those brief few seconds, she felt comfortable. He looked at her in a light that he never viewed her before. She seemed less aggressive and more delicate. Although he wouldn't dare admit it, her outfit even complimented her figure well.

"Well, it's always good to be missed. I can't say I'll be sticking around here much longer myself."

Julia scanned the breakroom to make sure no one else was within earshot.

"I hear that. Cheers to both of us then."

Halston finished his lunch in the breakroom with Julia. He enjoyed the moment and didn't feel rushed to leave the room, for once.

Julia sat down at the table with Halston. She exhaled deeply before she bowed her head for a quick moment of prayer.

She prays?

Halston felt hypocritical but he truly didn't remember ever seeing her pray. He always felt like she preyed on him instead.

"I really admire your resilience. You're a family man, dealing with all of this, maintaining your composure when many people would have flipped out. What do you think is next for you?"

Halston snapped out of his judgmental daydream to answer Julia's question.

"I appreciate that. Thank you. I'm trying. I'm not exactly sure yet. I have a couple of friends who have some strong connections with other firms. I'll start there first and just see how it goes, I guess. That's all I can really do at this point."

Halston and Julia talked for a solid 15 minutes before he reluctantly wandered back to his office. He knew that James was set to return from lunch soon. Plus, he didn't want to hear Mr. Bosniac's mouth. One more cross word from him and he really would lose his cool.

James entered Halston's office just minutes after he settled in at his desk.

Perfect timing.

"Hey Coach. I guess it's time to get started again. How was your lunch?"

Hey Coach? Who the hell did this wannabe hot-shot kid with no real work experience think he was?

Halston suppressed the first response that came to mind.

"You're too modest. I'm no coach, just showing you the ropes as much as I can before I'm out of here. Lunch was nice. How was yours?"

He tried to keep in mind that James was truly the least of his concern.

Hell, I'd take my place too if I were him.

"It was great. Nice to get out for some fresh air. I tried out the new Italian bistro down the street. Now, I'm having second thoughts since my food was more of a meal better served for a nap."

James laughed nervously and returned to a serious facial expression once he realized his error.

Halston didn't even have to tell James that he should have kept such a rookie comment to himself.

"I know the feeling. Well, let's get started. Shall we? You're catching on to everything quickly. I'll show you some of my filing tips and tricks for clients. Of course, you'll develop your own cadence after a while. This will at least…"

Halston didn't even finish his sentence before Mr. Bosniac entered his office without knocking.

"Oops, sorry. Didn't mean to interrupt. Just checking to make sure everything is on track. Looks like you guys have got it under control," he stated.

Halston paused for a few seconds and returned a cold stare that pierced through Mr. Bosniac like a burning laser beam.

"Of course, everything's on track. Why would it not be?"

He barely acknowledged Mr. Bosniac's presence and continued speaking as if he was only speaking to James.

James was no fool. He picked up on the hostility between the two gentlemen and intently watched the computer screen as Halston spoke. He didn't want to rock the boat any further than the tense tides that were already disrupting the water.

Halston drudged through the rest of the work day, despite his fuming anger. He wrapped up a little early with James to beat traffic on the way home and clear his mind before he broke the news to Kelly. He couldn't delay it any longer. She deserved to know and he felt guilty keeping his soon-to-be employment status hidden from her this long.

"Have a good night, Halston," Julia said to him on his way out of the office.

"Huh? Oh, I'm sorry, Julia. You have a great night too. My head was in another place."

"That's ok. Take care. See you tomorrow."

Halston exited the elevator and spilled into the front lobby. His every move felt surreal. Once he made it inside the parking garage, he turned down the radio and sat still in silence. He tried to get his story straight for Kelly. Nothing worked.

Shit.

It was going to be a long night.

Kelly cried tears of joy and fear, simultaneously. She slumped down to the cold tile on the bathroom floor as she looked at the pregnancy test for the fourth time. They tried to have a child right before she got sick. Although her health was nearly back to normal, they agreed they would wait at least another year before they tried again.

This was great news. They could start a family outside of just the two of them. She knew Halston would be a great father. She coached herself through all of the positives in her head: they were both of relatively good health, they were fairly young and they both had flourishing careers. Everything was seemingly aligned for such a beautiful blessing.

Why do I feel so apprehensive?

Kelly chalked it up to her nerves.

Should I tell Halston now?

Of course. She had to tell him tonight.

"Whew," she exhaled loud.

Kelly looked down at her watch.

5:39 pm.

Halston would be home soon.

She had to pull herself together so she wouldn't freak him out. Kelly wished she could just tell someone to get it off her chest before breaking the news to Halston. Oh well, she helped make the baby growing inside her. Now, she had to put on her big girl panties and tell her husband they were expecting.

Wait.

She couldn't just tell him on a random Thursday night. It had to be planned. It had to be special. She had to make him cry. After all, he was ready for kids more than she was lately. Her heart smiled at the thought of what a wonderful father he would be.

Her phone buzzed on the bathroom counter. She shuddered with nervousness, as she expected it to be Halston.

Melina.

Hell no.

Kelly couldn't engage in any communication with Melina right now. That would only heighten the situation and elevate her anxiety.

As she picked herself up from the floor and lightly touched up her makeup, she decided to peruse YouTube for pregnancy reveal ideas.

Maybe that's not a good idea after all..

The last thing she wanted was for Halston to see her search history for pregnancy reveals and she hadn't even broken the news to him.

Think. Think. Think.

She decided to cook him dinner instead. That was thoughtful and simple enough to whip up by the time he came home. Kelly reached inside of the refrigerator and pulled out the ground turkey, onions, bell peppers, garlic and cilantro. She never met a man that liked cilantro in his spaghetti. It was one of the idiosyncrasies she grew to love about her husband.

Her phone buzzed once more.

Melina messaged her again.

Kelly opened both messages to see what Melina messaged. Although she did talk to Melina occasionally after work hours, most of their hangout time was right after work or when she knew Halston was disposed with work or a night out with the guys.

Hey girl. You won't believe what I saw today. Hit me back if you can.

Hey, it's me again. Scratch that. What I told you can wait. I know you're probably getting in some time with the hubby. Talk to you tomorrow.

She smiled at the phone. Kelly didn't even try to guess what Melina was referencing.

Uh oh. Looking forward to hearing about this. Cooking for the hubby now. I'm off tomorrow but we should do lunch again on Monday so you can give me the tea.

Kelly placed her phone back on the kitchen counter and began to chop the vegetables.

6:17 pm.

She knew Halston would be home any minute. The grapeseed oil started to sizzle in the cast iron skillet as she tossed the vegetables in with some seasoning. The fragrant smell lifted her spirits and calmed her nerves.

"Will you like spaghetti too?" she inquired softly as she rubbed her non-existent pregnancy bulge.

The garage door suddenly opened. She was right on time. Kelly added the ground turkey to the skillet, sprinkled in more seasoning and some extra pieces of garlic. She then placed a large pot of water on the stove to boil the noodles.

The door cracked and Kelly heard Halston step inside. She could tell by the pause in the rhythm of his steps that he was either on his phone or preoccupied. Hopefully he hadn't picked up dinner on the way home.

"Babe?" Halston called as he walked into the kitchen.

"You rang?" she rebutted back playfully as she stirred the sauce and meat together in the pot.

A mild wave of nausea began to swirl at the pit of her stomach. No. No. No. She was not up for any pregnancy bubble guts tonight.

"Mmmm, that smells heavenly, baby. Can I help with anything?"

Halston hugged her from behind and kissed her on the back of her neck.

Kelly's knees buckled, both with anxiety and pleasure. The warm inviting smell of his cologne and his strong embrace made her feel sexy, safe and wanted.

"Not at all. I want you to relax and get comfortable. The food should be ready in about 20 minutes. How was your day?"

Kelly turned to face him and kiss his lips.

"Oh, it was alright. You know, just another day in the office."

Halston tried to hide his trepidation about telling Kelly about his soon-to-be unemployment status. He hoped she couldn't pick up on his uneasy demeanor.

"Ok, just alright? Are you sure? Somebody I need to come up there and fight? You know I will. All I need is an excuse."

Kelly laid the spoon against the rim of the pot as she gave an air karate chop to an invisible opponent.

"See, that's why I love you. I'll tell you all about it after we have dinner. How about that? Thank you so much by the way. It looks delicious and so do you."

Halston popped her on the backside with his left hand, as he loosened his tie with his right hand.

"Go on now before you make me burn this food. I may not be so tap worthy then," she giggled.

"Babe, you're always tap worthy."

"Well, I'm glad you still think so."

Kelly drained the water from the noodles and started preparing the salad for dinner. She added banana peppers and blue cheese (two of Halston's favorites) to the mix of kale, bell peppers, cherry tomatoes and walnuts. The meat sauce simmered as she turned the fire down on the stove to the lowest setting.

6:44 pm.

Perfect. She was ahead of schedule.

Meanwhile, Halston was in the bedroom. He undressed and changed into some sweatpants and a t-shirt.

At least I'll be comfortable if I have to deliver such shitty news, he thought.

He rehearsed how he would bring up his lay-off in his head. He convinced himself that it was better than getting fired.

Stop. It is what it is and it's not the end of the world.

"Whew," he exhaled as he strode with false confidence back towards the kitchen.

"I'm so sorry, babe. I didn't even ask if you had a good day. How was work?"

"I can't really complain. It was pretty good, even better that I won't have to be there tomorrow. I'll be so glad once the weekend is over and my dad's party is done; as crazy as that may sound."

"I understand that. You've been busy getting everything together for the party. I know he is going to flip once he sees all of the detail you've put into his big day."

"I really hope so. I'm happy my mom has really been easing up on me this week. I'll take all the wins I can get, big or small. Dinner is just about done. Do you mind grabbing the wine glasses and the merlot? Actually, you can have some wine but I'll just drink some juice.".

"Wait a minute. I've never known you to turn down a glass of wine. You feeling ok?"

Halston playfully placed his hand to her forehead to check her temperature. He hoped for something even stronger than wine to take the edge off the day and the conversation to come.

"You're so silly. Yes, I'm good babe. I just have a really faint headache and don't want the wine to take it over the top."

She lied straight to his face. Kelly didn't think about alcohol until now. She knew she couldn't wait much longer to tell Halston that she was pregnant.

"Ooh, yeah wine headaches are the worst. I get it."

He helped her set the table as he could hardly wait to dig into the delicious meal she prepared. He smiled widely as he glanced down at his plate with cilantro sprinkled on top of his spaghetti. The little things Kelly paid attention to are what really made him fall head over heels for her.

"Yeah, I do not want that at all."

Halston poured a generous glass of lemonade for Kelly and a separate glass of wine for himself.

"I'll drink in solidarity with you. Wine is overrated anyway."

He raised his glass to toast hers.

"Wait a minute. Now, you're pushing it."

"Touché, but this spaghetti…wow, it's amazing. You really out-did yourself. Thanks for adding the cilantro on mine too. I know it's weird, but I appreciate you adding it on for me. This salad, too…so good! Thank you, baby. It's delicious."

For a moment, he almost forgot about his anxiety of having to reveal his pending unemployment status.

"Nothing about you is weird; it's what makes you unique and made just for me. I'm so glad you liked the food. So, tell me about work. What happened?"

"Ah, yeah…..work. I guess there's no easy way to say this, but I got laid off today."

He didn't expect to spill the news so flippantly, but he was glad to get it out in the open.

"What happened? Baby, I'm so sorry. I never trusted that bastard Bosniac. He's a snake.".

"You can say that again. Turns out that kid James that I told you about was interviewing for my job. Mr. Bosniac has me training him for the next couple of weeks and then I'll be done there."

"Wait. So, he has you training the guy that took your role? That's bullshit."

She was fuming now. Thankfully, all of focus and anger was towards Mr. Bosniac and not Halston.

Does she really understand that I just lost my job?

"Yep, that is exactly what he's doing. I already put out some applications into some other firms. I'll make sure we don't have too big of a lapse between my checks. I'll make it work," he sighed.

"Baby, you've never given me any reason to doubt you. You've always provided for us. I have no fear. We're going to be alright," Kelly assured him.

She reached out to place her hand on top of his.

"Thank you, baby. I really appreciate that. I wanted to do something new but didn't think it would happen like this."

"You've been talking about starting your own business. What if this is your chance to do that? What if this is your out? Everything happens for a reason. We say that all the time. You never know."

Kelly was nervous but she couldn't let her true feelings surface. Only she knew the secret she was holding from Halston. If she wasn't pregnant, she truly would have no reason to worry about his job status. After all, they had a hefty savings account. Nonetheless, she was so happy she heeded to her better judgment and decided not to tell him about that she was expecting tonight.

elly popped an anti-nausea pill in the restroom of the recreation hall. She meant to take one earlier but forgot in all the hustle and bustle of making sure everything was perfect for her dad. Although she felt fine now, she didn't want to take the slightest chance of having any upset stomach issues.

Her phone buzzed inside of her purse; it was her mother.

We are in route. Should be there in less than 15 mins.

Everything fell into place nicely. Halston helped her get the last bit of the table center pieces together, the caterer was already in place for the food and Melvin showed up with the balloons on time; a bonus she didn't expect.

The birthday party was a nice getaway from reality for her and Halston as well. He was in positive spirits, but she knew he still felt uneasy about losing his job. She had full confidence that it was all meant to be and he would find something much better. She couldn't have been happier that he was on the brink of exploring a new role outside of that hellhole, maybe even a new career.

Her dad's party expected roughly 15 guests, including she and Halston. Their closest family and some of her dad's friends were expected to be there. As she made a mental note of all the guests she greeted, her aunt Monica was the only person missing.

Monica walked through the bathroom door, almost on cue with

Kelly's thoughts.

"Ooh, there is my gorgeous niece. You just look even more beautiful every time I see you. Give me some love."

Monica's perfume tickled Kelly's nose. She held back a sneeze as she leaned into her aunt's shoulder to hug her. Monica was her dad's younger sister. She was only 13 years Kelly's senior, so she often thought of her more like the big sister she never had. She also had the uncanny ability to read Kelly like a book, which sometimes didn't work to her advantage.

"Thank you so much, Monica. Look who's talking. You look gorgeous."

Monica always insisted that Kelly called her by her first name, since she didn't feel like she was old enough to be anyone's aunt.

"Well, you know, I try my best. I have to keep up with you younger ladies. Wait a minute," Monica paused. "You have an impeccable glow. There are only a couple of reasons for that and by the looks of it, I'd say your glow is due to an additional family member on the way."

"We are not ready for all of that yet. When it's time, you'll be one of the first to know. I'll take the glow, though: I won't reject that."

Kelly laughed as they both spilled out of the restroom.

Damn. She was spot on.

Kelly couldn't believe how accurate her aunt was about her pregnancy.

Her parents would be there any minute. Kelly watched as Halston stood in the corner, near the caterer, talking to her brother. She smiled at how happy she imagined he'd be to finally be a dad, despite all their previously failed attempts. She also knew how apprehensive he would be if she revealed the news to him before he had another serious job prospect.

"Baby? Kelly? Can you hear me?" her mother tapped her on the shoulder.

"Oh. Mom. I'm so sorry. I was in another world there for a moment. Where's Dad?"

Kelly tried to shake off her startled demeanor from being

awakened from her daydream.

"He's in the car. I told him to wait there for a couple of minutes. I wanted to see everything without him first. We got him good. He was just starting to suspect something on the way here, but he really has no idea," her mother gleamed.

"That is awesome. We really pulled this together. You look so pretty, Mom. I love you," Kelly replied, as she squeezed her mother tightly.

"Thank you, babe. I hope you noticed I'm wearing the earrings you bought me last Mother's Day."

Kelly's mother playfully pushed her hands behind both of her ears to highlight her earrings. She shimmied her shoulders to give an extra effect. If only she knew that Halston picked out those earrings she loved so much, not Kelly.

"Yes, I did notice. They look so great on you. Why do I feel nervous?" Kelly asked her mother rhetorically.

"Heck, I'd say maybe because you were the mastermind behind this whole thing. It looks gorgeous, just like you. Hmph, you are glowing. I love it. Let me go get your father out of the car so he can make his grand entrance."

Glowing.

There goes that word again.

Damn.

Was it that obvious? She barely even knew that she was pregnant. How could her aunt see it so clearly? Her mother didn't come right out and say it but her eyes may as well have shouted it from the DJ booth.

"Ahhh," she whispered aloud.

Kelly hoped that her newfound "glow" wasn't so obvious to Halston.

She turned to catch her mom and dad walking into the recreation center out of the corner of her eye. Her anxious feelings shifted from her own issues to make sure her dad had a great time at his party.

"Ooh, now don't you look mighty dapper? Happy Birthday,

Daddy.

Kelly dusted off her dad's shoulders with a wide-eyed smile as she hugged him tightly.

"Thank you, baby. Do you think an old man still has it?"

He spun around slowly so she could get a 360-degree view of his well-tailored black suit. He donned a royal purple shirt and a matching tie. He was an avid sock lover and his black and gray socks featured flecks of purple that matched his shirt perfectly.

"Umph, I would certainly say so. What do you think, Mom?"

"I think he did alright. I'll give him an A-. How about that?" she answered in a sarcastic, yet loving tone.

"Ooh, there's always a hater in the bunch, right?" Kelly's father laughed.

"Well, why don't you both come this way? I have something I want you to see."

Halston met Kelly at the entrance of the party room right before they walked through the doors.

"Oooh, Mr. Smooth's the name, right? Happy Birthday, Dad."

Halston wasn't incredibly close to Kelly's father, or even her mother, but they were the closest thing he had to parents since his own parents were deceased.

"Thank you, Son. Look who's talking. I'd say we can be the next stars of The Bachelor," her father joked.

"Oh, I'd say he is on a roll tonight," her mother mumbled.

Kelly and Halston escorted them through the double doors. A DJ on a large stage immediately cued up "Before I Let Go" by Frankie Beverly and Maze. Gold and silver balloons fell from the ceiling and showered them as they crossed the threshold. The aroma of the catered hors d'oeuvres, including beef BBQ sliders, shrimp pasta salad, grilled vegetable skewers, a mashed potato bar and assorted flavors of cake pops, added to the moment to make it a picture-perfect memory.

"Surprise!"

Everyone shouted in unison as Kelly's parents crossed the threshold inside.

Kelly glanced over at her father to check for the reaction she desired most, his tears. She always thought of her father as a man's man, but she knew she was his kryptonite. Now, she felt like all the hard work, spats with her mother, and last-minute changes were worth her effort.

Halston rubbed Kelly's back as she began to shed tears of her own. He couldn't be prouder of his wife. He felt like he had the most special woman in the room.

Melvin strolled up, hugged his dad, and join in the celebration.

"What? I have my favorite lady and my three beautiful kids here? You all planned all of this for me?" Kelly's dad asked.

He was truly flabbergasted.

Everyone began to dance, eat and congratulate Kelly's father on his milestone birthday. The DJ shouted him out on the mic and yelled, "Y'all can do better than that. Let's get this party jumping for the man of the night."

Kelly laughed as she watched her father give his best dance moves. He was much livelier and more outgoing than her mother. The yin and yang dynamic of their personalities was partly what made their marriage last so long. Even Kelly's mother got a kick out of how ecstatic her husband was for his party.

"I'd say he's pleased, wouldn't you?" Kelly's mother asked Kelly and Melvin.

"Yes, indeed. I can't understand all those dance moves, but I have to give it to him. He has his own rhythm," Melvin snickered.

"Oh, goodness. Where did you find these cake pops? They are dangerously delicious. If you see me grab more than three more, take them out of my hand," she laughed.

Kelly knew exactly what her mother was doing. She wanted to make Melvin feel included, even though Kelly did majority of the planning. Kelly didn't mind because Melvin failed to come around much. She was mainly glad to see him in one place with the rest of the family.

"Aren't they amazing?" Melvin chimed in. "One of my former coworkers owns a small cake shop downtown. I haven't tasted any cake pops better than hers. I always have to ration myself when I eat them too."

As Kelly made her way to the dance floor to join her dad, Kelly's mother thought it was the perfect opportunity to talk to Halston. She always found her son-in-law to be a bit mysterious. No matter how much she prodded and poked, he was a master at letting her know only what she asked; not a bit more information. She knew Kelly wouldn't approve of her subtle prying.

"How is my handsome bonus son doing?" Kelly's mother asked.

"I am doing great. I can't complain. How is my beautiful bonus mom? This is a great party. You, Kelly and Melvin really outdid yourselves," Halston replied.

He enjoyed speaking with Kelly's mother, although he was on guard to keep the discussion light.

"Thank you, darling. I'm just glad it's over and now he can get to really enjoy it all," she smiled.

A slightly uncomfortable silence arose as the music played in the background.

"I can imagine. You all worked hard on this. How are your yoga classes coming along?"

"Oooh, you sure do have a great memory. They are going well, baby. Thanks for asking. This ole lady has to hold on to her youth some kind of way. I love yoga. How are things going at work for you?"

There it was. The million-dollar question.

Halston doubted that Kelly disclosed his job status to her parents. Her dad's party was a nice diversion from that coming up in natural conversation. He took a gamble and answered with a vague, yet accurate response.

"It's going well. I think it will be time to look for something new soon; you know, continue to elevate.".

"I heart that. Nothing wrong with elevation. I love a man with a plan."

"Well, don't just stand there on the wall. If you're not dancing, you're not in the groove. If you're not in the groove, then you may as well leave. Let's keep this party going," the DJ commanded.

He cued up "Love Music" by Earth, Wind & Fire, one of Kelly's dad's favorite groups. However, Kelly's mom and Halston were one of the few people still not on the dance floor.

"I think we've been summoned. May I have this dance?" Halston asked.

He smoothly spun his mother-in-law around before they made their way to the dance floor.

She beamed with joy and said, "Certainly. I don't even have to look. I know her dad is really about to 'cut-a-rug' to this one."

Melvin soon joined them on the dance floor as well, with a cock-tail in hand.

At that very moment, everyone was all on one accord: celebration.

Only two weeks remained before Devin and Lynelle's big Halloween party. Kelly still needed to get a couple of things to complete her outfit. She and Halston decided to dress up as Ike and Tina Turner. She also planned on finally telling Halston that she was pregnant. Kelly had turned down alcohol a few times now in the past month and suspected he would question her soon.

Melina bugged Kelly about catching up. She needed to get some things for her costume too, which was Jessica Rabbit. Kelly laughed when her friend first shared her costume choice with her. She thought it was right up her alley for Melina's personality.

"Girl, are you ready yet? You know I still need to tell you about what happened a few weeks ago. I don't even know if I should show up to this party now," Melina confessed.

"Yeah, just give me five minutes and I'll be done. What are you talking about? These Halloween parties are always a blast. I'm telling you, you don't want to miss it," Kelly assured her.

"Umm hmmm. I hear you. I'll wait to leave here and fill you in," Melina replied, unphased by Kelly's declaration.

"You are such a mess. OK, I think I'm ready now. Let's go to Halloween City and then we can grab dinner, your pick this time."

"Ooh, sounds like a plan and I know the perfect place. There's a new hibachi restaurant nearby. Let's go there."

"Nice, I've actually had a taste for hibachi lately. I'll bring Halston some too. He's busy consulting with a client tonight."

"Nice. How are things going with his job search?"

Although Kelly barely felt comfortable telling her that Halston recently lost his job, she was tight-lipped about her pregnancy. Plus, she was a tad bit superstitious and didn't believe in telling anyone (besides Halston) for at least the first trimester.

"Yeah, he just had his last day at the old place last week. So, he's doing independent consulting in the meantime. If he keeps this cadence up, I told him he should just try that full time for a while."

"That is awesome. You really have a good one. I'm telling you, please let me know if he has a long-lost brother that he doesn't know about."

"Thank you and if he does, you know you'll be the first to know. Alright, that's a wrap. Let's hit it and go costume shopping."

"Yes, I'm ready. You think we should go eat first?"

"I'm fine with waiting after we shop, unless you're hungry now."

"I'm fine. I want to make sure I can still fit into this Jessica Rabbit dress after I eat. I can't show up embarrassing you or myself," Melina laughed.

"Shut it. Your curves are in all the right places. You have nothing to worry about," Kelly promised her friend.

"Hmph. I don't know about all of that, but I appreciate the vote of confidence."

"Come on, let's go. Is it OK if I ride with you?"

"You bet. I was going to suggest it. Let me tell you what I was texting you about the other day. Brace yourself."

"Yes, I need to hear about this tea. It must be piping hot because you have been begging to spill it."

They sauntered out of the elevator and into the parking garage. As soon as they were seated in Melina's car, she started telling what she knew. She couldn't even wait until they exited the garage.

"Alright, here it goes. Does your friend Devin tend to stray from home?"

"Wait. Do you mean is he a cheater? Of course not. He loves Lynelle. No way."

"Well, I saw what I saw. Unless he has a long-lost twin brother, I saw him out with some woman."

"That was probably Lynelle. How did she look?" Kelly inquired.

"Let's see. She was short. She had to be under five and a half feet. She had a blunt bob haircut, wide hips, kinda small breasts. Her skin was a dark olive tone, like an Egyptian goddess. Maybe it was his wife. Whoever she was, she was bad."

"Shit. Wow. Um…ok, let's think. Maybe that's just a coworker, a cousin … who knows? He does have a little sister too, but she looks nothing like what you described."

"Are you thinking what I'm thinking?"

"I just. I don't understand. Lynelle is pretty, but she doesn't look like that. How did he act when you saw him with her?"

"It was right outside of that new dessert shop XO CoCo. They didn't do anything overtly flirty, but he did have his hand around her waist. Something about the way she leaned into him too made it seem like they were 'familiar' if you know I mean."

"Wow, I can't believe it. I'm speechless," Kelly replied, in a daze.

Melina was surprised at the shock her friend exhibited. She firmly believed that most men cheated, so she didn't understand why Kelly seemed so caught off guard by the possibility of Devin cheating on his wife.

"You look a little flushed. Are you okay? I know you're much more hopeful of the male species than I am," Melina laughed.

"Girl……yeah, it's all good. I hate that for Lynelle, if it's true. I don't know if I should say anything," Kelly replied.

"For what? Hell, forget I even said it. Maybe I saw the wrong thing. You know my mind is jaded anyway. Don't pay any attention to me. Besides, don't you think Halston would have given you an inkling if he knew Devin was cheating?" Melina asked.

"I guess you're right, but Halston is like Fort Knox when it comes to his friends. He's not one to do a lot of pillow talk. I imagine he would let me know if he knew Devin was unfaithful. Cheating is pretty major."

She looked through the passenger window as Melina stopped at the light adjacent to Halloween. Suddenly, her mood wasn't so festive. She felt a small wave of nausea swirling in the pit of her stomach.

"Yeah, that is true. Oh well. Let's go find what we need for these outfits. We are going to be the baddest chics at the party. I'm excited to get out and try something different. I am usually such a bum for Halloween. I watch scary movies and eat popcorn by myself. That usually ends with me drinking one too many glasses of wine and dialing up an old flame to come to hold me from the boogeyman," Melina laughed.

Kelly was put off by how quickly Melina seemed to have gotten over the information she just shared with her.

Does she not realize she basically just told me that my husband's best friend is likely cheating on his wife?

She calmed her nerves as best she could and tried to live in the moment.

"The boogeyman, huh? I'm sure you acted scared on purpose so you could jump in his lap," Kelly chimed in.

"Well, a scared girl's gotta do what a scared girl's gotta do. Those big strong arms, that chest and those thighs. You know I love a man with thick thighs. Damn, I need to get laid, quick, fast and in a hurry. This is pitiful," Melina said.

Kelly and Melina enjoyed the rest of the week-day girls' night out and found the perfect pieces to accessorize their outfits for the Halloween party. By the time they left the store, both women had worked up a healthy appetite. They laughed and joked over food at the hibachi grill and Kelly placed an order of chicken and steak to bring home to Halston.

As Kelly drove home from her night with Melina, she was faced with the deafening reality of her uncomfortable silence. Although she flipped from music, podcasts and even what she liked to call "yoga music", nothing helped. She was faced with the possibility that her husband's best friend could be cheating on his wife, right before she planned to reveal her pregnancy to Halston. She really didn't need this type of drama in her life right now. Ultimately, she decided to make the most logical choice in her mind; just sticking to telling Halston she was pregnant and staying out of Devin and Lynelle's business.

CHAPTER 16

Kelly exhaled deeply as she recanted her plan to tell Halston about her pregnancy. Everything was all set. It was the weekend before the Halloween party and they both had a free weekend. Her plan was to take him to one of their favorite restaurants – Molten Lava; a chocolate fondue spot, on Saturday.

She planned to have them place a note inside of one of the chocolate pinatas that revealed she was expecting. Considering the delicate nature of their previous attempts of trying to have a child, she didn't even run her idea past anyone else. Plus, she was still very early in her pregnancy. She couldn't go through another heartbreak of a false alarm and then having to face the people she told, even her parents.

Kelly tried her best to hide her nervousness Friday night. Halston suggested that they go to the movies to see a new Angelina Jolie film. Perfect. They both loved the movies, but she especially loved the idea that night. It meant she could still spend time cuddled in his arms, but not have to engage in deep discussion for a bit: thus avoiding eye contact until she had to deliver the big news.

Although her justification was a bit juvenile, she jumped at the idea of stalling as much as she could until the very moment that she revealed their upcoming addition to their family.

Halston was still doing well with his outside consulting. Between his severance from Axl Corp and his side consulting gigs, they brought in slightly more income than when he worked full time. Despite their unforeseen future financially, things seemed to be looking up and stable at the very least.

"Babe, I am so excited about seeing this new movie. Angelina Jolie always kicks ass, literally," she giggled.

Angelina Jolie's films *Salt* and *Wanted* were some of their favorites that they could watch repeatedly.

"You know she will. I'm excited about seeing it too and even more excited about us getting some quality time together.".

Kelly melted. He always knew the right things to say. Sometimes, there was a side of her that wanted Halston to have a rougher edge, like a bad boy but without the drinking, cheating, drugs or domestic violence. Nonetheless, every time she looked in his eyes, she realized she had everything she needed.

"Aren't you sweet. Yes, I'm really excited about that too. Food, a movie and my baby sounds like the best Friday night ever to me."

They decided to go to a trendy new theater they visited a couple of times, called Gawk. Just walking into the building was an experience. Their walls had intricate crown molding with golden flecks in the cream-colored paint. The wall sconces that housed the lights along the walls were exquisite as well.

"Yes, that makes two of us. I just need to put on my shoes and I'm ready, if you are," he replied.

"Yes, I am all set. Can you believe it? Wait. Actually, let me bump up the top of my hair really quickly. It won't take long. I know we need to head out in a few minutes, so we don't miss the previews," she added.

Kelly tossed the longest pieces of hair in the front with her fingers. She attended beauty school for a couple of years as a side gig, while she was in college. Although she never became a beautician, she enjoyed the profession and learned valuable skills to maintain her own hair. She had just given herself a new cut and color, which she loved. Her hair was tapered at the sides and in the back, with shimmers of eggplant mixed into her natural dark brown tones.

The shape of her haircut formed a subtle mohawk: Halston loved it. He thought it was edgier and sexier than some of her more recent styles. Plus, he loved that she started to gain her confidence back. Lord knows she needed all the confidence she could get right now.

"Alright. Coming," Kelly exclaimed as she made her way to the living room.

"Gorgeous. I'm such a lucky man. Let's go, babe," Halston commanded as they walked through the kitchen to get to the garage.

The movie started in 30 minutes, but the theater was only 15 minutes away. Perfect timing. Halston and Kelly blasted a couple of throwback gems from Missy Elliott on their way to the movies. The songs brought back some of the early moments of their courtship.

Kelly felt a surge of hunger overtake her as she and Halton settled into their assigned seats. She chalked it up to pregnancy hormones, but she didn't want Halston to think she was being a pig. She ordered fajita chicken nachos and a side of humus, no alcohol, of course. She swallowed hard after she caught a glimpse of Halston's slightly surprised expression after ordering a turkey burger with sweet potato fries.

"Mmmm, this feels so nice. I love you, babe. Thank you for always making me feel so special," Kelly sighed as she sunk her head into his chest. She loved Gawk's theater seating because they were able to lift the middle armrest and cuddle together before and after the food.

"It's truly my pleasure. Thank you for always making me feel like a king. I love you too," he replied, as he kissed her forehead.

Suddenly, Kelly's position didn't feel so comfortable anymore. She shifted slightly, as not to alarm Halston. He may not have even noticed some of the strange things she had done lately, but she didn't want to add to the list, just in case he did.

The lights in the theater began to dim as the plush navy curtains retreated to their corners right next to the edge of the screen. Their food arrived about ten minutes later, just before the movie started.

Kelly tried her best to pace herself while eating her food. She felt bad when she realized Halston was full from his burger and fries.

However, that didn't stop her from continuing to eat her entrée and most of the hummus appetizer. She justified her hunger for the fact that she was eating for two. It made logical sense in her head if she could keep Halston from finding out until tomorrow.

During the next 90 minutes, she escaped in a dream world as she and Halston watched the action-packed movie. She didn't have a care in the world and she felt a small release of excitement leave her once the credits rolled. She and Halston always stayed until the credits ended, as if every movie had a Marvel surprise at the end. It was their quirky thing they enjoyed together.

Once the lights slowly ascended to their full brightness, they sat for another couple of minutes giving their critiques about the movie. Overall, they both thoroughly enjoyed the film.

That's when she saw them, just as they arose from their seats. Omar and some unknown woman that was accompanying him. Kelly knew him to be with no less than at least ten different women the entire time she knew him; that was on the modest side. The actual number was probably much higher considering how many women he had meaningless flings with that she never met. This woman must have been somewhat special, maybe not serious, but more than a one-night stand.

They didn't see her initially. Kelly was going to attempt to move past them until she saw that Halston noticed his friend too.

"Aye, Omar. Is that you?" he called out.

Shit.

She didn't have anything against Omar. He was a fun-loving guy. Kelly just wasn't in the mood for his wit or sense of humor tonight.

"Halston? Kells?" Omar yelled, from the other side of the theater.

Kells was his nickname for Kelly. He was the only person that called her that. Somehow after all this time, it still stuck. The woman he was with quickly changed her face to a friendly expression from one that suggested she was a doe-eyed deer caught in headlights.

Hell, I'd be nervous if I were with him too, girl, Kelly thought to herself as they both made their way towards she and Halston.

As they moved closer, Kelly did as all women do. She sized up

Omar's date. She was a strikingly beautiful woman. Although near-ly all the women Kelly had seen Omar with were pretty, there was something different about her. The corners of her eyes tapered off at the ends, like almonds, with dark, full pupils. She had a head full of naturally curly, brown hair that looked perfectly untamed. The top of her breasts played peak-a-boo just above the hem of her blouse to suggest she was only a nasty girl behind closed doors and noth-ing less than a lady in the streets.

"Well, look what the cat dragged in," Halston laughed.

"Small world, right. Halston, Kelly, this is Brandy," Omar said.

He seemed eager to introduce Brandy, which was slightly outside of his M.O. He was more enthused for them to meet her than any of the previous women they met.

"Nice to meet you both. So, what did you guys think about the movie?" Brandy asked.

Her demeanor was friendly, yet somewhat cautious.

"It was great. We loved it. Then again, we are practically Angeli-na Jolie groupies," Kelly laughed.

"So are we. That woman can do no wrong," Omar said.

We? Halston thought.

Although he had a hard time keeping up with his friend's flavors of the month, he didn't recall hearing anything about Brandy. He was anxious to know when they started moving towards "we" status.

"Most definitely. It's good to see you, man. It's really nice to meet you too, Brandy," Halston added.

"Likewise. It was really nice to meet you both too," she said.

"Well, I know you two lovebirds can't be going to bed this early. You want to meet us at the Screaming Coyote? That place finally opened last week. Have you seen the pictures online? It looks sick; really nice ambiance," Omar said.

Omar was always up for a new adventure. That's what Kelly ad-mired about him. She credited him for some of that attitude rub-bing off on Halston. Although she had also seen some amazing photos of Screaming Coyote on Instagram, this was not the night she wanted to go to a trendy new bar downtown. Against her better judgment, she suggested that she and Halston join them.

"Sure, that sounds like fun. What do you say, babe?" she glanced at Halston for approval.

She basically volunteered them to hang out with Omar and Brandy, but she knew he wouldn't mind.

Now, she just had to think of another lie not to drink or at least slip in a virgin cocktail.

The bottom of Halston's feet tingled with a burning sensation. He wiped his slightly sweaty brow in his sleep. A woman's calm voice whispered in his ear. She sounded familiar, yet distant.

"Be careful," she muttered.

He was still unsure of the woman's identity until her hand graced his face. Her calming touch, mixed with the relaxing scent of lavender and vanilla jolted his memory. His mother. Halston's parents both died in a fire, due to a faulty gas line when he was only six years old.

Although he didn't have many memories of her, the way she smelled was something that remained imprinted on his brain. His father was in and out, so they barely had a relationship, but he remembered and revered the love of his mother.

"Be careful," she repeated.

This time her tone was more resounding and cautionary than her first utterance.

"Go!" his mother shouted.

"Ah, what? Huh?" Halston woke up in a dizzy stupor.

He panted wildly and looked around the bedroom. He tried not to awaken Kelly, but it was too late.

"Baby. Baby. It was just a dream. Wake up. It's ok," Kelly said.

She held Halston in her arms to try to calm his bewilderment.

"Thank you, babe. It was just a bad dream, that's all. I'm sorry. I didn't mean to wake you up."

"Don't worry about that. It must have been a horrible dream. What happened?"

"Someone touched me in an eerie way. It was a woman and felt the need to warn me about something. The whole thing felt so real," Halston replied.

He flat-out lied. He didn't know why, but he felt uneasy telling Kelly that his mother gave him such a staunch warning in his dream.

"Mmmm, that does sound strange. Well, the great thing is it was all a dream. I've heard bad dreams can sometimes have good meanings. Maybe it was a sign of something good, in disguise," she replied, with slurred speech, in a positive tone.

Halston and Kelly soon drifted off to sleep again. The last thing Halston remembered was looking at the clock before he closed his eyes again. It was 3:36 am. The sun soon peered through their bedroom curtains, signaling the morning.

Kelly got out of bed shortly after 8:00 am. She wanted to sleep in a bit longer, but her nerves wouldn't allow her to be still.

Halston slept soundly until shortly after 8:45 am.

Kelly was grateful for the short time to be alone with her thoughts and mentally prepare for the excitement of the day. She smiled as she peered out of the window in their kitchen and sipped a steaming, delicious cup of coffee. The warmth eased her body and her mind simultaneously.

Halston stretched his arm across the bed and realized Kelly was already up. He brushed his teeth and walked into the kitchen to join her.

"Good morning, beautiful. Did my nightmare drive you to drink first thing in the morning?" Halston joked.

"Yes, I'm afraid it did. 'The best part of waking up' they say," Kelly laughed as she raised her mauve-colored coffee mug to signal an air toast to Halston.

"I may have to join you in this early morning happy hour," he teased her.

Kelly flashed him a mischievous grin and fought the sudden urge to rub her hand across the growing life inside of her belly.

"I'm not sure if you plan on going to the gym before we go to Molten Lava, but I can cook a light breakfast for us," Kelly said.

"Thank you, baby. That sounds great. I think I'll skip it today and stay in with you," Halston replied.

"Sounds great. Well, in that case, breakfast will be served in about 30 minutes," Kelly beamed.

·

The time drew near. Kelly and Halston were almost finished with their lunch. Kelly ordered a Thai chicken salad and Halston ordered a tuna melt with fries. They both loved Molten Lava and talked about the exquisite ambiance like it was their first time dining there. Plus, it helped pass the time before the big reveal. Kelly's anxiety continued to build up, although she tried not to let it show.

"Did they add more geishas on the ceiling?" Halston asked.

The restaurant was immaculately decorated with various Asian artifacts and characters that lined the walls and the ceilings. Even the sconces were strategically placed to accent the art on the walls.

"Ooh, I think you're right. It looks like they did. I'm almost certain the one above us wasn't here the last time," Kelly agreed.

Kelly glanced down at her watch to check the time.

2:37 pm.

The dessert (and more importantly, the surprise revealing of her pregnancy) should be brought out any minute.

Just as she finished the last bit of her salad, three servers made their way towards the table. One server held a medium-sized golden gong and a mallet, while the other server on the left side held glittering streamers that sparkled brighter with each step. The server in the middle held the golden chocolate sphere that swung delicately above a bed of strawberries, with milk and white chocolate truffles.

Kelly was positioned perfectly to see the men approaching the table, as Halston had his back towards them.

"Hello there, beautiful couple. I have a special fondue for the man and the lovely lady," the waiter in the middle said, as he placed the delectable chocolate centerpiece on the table.

The waiter on the left hand of the gong to Halston, while the waiter on the right? added the streamers on either side of the edible masterpiece.

Halston looked pleasantly perplexed as Kelly looked on in anticipation. The presentation of the idea was even more gorgeous than she expected. She unlocked her phone to prepare to capture action shots as she revealed the news of the upcoming addition to their family.

"One. Two. Ooh, Fondue. Three. Four. Wait, there's more. Give it a crack. Give it a go," all three men chanted in unison.

"Wait a minute. Something tells me you were behind this. It's not my birthday or our anniversary. Are there any other important dates I'm not thinking about?" Halston asked.

"I have no idea. Maybe you should open the sphere and see what's inside," Kelly replied with raised eyebrows.

She acted like she had no idea what would happen next. She released a huge sigh of relief. Everything happened perfectly so far; even better than she envisioned.

"Ok. You're up to something," he grinned.

Halston took the mallet from one of the waiters and used it to crack open the chocolate sphere. A small baby made of white chocolate lied nestled inside of the bottom of the milk chocolate sphere.

"Wait. Does this mean...? Are you.....? Are we expecting a baby?" Halston asked.

Kelly could tell he needed confirmation before he felt fully confident to say what the surprise told him.

"Yes, Halston. We're having a baby. I know, I can't believe it's finally happening," Kelly said as tears formed in the corners of her eyes.

"This is the best news ever. I love you," Halston cried.

"I love you too," Kelly exclaimed.

Her tears were now free flowing as well. She knew Halston
would be an incredible father. They were finally about to have a
family.

ow, ok. I can see how your wife's pregnancy would have been a big life change for both of you. I imagine there was even some trepidation about the status of her health throughout the pregnancy. Was that what had you troubled?"

"Not exactly. I'd say it's a little deeper than that," Halston paused.

"Well, do tell. That is if you feel comfortable to do so," Sharon tread lightly.

"I decided I would move my yearly physical up a bit and go get tested," he replied.

"Tested? Did you suspect your wife gave you some type of venereal disease? Did she show signs of being unfaithful?"

"You know how something seems off, but you don't have the evidence to back up your thoughts?" he asked rhetorically.

Sharon nodded and kept quiet, as not to interrupt him. She could tell he needed to get his thoughts out in the open, even if it was only to her in their session.

"So, the reason why I moved my physical up was because I started to question how we were able to get pregnant so easily. Right before Kelly got sick, we tried to have a baby but failed. I felt like it was mainly my fault because my sperm count was too low. Nothing had changed in my condition during that initial time and when she got pregnant again. I guess something about it didn't feel right," he said.

"Hmmmm, ok. That's a lot for anyone to handle, not to mention the possibility of infidelity in a marriage. I don't mean to sound sexist when I say this, but this is a rare case for a man to be in this position. At least in my line of work, I haven't come across it much if at all."

"No offense taken. I haven't heard of it much either."

"Once you found out that the possibilities of getting your wife pregnant were still slim, how did you move forward in sharing that news with her?"

"Things came to a head the morning after my friend Devin's Halloween party. He and his wife, Lynelle, hosted a party: they hosted this lavish party every year. It was a big deal. Costumes, food, drinks, the whole nine yards. I'll never forget that night," Halston trailed.

.

"'Anna Mae? Anna Mae Bullock?' Are you ready or what girl?" Halston called from the living room.

"'Oh, ah yes, Ike.' I'll be there in 45 seconds. I'm just teasing my hair a bit, babe," Kelly replied.

"Well, hurry up, now. You know all the good food and liquor will be gone if we keep waiting on you and those wigs. That's what set us back now," he replied, as he grabbed a few chips from the pantry.

"'I'm sorry, Ike.' Here I am. I'm ready," Kelly replied, as she pranced into the living room to join Halston.

"Damn, now that's more like it, 'Anna Mae'. Tina Turner, eat your heart out. Let me see you shimmy with those fringes," Halston commanded.

"Boy, you are so silly. Come on, let's go. You are looking mighty fine and groovy too, Ike. I'm totally with you on the snacks and drinks. We don't not need to miss out on that, especially since we're eating for three now," she smiled.

Kelly still gave him the shimmy he requested before they walked out of the door. She checked her phone to see a missed text from Melina.

Are you sure it's ok for me to bring a date? I don't want to intrude on Devin and Lynelle's space.

Yes, you are fine. The more the merrier with them. I'm excited to meet this mystery man, Kelly texted her back.

Ok, cool. I'm excited for you to meet him too. I'll be there in about 30 mins, Melina replied.

Kelly glanced at the clock in the car. They would be at Devin and Lynelle's house in less than 15 minutes. The timing was perfect. She joked and laughed with Halston about memories from some of the parties Devin and Lynelle hosted from years prior. Before they knew it, they had arrived.

Cars lined the side of street and around the block when they pulled up to Devin and Lynelle's house. By the looks of the cars outside, it appeared the party had a lot more guests than normal; that or several other people showed up relatively on time.

The outside of their house was decorated with ghouls and goblins placed strategically along the path to their front door. They had two large trees near on either side of the lawn that were perfect for Halloween, since they already looked like weeping willows. Cobbed webs were strewn between each tree and across the edges of the roof. Two large trick mirrors were placed by the archway leading to the front door. Dancing orange and white lights could be seen from the outside of the window. The bass from the music inside was just loud enough to know that music was playing, but quiet enough not to disturb the neighborhood.

Kelly and Halston turned to each other with excitement as they rang the doorbell and waited for either Devin or Lynelle to welcome them inside.

A ghastly laugh mixed with the thumping bass of Michael Jackson's "Thriller" greeted them as an undisclosed person swung open the door.

"Step inside if you dare," the female voice said.

"Ooh, yes, mam. You are looking fierce in that Cat Woman suit. Do you promise to whip me?" Kelly asked as she and Halston crossed over the meticulously decorated threshold.

"If you're a good girl, I might give you a spank or two, Tina. I am loving the hair and those fringes. Just shimmy for me," Lynelle said.

"Have you been peeping through our window? You sound just like Halston," Kelly laughed.

"Great minds think alike. Hey Lynelle. Great costume," Halston added.

" 'Why, thank you, Ike.' Devin is somewhere running around here. Look for Batman and you'll find him. Make yourselves at home, as usual," Lynelle replied.

Thriller began to fade out, just as Devin turned the corner.

"Ike and Tina. My favorites," Devin shouted as he walked into Kelly and Halston.

"You know we had to come correct. This is the event of the year. You make a pretty dapper Batman," Kelly hugged Devin.

Halston greeted Devin as they had a playful male ego competition of whose costume was better.

"Take these. I knew you two would be here soon, so I made these special drinks for you. They're strong, so proceed with caution," Devin laughed.

"Nice. Yes, thank you, brother. I will take that off your hands," Halston replied excitedly.

Kelly paused.

"I'm going to be the designated driver tonight. I hate to be the party pooper, but I'll pass. Thank you," Kelly replied.

She didn't want to reveal her pregnancy right there in front of Devin, especially since he would be the first person to know outside of her and Halston. Kelly didn't think Halston would have minded, but she opted for the easier route of avoidance.

"My, how things have changed. You know we have an extra room here but suit yourself. There's plenty of food in the kitchen and little kiddie drinks for you, Tina," Devin joked.

"Haha. Sounds good. We don't want to keep you from the party. We'll get our plates and make our rounds to say hello," she told Devin.

Kelly and Halston stepped further into the kitchen as Devin

moved towards the living room. There were strobe lights at the corners of the kitchen that shone up to the ceiling with different colored lights. Kelly had to look away from the lights quickly to avoid feeling dizzy.

"Whew, great save on the drink, babe. I figured you may not want to let them know about our little secret yet," Halston stated once Devin walked out of the kitchen.

"I know, right. I might not be able to drink, but I'm starving. This food looks delicious. Lynelle went all out," Kelly glanced at the counter in awe and didn't know what to put on her plate first.

There was a bowl with a mound of dirt cake (Lynelle's special recipe of vanilla pudding, cool whip, crumbled graham crackers, Oreos, and a hint of almond extract) with gummy worms hanging out of the side of it. On the side of that were chicken strips drizzled with an Asian zing sauce (for fake blood), beef sliders with toy knives stuck in the middle of them, and a purple punch with candied beetles floating inside of it. Plus, there was a large pan of chicken and vegan enchiladas, each with generous splatters of sauce and tombstones standing at the edge of the pan.

Melina entered the kitchen almost on cue to the beginning of Taylor Swift's "Bad Blood".

"Hey girl, hey. Oooh, I see you, Ms. Tina. Hey Halston, I mean, Ike," Melina exclaimed as she reached out to hug Kelly.

"Look who's talking. Damn girl, you are wearing that Jessica Rabbit outfit. You did not come to play," Kelly bellowed.

Kelly subtly motioned for Melina to introduce her to the man in the car mechanic costume by her side. Even in the slightly baggy outfit, Kelly could tell he had a nice build.

"This is my friend, James. He loves a great Halloween party just like me," she grinned.

"Nice to meet you, James," Kelly replied.

Halston looked intently at James's face for a moment. Then it hit him.

"Oh, where are my manners. I'm sorry. It's like sensory overload in here. James, this is my good friend, Kelly, and her husband,

Halston," she said.

"Well, well. It's a small world. I was wondering where I knew you from. I couldn't quite recognize you with the costume but it's good to see you again, man. How's the job been treating you?" Halston asked.

It took James a moment to realize who Halston was as well, and then it clicked.

"Halston? Man, it's good to see you too. Digging the Ike costume. It's been going well. You know, just still getting acclimated to everything but I'm enjoying the role. How has everything been going with you since you left?"

He knew that Halston was laid off from his position and wished he could have taken that last question back. He didn't want to make the moment any more awkward.

"Awesome. Glad to hear that. I'm doing well. I'm doing some independent consulting right now, so that's been working out well."

By this time, Kelly was fully aware of James's identity. She didn't want Halston to feel the least bit inferior because of what happened at his old job. Although he didn't need her validation, she beefed up his current status to help drive home the point that Halston was better off without the dead-end job.

"Yes, James. I recall Halston telling me about you now. Nice to meet you. Yes, thank goodness Halston is out of that place now. He had been trying to leave for quite some time, so everything fell into place nicely. The consulting has been a blessing in disguise," Kelly added.

"Well, look at that. Now that we've all gotten reacquainted with each other, let's dig into some of this grub. Kelly, thanks again for passing the word to Devin and Lynelle for the invite. This house is beautiful. They really went all out. This is a real-deal Halloween party," Melina said.

She wanted to hide under a rock. Melina knew there was a new guy that took Halston's place at work, but she didn't make the connection that it was James.

They all grabbed their snacks and migrated back towards the

living room. Melina scanned the room and noticed there were about 15 other people there, besides James, Kelly, Halston, and herself. She was glad to get out of the house and try something different.

Melina had just met James a couple of weeks before the party, but she thoroughly enjoyed his company. He was ambitious, easy on the eyes, and more importantly, great in bed. Despite going against her better judgment and sleeping with him so quickly, she needed a release. She needed to feel wanted again; hunted even.

As they all entered the room, Lynelle announced that everyone would introduce themselves before they started the first game of the night. Each person gave their name, where they were from originally, and a quirky, interesting fact that other people may not know. Kelly and Halston knew most of the people in the house, except for a handful.

"Alright, now that we're all cozy and familiar with each other, we're going to play a little game of Never Have I Ever. We have shots prepared for everyone to take. Does everyone know the rules of the game?" Devin asked.

Everyone nodded or responded in excitement, eager to let the game begin.

Kelly thought this was a good time to throw away her plate in the kitchen and then go to the restroom. She needed to think about how she could get out of the game.

A headache?

Nope. That wasn't good enough.

A medical condition?

She technically wouldn't have to lie with that one. Still, it didn't sound believable. Plus, that could start a firestorm of other questions she didn't want to get into, considering the cancer she beat.

A queasy stomach?

Yep. She threw her plate away in the kitchen and decided to go with that one.

Kelly ran straight into Devin as she entered the kitchen.

"Oh, I'm sorry. I told Halston this wig was too much. I should have clipped the front. I can't even see where I'm going. You and

Lynelle have really outdone yourselves this year," Kelly said.

"No worries, Tina. Batman has it all together. I'll have your shot ready for you. I know you prefer light over dark," Devin replied.

"Oh no, I'll still play but do you have some Sprite or Ginger Ale? I should drink that instead. My stomach is feeling a little swirly," Kelly rebutted.

"Are you kidding me? You have to play the game. Come on, it will be fun. Plus, a little alcohol will knock whatever that is right on out."

Kelly smiled and looked into his eyes without responding, before glancing back down at the floor.

"Wait. Hold on. You mean to tell me.....are you pregnant? I thought that you and Halston couldn't...."

"Will you keep it down? We're not exactly trying to make any baby announcements at your party. I'm not sure yet. I mean, I am but we're keeping it a secret for now."

"Ok, I get it. You know all of your secrets are safe with me," Devin replied, as he brushed his hand against her cheek.

"Um, yeah. Thanks. I'm going to go to the restroom for a minute."

Kelly peered towards the living room to make sure Halston and Lynelle were still occupied.

"Goodness, that was one hell of a party last night, wasn't it, babe?" Halston asked.

He had a slight hangover when he woke up, something he and Kelly typically experienced together after the annual Halloween party.

"Yes, it was. I had a good time, as always. I was a little sad I couldn't drink, but in due time," she smiled, as she rubbed her soon-to-be baby bump.

"I'm quite sure I had enough for the both of us. I'm still feeling it," Halston laughed.

He checked his phone and noticed a missed text message from Devin.

Thanks so much for coming last night bro. Had a great time. We should catch up next week.

He got out of the bed and rushed to brush his teeth, as he continued talking to Kelly. Halston replied to Devin and let him know he and Kelly had a fun night.

Of course, bro. Anytime. As long as you and Lynelle have it, we'll be there. I'm paying for it a little bit this morning lol.

Kelly peered around the corner to make sure Halston was still in the restroom before she checked her phone. She also had a missed text message from Devin.

So, did you tell Halston about our little conversation in the kitchen last night? I haven't said anything to Lynelle.

You know I didn't. I like keeping as much stress out of my life as possible, Kelly replied.

I got you. Just making sure. You don't think there's a chance it's.....?

Kelly was just about to put her phone down before she got the last text from Devin. She couldn't let that text go unanswered. She hurriedly responded back to him to avoid a back-and-forth exchange. Plus, she didn't want to discuss something like that via text.

What are you talking about, Devin? Of course, this baby is not yours.

Kelly immediately deleted the text.

Halston finished brushing his teeth and washing his face before he walked back into the bedroom.

Ding.

Another text message. He suspected it was Devin reaching out to him again.

What he read changed the trajectory of his life forever. He scanned it twice to make sure his eyes weren't deceiving him.

What are you talking about, Devin? Of course, this baby is not yours.

The text was sent to him, obviously in error.

From Kelly.

His wife.

"Hey babe, um......I thought Halloween was over," Halston said calmly as he stepped back into the bedroom.

He visibly trembled as he awaited her response.

Kelly paused for a moment.

She was unsure what her husband meant by his statement and thought maybe he was playing some type of game.

"Ha. Well, last I checked it is November 1st. Did those drinks hit you harder than you realize, babe?" Kelly laughed nervously.

If Halston was playing a joke on her, he had a spectacular poker face. She saw fire in his eyes; the kind of fire that was only present when he was angry with her.

"Oh, I'm as clear as a bell. I'm just having a little trouble processing this," he said.

Halston tossed the phone in Kelly's direction. It landed perfectly in her lap, face up.

She gasped as she saw the text message on his screen.

"Baby, that's…." her voice trailed off.

There was no way she could casually talk her way out of this one.

"Baby, that's what? Some bullshit? Ludicrous? A mistake? Do you want me to tell you what the fuck I think it is?" he commanded.

Kelly never knew Halston to speak to her in this manner. In fact, she only witnessed him speak to other people like that only a handful of times since she'd known him. This was incredibly serious and she feared for what he would do next.

"I uh….I didn't mean to send that to you.".

"Really? No shit! Thanks for stating the obvious."

The dreadful tone of his voice ricocheted against their bedroom walls like a dreadful game of ping-pong.

"I didn't mean for you to find out like this. I'm not proud of it," she said, as she removed the comforter to rise from the bed.

"Please, don't come near me right now. Just stay right there. I think what you meant to say is you didn't mean for me to find out. Period."

"You're right. I decided we should break it off. I wanted to tell you, honestly. I just haven't been able to work up the nerve to do it yet. I know, I'm a coward and you have every right to feel however you choose to feel about me right now."

"Break it off? Do you know what that tells me? This has happened more than once. Was it that good? When was the last time?"

The sound of their heartbeats was the only audible noise in the room. Their rhythm rivaled that of a college drumline.

"It started before I had that last long bout in the hospital. A few times then and once when I got out, a couple of months ago," she muttered.

"A couple of months ago. I see. Well, what kind of flipping fucking idiot am I? I'm playing basketball with him, in his house. Hell, he was my best friend," Halston ranted.

"I know. I know. I'm so sorry. Please believe me. It doesn't mean anything. I don't love him. I love you," Kelly pleaded.

She moved towards him but Halston moved back with every forward step she made.

"Stop. Don't touch me right now, please. I really don't want to know the answer to this question, but I'm gonna ask it anyway. Are you even sure this is our baby?"

nock knock.

Devin waited on the other side of the hotel room door. He waited for Kelly to complete two knocks from the inside. That was their thing. He knew it wasn't right but once they started, he couldn't stop.

He glanced down at his phone to make sure he was at the right room number. Yep. 236.

Then he checked the previous two texts they exchanged.

Say man….. Kelly said.

Say what? Devin replied with his usual response.

This was their thing when they needed their fix to see each other. Well, more than just see each other.

The doorknob finally turned from the inside.

"Hey, come on. Get inside," Kelly said.

She peered around the corner nervously before she closed the door.

"You seem a little tense. Let me help you relax," Devin said.

He moved his hands towards her shoulders to give her a massage.

"Devin. We can't. I know I've said this before, but I really mean it this time," Kelly said.

"Um, okay. What brought all of this on?" he questioned.

Kelly looked at him blankly before replying. She was fathomed at how he could be so oblivious to the mess they made. Then again, she was forced to see the light. Ignorance really is bliss.

"Devin, he knows."

Devin stared back at her in confusion and disbelief. The room seemed to sink into the ground, enveloping both him and her in despair.

"He knows? What do you mean he knows? How did he find out?" he shouted.

"From our text exchange the morning after the Halloween party. I accidentally responded to him and not you when you asked about the baby," she sighed.

"Oh my goodness. We are fucked. This is not good. What am I going to tell Lynelle?" he asked.

"Hell if I know. You need to think of something quickly. Halston has been gone for the last few days and I don't know where he's at or where he's going," she admitted.

"How did you accidentally text that to him and not me? Ugh, this is a mess."

"Look at the fucking pot calling the kettle black. You've got some nerve. Who started this whole thing in the first place?" she shouted.

"I…I'm sorry. That was out of line. You're right. We both made this bed and now….I guess we lay in it.".

"I don't know what I'm going to do. I can't lose Halston. I know I messed up but he can't leave me."

"Why?"

"Huh? What do you mean why?"

"I mean, you know how we talked about in a perfect world, it would be nice if we could have started something together. Maybe this is our out. This could be our time," Devin pleaded.

"Seriously? Is that all you can think about right now? Our lives are forever changed as we know them. That may have been a nice fantasy at one time, but I'm not leaving Halston."

"Can't blame a man for a trying. We should make love at least one more time."

"Shit. You are unbelievable. I'm in a hotel room talking to my husband's best friend about how he and I got caught cheating, oh and possibly with his baby. After all of that, you're thinking about sex right now? Just get out. Out!" she screamed.

"Not so loud. We don't want to attract any unnecessary attention," he warned.

"I think I've already made that mistake. I only called you here to tell you that the secret's out, nothing more than that."

"I'm sorry, Kelly. I really am. I'll be here to do whatever you want or don't want me to do for you. I mean that."

"Thank you. This is just so much for me to process right now. It's a lot for both of us to have to process," she admitted.

"True, it is. Just know that if the baby is mine, I'm willing to walk away from Lynelle and handle my responsibilities, if you'd have me."

Kelly sighed deeply as they embraced one last time. She knew Devin meant every word. Nonetheless, she wondered how she could ever forgive herself if she walked away from Halston.

Hmmm, wow. Halston, I must say in all my years of being active in my profession, I have never heard of a situation quite like this before, especially from a man's perspective. I don't mean to sound sexist when I say that. There's a lot to unpack in this situation," Sharon gathered.

She was impressed at how deep their sessions had gotten after just a few visits. Nonetheless, she had to remember to keep her composure and more importantly her professionalism. She didn't want to alienate Halston in any way and make him regret opening up to her. Sharon also found him quite attractive. Despite her physical attraction to Halston, she had a no-sex-or-dating-with-a-client policy.

"No sexist offense taken at all."

"Good. I don't mean to pry here, but you seem extremely calm and collected when recalling these situations. Was there any type of breaking point that you had during this time?"

"That's funny. I've always been dubbed as the cool guy. Cool Mr. Pointe with no breaking point. Yes, I broke. When I did, it was typically explosive."

"Explosive. That's a harsh descriptor. Although, I will say anything short of breaking the law, causing anyone harm or yourself harm, may be a good thing. Keeping our emotions bottled up inside of us without an outlet often has a toxic effect."

"I'd say so too, under most circumstances. I had my share of unruly moments. That's part of what drove me here. I know I need to get my feelings and anger in check. I'm a work in progress like I guess we all are."

"That is true. We are all a work in progress. If you don't mind delving into the details a bit, how did the pregnancy go with Kelly during that phase of your life?

•

"Oooh, girl I am too thrilled about you having this baby," Melina said.

"Thank you so much. My bulge is starting to show a bit now, so I guess I'll have to actually start telling people now," Kelly replied.

"Bulge? Hush. You are almost four months pregnant and barely showing," Melina exclaimed.

"I appreciate the vote of confidence. I'm telling you, I've already had to buy some bigger clothes. My dresses don't fit like they used to and neither do these pants I have on now," Kelly laughed.

"Well, what does Halston have to say about it? Has he noticed?"

Kelly paused for a moment.

Halston had still been in and out of the house for the last few weeks. He was still upset and rightfully so. However, he didn't necessarily blow up at Kelly because of her indiscretions. That was his way. Even when he should have, he kept his cool – at least more so than many people would in the same situation.

"Ah…."

"Hello-oh. You still there?"

"Oh. I'm sorry. Pregnancy brain must be a real thing. He hasn't said a word."

"I know I tell you this all the time, but you really don't know how lucky you are. I would do almost anything to be in your shoes."

"Thank you. I really appreciate that. I learn to appreciate Halston more and more every day. I am blessed to have him. But, enough about me. How are things going with you and your new beau, James?"

Kelly was almost home from work but then decided to stop and pick up some food from one of Halston's favorite Italian restaurants. She was glad he was at least back home every night. Although, she suspected his now consistent availability (despite his mental absence from their marriage) was only due to their unborn child.

"I don't want to jinx anything but it's going pretty well between us. You could have bought me for a penny when I realized James was the guy that took Halston's spot at his old job."

"Don't sweat that. I promise you. He was fine. His beef wasn't ever much with James anyway. It was with his shady ass ex-boss, Bosniac. I'm happy for you."

"Ooh, good. I'm glad I didn't cause any smoke there. That was the last thing I wanted to do. Hey, do you think Devin acted a little strangely at that party?" Melina asked.

"Mmm, not that I could see. What exactly do you mean?" Kelly inquired cautiously.

"I mean, you know that thing I told you about. I hope he's being faithful. Lynelle seems so sweet. He just seemed a bit on edge. You know him much better than I do, but he just seemed off that night."

"You may be on to something. Hell, who knows? You've always had good intuition. I didn't notice it, but you might be right."

"Yeah, just a thought. Well, I hear that garage door opening so I know what that means. Go ahead and get in there to Halston. Have a great night, chica. I'll talk to you tomorrow."

"Alright then, lady. Sounds like a plan. You have a great night too."

Kelly gathered her purse, her laptop bag, and the takeout before she got out of the car. Halston's car was in the garage, so she knew he was home. Although she was glad he was back at home, every day felt like tipping on pins and needles.

"Hello, babe. It's me," Kelly said, as she walked through the door slowly.

The lights were dim in the living room and it was eerily quiet. She placed the food on the dining room table and placed her bag and purse on the couch. Kelly peered around the corner and saw that the guest bedroom door was closed, with the light on. She figured Halston must have been working with a client.

A few minutes later he surfaced from the room. She was right.

"Oh, hey. Sorry I missed you. I didn't even hear you come in. I was just on the line with a client. I looked up some jobs earlier too, but no luck yet."

He kissed her on the forehead; not on the lips as she longed. Although he had been visibly frustrated lately with getting back into the workforce (since his stream of consulting opportunities had slowed down), she couldn't help but sense that part of the lack of his affection was a direct result of her uncovered indiscretions.

"Don't worry, baby. It will come soon. Everything happens for a reason. That just means there is something better around the corner."

"Thank you, baby. Mmmm, what a minute. I know that scent. Well, both scents. Your Chanel perfume and the food."

"Well, I must say I do love a man with a good appetite and great taste," she smiled.

She loved his taste and she made it a point to wear the shoes and perfume he bought for her over the last couple of years, every chance she got.

"Thank you, babe. You beat me to the punch. If my call hadn't run so long, I was planning to get dinner for us."

"In that case, I'm glad your call ran long. How was your call?"

"Well, that one was promising at least. It will be great for the books next month if they sign on. I'm walking that fine line of follow-up and not pissing them off," he laughed.

"I'd say you're walking that line quite well. If you don't mind, I'm going to get out of these clothes and throw on some sweats before we eat," Kelly said, as she kissed him on the cheek.

"Ok, I'll get the food on the table and pour some drinks for us in the meantime," Halston replied, as Kelly sauntered lazily into the bedroom.

Kelly removed her work clothes and hung them up on the back of the bedroom door before changing into her t-shirt and sweatpants.

She entered the restroom and splashed a handful of cold water on her face.

Then, she stared.

She looked at herself in the mirror and didn't recognize the woman she had become. A part of her felt unwanted when Halston just let her walk into the bedroom to change clothes. There was a time when he would have been all over her and she wouldn't have even been able to step foot into the bedroom, because they would have made love right there on the couch.

Those days, as she had once known them, were gone and may never return. It was all her fault.

"Babe, the food's getting cold. You still coming?"

"Oh. Yes, sorry babe. Here I come."

She hurried into the living room.

Halston greeted her with a warm, genuine smile.

Kelly hadn't seen him look at her with such adoration in a while.

"You're glowing," he said, in a matter-of-fact tone.

"Ah, um, thank you. I don't feel it, but I will take your word for it," she responded.

"You're welcome. I love you. Now, have a seat so I can share a meal with my favorite lady," he said.

Favorite?

Kelly found herself questioning everything in her marriage after her unfaithfulness was revealed.

"Alright, if you say so," she blushed, as not to let him on to her inner thoughts.

"Thanks again, babe. This is really hitting the spot. I was so hungry. So, tell me about your day," Halston exclaimed.

"Oh, it wasn't anything spectacular. I finished a quarterly business review with one of the most demanding clients in my portfolio. I'd say that alone made it a good day. Other than that, just ate lunch with Melina and listened to all of her wild tales."

"Nice, I know you knocked the meeting out of the park. I don't blame you. I'd be glad to have that done and over with too," Halston agreed.

Kelly could see there was a look of disdain resting just beneath his surface expressions. He seemed troubled and uneasy. She battled in her head whether she should pry into his thoughts.

What the hell? Things are already awkward anyway.

"Thank you, babe. I don't mean to spoil this nice vibe we're having right now but is anything on your mind that you want to talk about?"

"Oh, nothing major. Just a lot of thoughts have been running through my head. That's all."

"Ok, well do you want to talk about the minor things that are on your mind? I know I'm not perfect, but I do want us to stay connected if that doesn't sound too selfish."

"I….I don't really know how to say this. Kelly, what are we going to do if the baby is Devin's and not mine?"

Push! Push! Come on, you've got this. Push for us one more time. That's it. Yes," the doctor instructed Kelly.

Her pelvic area felt like it was on fire and she panted for every breath. Tears streamed down her face as she looked at Halston for comfort. She gripped has hand harder with each push. Kelly knew that although he was there for her the entire time, their lives were changed forever.

"You've got this. He's almost here, baby. Our boy is on the way," Halston exclaimed.

Hearing Halston say that one simple word, "our", felt like a warm honey salve for her labor pains.

"You're right. OK. OK. I'm trying," she whispered as she continued to push as the doctor instructed.

"Mrs. Pointe. Wait. Please. Stop pushing for just a moment. His umbilical cord is wrapped around his neck. If you keep pushing, he won't be able to breathe," the doctor stated.

Halston felt a lump form at the back of his throat.

He didn't want to make Kelly nervous, so he kept a straight face; at least as best as he could.

Kelly looked up to the ceiling and prayed to God.

Please don't let this be my punishment. I can't lose my baby.

"Just a few more turns. We have to turn the baby around inside.

This may feel uncomfortable, but it won't last long. You're almost there," the doctor assured her.

The doctor had a soothing tone that was perfect for the current situation. She almost lessened the severity of the moment with her gentle words. Suddenly, everything was okay.

"Alright, Mrs. Pointe. Now, we need you to push again. He's fine now. We just need a few more strong pushes and your baby will be here before you know it," she assured Kelly.

Kelly cautiously resumed pushing and whispered a "thank you" to God. She lost track of time but she had to be in labor for over ten hours at this point. Her head felt light and her mouth was as dry as cotton. Nonetheless, she kept pushing.

"I think you two have yourselves a happy baby boy," the doctor said.

Finally, it was all over. Their baby boy had arrived.

Matthew was the name Halston and Kelly agreed upon. Way before she got pregnant, they both toyed with the idea of naming him Halston Jr., but that hadn't held up well with the most recent circumstances.

"Ah, there he is. He's so beautiful. I love you," Kelly turned to look at Halston as she waited to hold their new baby boy.

"I love you too," Halston replied as he stroked Kelly's forehead.

It was a beautiful experience being able to witness her give birth to their child, or at least give birth to who he hoped was their child. Perhaps it made him hopelessly in love, but he desperately hoped that Matthew was truly his son. He looked at his son's face as the doctor cleaned him up and wrapped him in a blanket to pass him to Kelly.

He saw a resemblance to himself in Matthew's eye area. Then again, he knew it was too early to really be able to tell his full features. The complexion almost matched his, but he knew that would change over time as well. Halston hated this euphoric and paranoid mix of feelings about the birth of his son. The situation was something he never thought he would have to endure.

"Shhh, Momma is here. Yes, she is. Daddy is here too. Can you see us?" Kelly cooed with a childlike tone.

"Hey there, son. Yes, your Daddy is here. We love you," Halston said.

Matthew looked up and grinned as Kelly and Halston rubbed him.

"You see that? Looks like he's going to be a happy baby." Kelly smiled.

"I think so too. Yes, I thought it was just me but I did see him smile too. Ooh, let me get a picture of you holding him," Halston said.

"Ok, well this one will just be for our private archive. I'm sure I look a mess," she cautioned.

"Nope. You look as beautiful as ever. I won't post it though. This one will stay with us. Can you give Daddy another smile, Matthew?" Halston asked.

Halston took a few snapshots of Matthew and Kelly together. No matter what the outcome was in the future, Halston decided he would focus on one thought: living in the moment.

•

Sharon checked her watch to see how much time she had left before Halston arrived. Only two minutes, if he arrived as promptly as he usually did.

Her phone buzzed on her desk.

She glanced down to see an incoming text from Halston.

Hi Sharon, I'm stuck behind a wreck on the freeway. I'll be just a few minutes late.

Thank God. She was grateful for the extra time to go to the ladies' room before their session.

No worries. Thanks for letting me know, Halston. I'll see you soon!

Sharon went to the restroom and grabbed a Nutri-Grain bar. She was hungry and her schedule was off, due to back-to-back sessions. The snack would sustain her at least until the end of Halston's session.

Two knocks ensued on the front side of her door, just as she took her last bite of the Nutri-Grain bar.

"Yes, come in," she replied.

She looked down at her watch: 4:06pm. Even with the delay, Halston was still relatively on time.

"Hi Sharon, I apologize for my tardiness. You never can predict these roads after 3:00pm on a weekday. How are you?"

"Look, no worries. Trust me, I totally understand. I'm doing well and you? You look mighty dapper today. What's the special occasion?"

Sharon noticed that Halston was a stylish dresser since their first session. However, he was dressed particularly well today. His navy-blue pants were a shade off from a typical business casual color, but in a good way. His shirt was a lilac, stiff-collar underneath with a fuchsia tie. He topped off the outfit with a pair of brown leather boots with a belt of the same shade of brown.

"Ah, thank you. I just met an old friend at an art gallery. Nothing major. I've never come here from that location before, so I guess that and the wreck tripped me up a bit," he admitted.

"I see. Well, it's been a while since our last session. I know we both have been busy people lately. I do have an extra 30 minutes available today if you would like to extend our session to get back on a regular cadence, free of charge. No pressure."

"Thank you, Sharon. I may take you up on that today. I appreciate the offer."

"Sounds good. Here's a bottle of water for you. Let's get started then, shall we?"

"Yeah, it almost feels like the first time again. I guess it's been a little strange getting out of the routine."

"That is totally understandable. This isn't a race, but more so a long walk. Let's start by picking up where you left off last. We talked about Kelly's pregnancy and her finally giving birth to the baby. How were things for you after the new addition to the family?" she asked.

Halston exhaled and paused before he answered. He felt somewhat ashamed and less of a man recounting certain parts of his story. Nonetheless, he knew this was for his greater good.

"It was a fucking nightmare if I'm honest," he said dryly.

•

"Hey, look who's here. The new dad! Congratulations again man. I'm so happy for you and Kelly," Omar exclaimed.

Halston had just walked into the bar to meet Omar and Devin. Although he had talked to Omar a few times during the latter part of Kelly's pregnancy, their interaction was limited. Devin was a different story. Today was the first day Halston had seen him since last year's Halloween party.

Devin did call Halston and admitted that he slept with Kelly, a bitch move as far as Halston was concerned. He expected an in-person apology instead. Their interaction today would be unpredictable, to say the least.

"Thank you, man. It's been amazing. Nobody warned me about my sleep pattern getting knocked around like this though. Hey Devin," Halston replied, as he barely even looked at his old friend.

"Hey man. Yes, congratulations are in order. Can't wait to meet the little guy," Devin added.

"I'm sure you can't," Halston replied.

A cold chill hovered over the table as all the men took a sip of their drink. Omar looked at both of his friends, dumbfounded by the awkward exchange he just witnessed.

"Um, I thought we were all here to have a good time. What's going on with you two?" Omar inquired.

"Ha, should you tell him or me?" Halston laughed.

"Man, please let's not do this here," Devin pleaded.

"Do what? Tell Omar how you fucked my wife? Is that what we're not doing here?" he asked.

"Wait. What? Please tell me that isn't true," Omar looked at Devin.

Omar was the self-proclaimed whore of the group. Nonetheless, Halston doubted that he would have stooped so low as to sleep with Kelly.

"It was a mistake. I'm not proud of it. I apologized Halston, but I know we haven't talked in person yet. So, I will say it again here,

'I'm sorry'," Devin replied, in an agitated tone.

"Well, this is going smoothly. I can't believe this shit," Omar muttered sarcastically.

"You're sorry. Well, thank you for the fucking apology," Halston laughed.

"Man, I'm already catching enough heat at home from Lynelle. She threw me out twice already. I just got back in the house a couple of weeks ago," Devin ranted.

Halston gave Devin a long, piercing stare that burned smoking holes straight through him.

Devin avoided looking his former friend in the eyes.

Omar looked at both men with a heightened sense of anxiety. He didn't know what to expect next.

"So, let's try to break the ice here. Obviously, this is not an ideal situation. Let's just try to….," Omar ranted.

He couldn't even finish his sentence before Halston leaped from his seat and landed a solid, forceful punch to Devin's face.

Devin flipped backward out of his chair as a result of the brute force. He couldn't even get up from the ground before Halston landed another punch to his jaw on the opposite side.

"How about that? Save your weak-ass apology. I'm out of this motherfucker. Move out the way," Halston said, as he pushed past Omar.

Omar quickly stepped to the side. He didn't want to be the next casualty of the night. Everyone around their table gasped loudly. Several of the workers came to Devin's aid.

"This can't be real. We're too old for this high school bullshit. Get your ass up," Omar grunted, as he extended his hand to pull his friend up from the ground.

"Did you not just see that?" Devin asked as he held his rapidly swelling jaw.

"Hell yeah, I saw it. That's why I said what I said," Omar rebutted.

"He hit me, unprompted. You know that was uncalled for," Devin ranted.

"Just stop. Let's get out of here before you embarrass us more than you already have. You fucked Halston's wife. I'd say you got off pretty easy if all you got is a couple of cold decks to the face," Omar replied.

Devin looked at his friend and sighed. They walked through the double doors of the bar and towards the parking lot where their cars were parked.

"You gotta be kidding me," Devin said as they turned the corner.

He had recently purchased a new black-on-black Range Rover, a vehicle he had been ranting about to Halston and Omar for a few months prior.

The back window was shattered by one of the stones along the side of the building.

alston pulled into the driveway at home and sat in the garage for a few minutes. He needed to release the energy from seeing Devin before he welcomed his wife and his newborn baby. Something still didn't feel right. He decided the night couldn't possibly get any worse. Halston needed to tell her that he wanted a paternity test.

He unlocked the door and walked through the kitchen. He felt a push back against the door before Kelly peered around the door. She placed her finger over her mouth as he walked through the door quietly.

"Is he sleeping?" Halston whispered.

"Yeah, I just put him down about ten minutes ago," Kelly smiled and stood on her tip toes to kiss Halston.

She felt him pull back a tad bit. Her instinct instantly told her something was wrong. Then again, she didn't expect the night to go totally smoothly since he met up with Devin and Omar.

"Oh, yeah we don't want to wake up little man. I'll take over when he wakes up," he offered.

"Thank you, baby. I'll take you up on that. You had the right idea when you said I should take my bath before you left. I'm so glad I did. How was it tonight?"

"It was ok. No, it was euphoric. It felt really good."

"Really? Ok, what made it so euphoric? I'm all ears."

She had no idea what he was about to reveal to her. Kelly held her breath in anticipation of Halston's answer.

"I decked the shit out of his ass, tonight. It felt good too. I dare his ass to show up here too. He's such a coward."

His voice elevated as Kelly peeped around the corner to make sure Matthew was still sleeping soundly.

"What? I mean, I get that it was justified but did he hit you first?"

"No, I hit him first. He kept talking shit and I socked him. Please don't tell me after all of this, you're taking his side?" Halston asked with a furrowed brow.

"Well, what can I say? He deserved it. I'm so sorry I got us into this mess. I hope you can find it in your heart to forgive me one day. I know I have a lot to prove, but I'm changing. I promise."

"I forgive you, baby. I just..." his voice trailed.

"What? Whatever it is, I'll do it. I can't lose you."

"I need a paternity test. We've talked about it, but to really move on from this, I need it."

"Ok, we'll make it happen. I just don't want you to have any reason to mistrust me again."

"Thank you."

"Of course, it's the least I can do. Matthew and I need you. You and only you."

"I love that little man in there. I love you too."

"We love you too. I'll check first thing in the morning and schedule an appointment."

•

Meanwhile, Devin pulled into the driveway at home. The wind from the open-air through his back window whipped against his neck the whole way. The breeze was a nice distraction from the sucker punch Halston delivered to him.

Omar called him twice after they left the bar, but he didn't answer. He didn't want to hear any judgments from his friend. Especially since Omar was revered as the least responsible of the group. The tables had drastically turned.

Devin pulled into the garage and turned off the ignition. He sat in the car for a moment and decided to open the door. There was no sense in him stalling. He was already catching hell with Lynelle for his unfaithfulness. Now, this would only up the ante. He was sure that a piece of her would be glad that Halston punched him.

He walked inside the house and stopped inside the guest bathroom to get a good look at his face. His light-brown toasted skin was different shades of brown, blue, and a slight purple at the point of impact. There was no way he could hide the scar.

"Hmph," he muttered aloud to himself.

Devin was somewhat proud of Halston for standing up for himself like that. Halston was always so cool, calm, and collected. He rarely lost his temper, but when he did it was never pretty. Devin just didn't feel too good being on the receiving end of his friend's wrath. He understood. If it were him, he probably would have done the same to Halston or even worse than that.

He could hear Lynelle moving around in the living room, but she didn't come to check on him. They were merely roommates since she found out about him cheating.

"Hey, is that you in there?"

Her tone was direct and nonchalant. Her question sounded like more of a check that there wasn't an intruder inside the house, rather than excitement that Devin was home.

"Hey, yeah it's me."

Lynelle must have sensed something was off, even more than their new normal. She entered the guest bathroom before he could flip off the light switch and caught a glimpse of his jaw.

"Oh, wow. Um, what happened to your face?"

"I met up with Halston and Omar at a bar. Let's just say Halston wasn't too happy to see me," he muttered.

"Hmph. Rightfully so. Can you blame him? Look, I know this is the worst timing for this, but I can't keep pretending like I'm okay with this," she rebutted.

Lynelle handed Devin a manilla envelope.

He knew exactly what it was without even opening it.

"Whoa, I'm a changed man, Lynelle. I know I don't deserve another chance, but I'm not the same guy. I promise. No more lies."

Devin flashed her that million-dollar smile that she used to be unable to resist. He knew she was really done.

"I get it and the crazy thing is, I actually believe you. That probably makes me stupid. I understand that you're a changed man, but I'm also a changed woman. I don't want to always wonder "what if?" and "why?" I can't do that to myself. I love you, Devin. I'm sorry, but this is the end of us," she replied.

She gently placed her hand on his shoulder and helped him wipe some of the blood that he missed from the side of his face.

Halston sighed as he hovered over the crib and glanced down at his son. He studied Matthew's breathing and facial features as he slept, obliviously unaware of the controversy surrounding his existence. He replayed his doctor's words in his head about his extremely low chances of being able to father a child.

Was this a miracle?

Was he being naive?

Did he hopelessly believe that he and Kelly would last after she carelessly revealed her indiscretion?

All those thoughts ran through his mind. Each one competed for validity, as he explored its reality.

"Hey little man. Your Daddy loves you," he whispered.

Halston decided he would just relish in the moment of being a father for now.

Kelly was able to schedule a paternity test for Thursday of that week.

Now, he just had to wait.

Plus, he had to find a steadier income. If he and Kelly split up, he would have to live off one income, which was barely non-existent now. He dipped into the pot from his previous consulting opportunities, but even that was low. If he stayed with Kelly, and Matthew was really his child, he would still need a better job to take care of his family.

"What are we going to do, little man?" he muttered rhetorically.

Halston quickly walked into the living room to grab his phone. 2:20 pm. At least he served as a free babysitter while work was slow.

He searched through his contacts for Julia's phone number. Although he didn't believe it was the best thing to do, he had to figure something out. He wasn't about to just sit on his ass.

Hey Julia. Hope all is well. This is Halston. I know this is a strange request, but do you know if any other departments in the company are hiring?

Halston waited to get a response from her. He put his phone on vibrate and placed it in his pocket before he stepped back into the room to check on Matthew.

As soon as he walked into the room, his phone vibrated. He took it out of his pocket.

Great.

It was just a loyalty message from Banana Republic. He dismissed the message and place his phone back in his pocket.

His phone buzzed once more.

Halston! What a nice surprise. We should have lunch soon, so I can catch you up. Long story short, I'm not there anymore. I'm also in the market for a new job.

He let out a sigh of disappointment before he responded. Damn, she couldn't even help him out. Now, he really felt like he made a mistake reaching out to her, but he proceeded to text her back.

Ah ok then, I totally understand. Sounds good about the lunch too. I think I can make Wednesday work, if that's cool. I'll let you know by tomorrow morning.

Julia responded to him immediately.

Alright, sounds like a plan. Have a good one. Talk soon.

Now, he had to make an excuse to have someone watch Matthew. Kelly's parents were obsessed with their new grandson. He was sure they would be elated to watch him for a little while.

He decided he would just tell Kelly that he had an interview on

Wednesday. It was a little white lie, but she lied about far worse than a lunch meeting.

He looked back at his phone and saw he had a missed call from Omar. He checked his voicemail and listened to the message.

Hey man. Just seeing how you're doing since the other night. Also, I heard about an opportunity you might be interested in for work. Give me a ring when you can.

Halston deleted the message after he listened. He could tell that his friend was stuck between a rock and a hard place. Omar was equally close to Halston and Devin. However, he was a strong proponent for standing up for what was right. For that reason, he seemed like he sided more favorably towards Halston's side.

He stepped outside of the room where Matthew slept and called Omar back. He stood close enough where he could keep an eye on his son's movements.

"Hello? Hey man. What's going on?" Omar said when he answered the phone.

"Thanks for checking on me. I'm ok, just trying to process all this craziness right now. I appreciate the lookout on the job front too," Halston replied.

"No doubt. Of course, I know you're fine after the other night. Hell, you walked away without even a scratch. The broken window might have been a bit extreme. I can't say he was undeserving of it though. You don't play those kinds of games, especially with a friend. We're like brothers, man. We gotta move past this."

"Maybe I should, but I don't regret any of it. As a matter of fact, that bastard got away easy compared to all the things I've thought about doing to him. So, what's up with this job? Things are getting tight around here. My consulting has dropped off lately too."

He quickly changed the subject to the more pressing issue at hand. Although he knew Omar had a point, he wasn't in the mood to hear about his moral majority.

"I'm sorry to hear that. This might be your lucky day. That new rival company that's the competitor for the place you just left is hiring for your exact role. Melina told me about it last night."

"Okay, uh a startup. That can be brutal but oh well, I need the money. I'll look into that. Oh, and don't just slide in Melina like that. Sounds like you two are kicking it pretty strong."

He looked down at Matthew and saw him squirm slightly. It was after 4:00 pm now. He probably should wake him up soon so they could have a better chance of sleeping soundly through the night.

"Yeah, I guess you can say that. It's nothing serious yet but I guess you can say we're exclusively dating."

"Exclusively? Man, you may as well say you're married. I don't think I've ever heard you use that word in reference to a woman," Halston laughed.

Matthew squirmed harder and began to cry.

"Uh oh, sounds like little man is waking up. I don't want to hold you, man. I'll keep you posted about any news about other jobs. Have you heard about that crazy pandemic that's making its way here from Australia?".

"Yeah, let me put you on speaker for a minute while I pick him up. 'Daddy's here, little man. Yeah, yeah, yeah.' Um, I heard about that pandemic, but I didn't know it hit the U.S.."

Halston's attention was now split between tending to his son and juggling listening to his friend.

"Yeah, I just saw it on the news this morning. It hit New Hampshire this week. I know that's far from us but be careful out there. This stuff is hitting much closer to home."

"Wow, that's pretty scary. I didn't realize it was heading here that quickly. Thanks for the heads up. Let me get Matthew settled, but I can call you back in a bit."

"Oh yeah, for sure. Handle the nephew, man. I'll get that link for the job and send it to you. The company is called Fugen, if you want to look them up in the meantime."

"Awesome. Thanks, man. I appreciate you. I'll talk to you later."

Halston rocked Matthew in his arms as he walked towards the kitchen to prepare dinner for Kelly before she arrived. They both talked about eating less meat, so he decided to prepare eggplant parmesan with marinara and pasta. There was also some squash and zucchini in the refrigerator. He decided to dice those up and save them to sauté once the eggplant was almost done.

"Hey there, little man. Are you going to stop fussing for Daddy? Yeah, I've got you. Soon, you'll be able to eat food like this too. Are you ready for that?" he cooed in a childlike voice.

Halston waited until Matthew was calm and then gently placed him inside his baby chair while he started to prepare the food. He decided to turn on the news while he cooked. The TV served as a dual purpose for Halston to have some background noise while he cooked and to keep Matthew awake.

"Coming up at 5:00, New Hampshire is the first U.S. state hit with what medical experts say could be a widespread, deadly virus," the news anchor reported.

"Guess Omar was right," Halston mumbled to himself.

Although the thought of a pandemic sounded frightening, Halston felt somewhat secure that they lived in Texas, far away from where the outbreak was.

Matthew had calmed down for the moment, as he peered at Halston cutting the eggplant for dinner.

Halston loved Matthew's inquisitive, yearning gaze. Truth be told, he was glad that he didn't throw a fit when he woke up. Halston preheated the oven while he sliced the eggplant in half and prepared the egg wash for the batter.

4:42 pm.

He seasoned the batter for the eggplant and placed it on a wide, empty plate. Then, he diced the squash and zucchini, a few red onions, bell peppers, and a few banana peppers for spice. He halfway listened to the news as he waited for the oven to preheat.

"Yes, Jim, something tells me the entire country better sit up and take notice. My heart goes out to the people who have already been affected by this monstrous virus. I'm Kiely Cole, reporting live," she said.

Halston shook his head in disbelief as he continued to prepare the food.

He heard the garage door open as soon as he finished breading the eggplant.

"Uh oh, do you know who that is? That's your mom coming in. I bet you're happy to see her," Halston said, as he played with Matthew in the chair.

Halston unlocked the door from the kitchen to make sure she was able to easily get inside.

"Oh, hey babe. Thank you for getting the door for me. How are my two favorite men?"

"Better now. How was your day?"

"Ah, oh my God. Is that eggplant? That looks so good. Ooh, we haven't had that in forever and it's healthy too. The best of both worlds," she replied as she picked up Matthew from his booster chair.

"Yeah, the little man and I decided we would try something different tonight. Isn't that right?" Halston asked as if he was waiting for Matthew to reply.

He kissed Kelly on her cheek, in between completing the finishing touches on the meal.

"It sure is. Your daddy is an excellent cook too, so I'm sure you've been taking some good notes, cutie pie," Kelly added.

She kissed Matthew's plump cheeks as he cooed softly.

"I'm glad your mom thinks so."

"I sure do. How was your day?" she asked.

"It was pretty good. The consulting has still been a bit slow, but I have a lunch meeting tomorrow with one of my old coworkers. He recently left the company and said a new opportunity came up. But I'm not sure if I can make it yet. I know we would need someone to watch Matthew. Do you think your parents would be able to watch him?"

"Look at you, big time. Congratulations. That is awesome. I'll do you one better. I just got off the phone with my mom and she and my dad have been itching to keep him. I told her I'd let her know once I talked to you. She can come pick him up tonight."

"Oh, really? Ok, that will work. Omar told me about a job that he's supposed to send me some info on too. Enough about me.

How was your day?"

"Look at you. Okay, I see you have some options lined up. I'm so proud of you baby. My day was a breeze for a change. I'll take it."

"Thank you, baby. Oh, the food should be done in about 20 minutes. We'll have enough for your parents if they want some food too."

"Hmmm…." Kelly sighed as she removed her navy-blue blazer and draped it over the back of the kitchen chair.

"What's wrong? We can save the food for ourselves if you think that's a better idea."

"No, it's not that at all. Thank you. I'm sure they would love to have some of the dinner. I'm just even more grateful for you more and more each day."

ulia ambled towards the quaint booth that the waitress chose for her and Halston. The placement couldn't have been more ironic. The lighting seemed to be the dimmest in the corner where he waited for her to arrive.

She wore a thin khaki jacket that rested strategically upon the curves of her gracious hips. A purple cashmere, low-plunging blouse that made her breasts sit up like two perfectly round grapefruits, waiting to be devoured. Her form-fitting jeans and brown, knee-high boots completed the outfit perfectly. She seemed to glide across the floor as she advanced towards him.

"Well, hello there, stranger. Long time no see. How are you doing?" she asked with outstretched arms before she took her seat.

"It has been quite a while, hasn't it? I know you like sweet tea, so I ordered you one. This was a great choice. I've been in the mood for sushi for a while. I've heard great things about this spot."

"Yes, far too long and thank you for the tea. You remembered. I'm impressed," she smiled, as she removed her coat before taking a seat.

"I did. So, what's new with you? Did you finally get tired of the old ball and chain and send them your regards?"

"Not exactly. Let's just say they pushed me out before I could really make my own decision," she smirked.

The waitress interrupted before Halston asked what happened.

"Hello, welcome to Sushi Paradise. My name is Tish and I'll be taking care of you. We are thrilled to have you today. May I interest you in our mystery roll of the week?"

The waitress had a short, pixie-style haircut, with minimal make-up and a fresh, youthful face. She couldn't have been a day over 22 years old, with a petite, yet curvy frame.

"I can't speak for her, but I think I'll try something else. Thank you."

"I'm a sucker for a good bento box, so I'll likely have one of those instead. Thank you for letting us know," Julia added.

"I must say, we do have the best bento box in town if you ask me. I can give you a few moments to look over the menu for your entrees. Would you like any appetizers in the meantime?"

"Oooh, yes. Halston, I remember you like edamame. Can we have that and the potstickers?" Julia requested, in a chipper tone.

"Sure, I will get that in for you and top of your drinks as well," Tish replied, as she walked away.

"So, where were we? You were just about to tell me what happened with the old job. I'm impressed that you remember I like edamame too," he smiled.

Julia liked Halston's less guarded demeanor, versus their prior in-office interactions. Perhaps he was just more comfortable outside of the workplace. Either way, she enjoyed the new, laid-back side of him.

"Yes, of course, I remembered. Oh, the job. Yes, let's just say it was a textbook #MeToo situation," she sighed.

"Wait. Are you saying that Bosniac touched you inappropriately?"

"Oh, you wouldn't see me here in person if that happened. I'd be behind bars. He didn't do that, but he called me into his office one day for an impromptu "one-on-one". He spewed bullshit about me asserting myself more and stepping into my talent as an employee at the company. He said that if I was willing to go outside of my comfort zone, I could really be something special."

"What the hell? He really has some nerve. I always knew he was a damned pervert."

"You can say that again. That's not all. Right after he told me how great I could be, he opened his legs wide in his chair and slipped his hand over his crotch. I didn't say a word and I stormed out of his office."

"He wasn't even your manager. Did you report it?"

"Martin was always a wimp. Bosniac called me into his office three days after I filed the complaint. Martin was there too. He made up some foolishness about how the company was going in another direction and thought it would be best for us to part ways. So, I'm taking legal action against the whole company. Turns out the same thing happened to several other women that worked there too.

"Wow, I'm so sorry Julia. That's ridiculous. I didn't realize all of that happened."

"Yep, so that's where I am in my life right now. Things are going well, considering that. I can't complain. Just taking it one day at a time," she sighed.

Tish returned to their table again before Halston could respond.

"Alright, here are your appetizers and I'll top off your drinks. Do we need a few more minutes to decide on the entrees?" she asked.

"I think we're ready now," Julia answered.

"Fantastic. What can I get for you?" Tish asked.

"I'll have the teriyaki chicken bento box. I'd like to substitute the shrimp for double volcano rolls if that's ok," Julia requested.

"Yes, we can certainly do that for you. How about for you, sir?"

"I'll have one Las Vegas roll, miso soup and a side salad."

"Perfect. Sounds good. I'll get these orders in and your food will be out shortly. I'll take these plates out of your way too."

"Well, sounds like you really dodged a bullet. I hope everything goes well with the lawsuit. God knows someone needs to take that jerk down. So, what are you doing for work now?" Halston ranted, after Tish left the table.

"Yeah, I hope so too. It may take a while to get everything settled. In the meantime, I have to make my own moves. I am.....

diversifying my portfolio with some special investors for a new startup," she sounded off, almost as if she read from a script.

"Hmmm….ok. What company? That sounds interesting, but I must say I'm not exactly sure what it means."

"It's a long story. I don't know if you really want me to get into it. Let's just say it's an O.P.P. type of situation if you catch my drift," she smirked.

"Wait. I…..um, are you saying that your new gig is a scheme that's ripping people off?"

"Tell the whole restaurant, why don't you? I wouldn't exactly say that, but it pays the bills and no one is hurt in the end. It's safe," she promised.

"Hey, to each his, or in your case, her own. I'm not knocking it," he laughed.

"I'm telling you. You may be calling me soon to find out more about it. This 9 to 5 life is not for me."

"I will definitely keep you posted. I may have to join you in the scheme. This job search definitely isn't yielding any positive results for me either."

"So, how is married life? Your wife? How is she doing?" Julia asked with a slight smirk.

"She's doing well, still healthy. We just had a son, so getting adjusted to living with the little man."

Halston put on his best poker face, as not to reveal the actual issues going on at home.

"What? You should have led off with that great news, silly. That is awesome. You're a lucky guy. Congratulations," she replied, with warm, genuine enthusiasm.

"Thank you. I'd like to think so too. That's why I really need to get this job situation straightened out."

Halston battled the thought of whether he should share his real situation at home with Julia. He had self-control and he knew he wouldn't try anything inappropriate. Then again, Kelly did cheat on him. She was unfaithful and with his best friend, of all people.

Julia seemed to sense he was hiding something, even without

him spilling all the gritty details. She smiled as she looked deeply into his eyes, as if to search for the real answers to some of her questions.

"I understand that. With more blessings come more responsibilities. So, if the food is bad, it's on you since you picked the place. I will say, the potstickers were a winner," she laughed.

"Oh okay, I didn't know I was on a food trial," he grinned.

They laughed and caught each other up on other details of their lives before the food arrived. Everything was beautifully plated and the food tasted amazing.

Tish came back to check on them midway through their lunch. Her attentiveness was impressive for someone who appeared to be so young. She handled her waitress duties with the ease of a seasoned veteran.

"How does the food taste? I hope you're enjoying your meals. Also, here is another refill for your drinks," she said.

"Oh, this is wonderful. These volcano rolls are amazing and the chicken is seasoned perfectly. We'll be back. I told him that he would have some explaining to do if I didn't enjoy it," Julia giggled.

"Well, I'm glad we passed the test and we would love to have you back. I forgot to ask if either of you has ever dined with us," she glanced towards Halston.

Her eyes quickly moved to his wedding finger and back to Julia, who obviously didn't have a wedding ring on her finger. She fixed her gaze and looked Halston squarely in his eyes again.

"It's actually my first time dining here too. I've just heard great things. I can see why. The food was great," he said.

"Ah, nice. That's what we love to hear. No rush, but I will prepare your check and bring it out shortly. Will it be separate or together?"

"Together," Julia exclaimed, before Halston could utter a word.

"I'll give you the money for it. You didn't have to do that. I called you."

"I know, but it has been my pleasure. Consider it a late baby shower gift for the baby. We'll have to do this again sometime. This was wonderful."

"Yes, I agree. Let's do that. It was really nice to see you too and thank you."

As she leaned forward to grab her drink, the upper curvature of her breasts seemed to rise higher from the top of her blouse.

Halston fought the urge of another rising inside of his pants.

CHAPTER 25

So, how did you feel when you found out that Matthew wasn't your child?" Sharon asked, almost rhetorically.

How can you measure that type of pain? She thought. Nevertheless, she had to do her job and ask the hard questions to lead to Halston's healing.

"How do you think it felt?" he asked sarcastically.

"I didn't mean any disrespect or harm. I just want to get to the root of your feelings. We can't heal what we won't reveal. We can come back to that later if you prefer," Sharon suggested.

"I'm sorry, I didn't mean that you were being insensitive. I'm truly curious. How do you think it felt?" he inquired.

"I can imagine it was quite devastating, heart wrenching, unreal. I'll be honest. I've been through my share of hardships in life, but I can't exactly tell you how that feels. I've never been through it. I can only speculate," she sighed.

"The best way I can describe it is like sudden, shooting pains but to your soul and not your body. It feels like somebody is stabbing you countless times in your spirit, taking a piece of you with each jab. Honestly, I still haven't quite recovered from it," he admitted.

"If you feel comfortable, do you recall exactly how she told you or how you found out? Sometimes how we receive information has an even greater impact than the information itself," she said.

"Hmph. Looking back, that's so true. We did one of those rapid tests to get the results back quicker. She got the call first and she told me when she got home that day after work. I was there the whole day, taking care of Matthew. I remember him being so fussy that day. He was typically a really calm baby, but it was almost as if he knew something wasn't right," Halston recalled, as his voice cracked.

"Remember, only share what you are comfortable to share right now," she assured him.

"Thank you. This is…..a lot. I haven't talked about it in this level of detail with anyone. Um, but she came home and I already knew the answer as soon as she walked in. I could see it written all over her face. I guess when you've been with someone as long as we were together, you anticipate their actions."

"Hopefully she didn't try to prolong telling you."

"Not exactly, but I get the feeling she probably did know earlier that day and just didn't mention it until she came home. I'm a stickler for people telling me certain things to my face instead of over the phone. She knew that couldn't have been a phone call on the way home type of situation. That's when she said it. "I'm so sorry," he recanted.

"Oh, my goodness. So you had to console her during one of your lowest moments?" she asked.

"Yes, she almost passed out. Her knees buckled and she started wailing. I grabbed her and hugged her. Matthew was asleep when she first got home but he started screaming almost as soon as she said it. That's when she uh, dug the knife a little deeper and said it would be best if we get a divorce. She didn't think we would be able to recover from our truth," he added.

"What did you think? Do you believe the two of you could have survived her infidelity and raising your best friend's child that you thought was yours?" Sharon asked.

"I thought we could. I mean, I knew the chances were slim to none but I did think there was at least some hope. Apparently, I was the only one who thought it could work. Maybe I was just living in a fantasy, you know?"

"Sounds like you were just trying to hold up your end of the bargain as a husband. People don't always take vows seriously, especially when better turns to worse. That's when the real test comes."

"You know what? If I'm being completely honest, I didn't want her to make the first move towards the divorce. Deep down, I knew it would happen. I felt like since she cheated, I should have been the one to end the marriage. She owed me that much," he sighed.

"Yes, now we're getting somewhere. Resentment is a powerful thing that can really tip us over the edge if we're not careful," she warned.

"Very true. I'm a living witness," he laughed.

"Ok, so you went through the divorce process which is so different for everyone. How did that look for you?" Sharon asked.

"A lot happened during that time. I don't even know where to start, her paintings were a turning point. She's a great artist. I can't take that away from her. I guess you can call it poetic justice," he began.

·

"Ok, I think that's everything. I uh….guess this is it. Maybe we'll see each other around sometime. Halston, I'll always love you. I truly regret my mistakes and how this all turned out."

Kelly reached out to embrace Halston.

Part of him didn't even want to touch her. Another part of him wanted to capture her and never let her go; tell her they would find some way to work out everything.

"I'll always love you too, Kelly," he replied.

A thick moment of silence wedged its way between their bodies as a symbol of the death of their love.

"Mmmm," Kelly exhaled, as she pulled back from Halston.

"Hey, the anniversary painting is still in the garage. I'm not sure what you want to do with it. There's that one and a few others in there too."

"Ah, I'll leave them in your hands. I'm sure you'll find a good home for them."

"Ok, suit yourself.".

"Melina just texted me. I think she's going to pull up and get me in a second. I'll just wait outside," Kelly replied.

"Alright. Well, I guess I will see you around. You take care of yourself. The buyers should be here in a bit. I'll load the paintings in my car and take care of everything here."

"OK… bye, Halston," Kelly said.

"Goodbye, Kelly," Halston replied.

The hollow sound of the click of the door closing signaled a painful reality.

It was really the end.

That was it.

Some separations lead to reconciliation, but Halston and Kelly both knew it was over. Now, he had to move on with his life and pick up the pieces.

Halston paced each of the rooms in the house and grazed his hands over the wall over the walls. He paused in the bathroom, where he found out about Kelly cheating on him with Devin. He replayed the beginning of his friendship with Devin and realized he shouldn't have been so surprised with how everything turned out. He was friends with Omar first and met Devin when he was a transfer student in college. It was one of those associations that brings assimilation types of friendships.

Halston heard a knock at the door that snapped him out of his daydream. It must have been the new buyers for the home.

He grabbed the paintings out of the garage and stacked them by the kitchen door before he let them in. The Bartners were a loving couple with no children. They appeared to be about ten years older than him and Kelly.

"Hello, good morning, Mr. and Mrs. Bartner."

"Good morning. Please, call us Sonya and Isaac. I can't believe it. It's finally closing day. Where is your lovely wife?" Sonya asked.

"Oh, you just missed her. She extends her regards. We are actually in the process of a divorce, so we're parting ways after the sale of the house," Halston revealed.

"We're sorry to hear that. You all seemed like such a nice couple. We know a thing or two about marriage and every day is not easy, but if you can, you make it work. I'm sure you both will decide what's best," Isaac added.

"Yes, love is a complicated thing. We are sorry to hear that," Sonya chimed in.

"Thank you; it's okay. That's life. We are thrilled that you both love the house. We decided to throw in the deep freezer that's in the garage if you would like that. It's practically brand new. We just bought it last year," Halston said.

"Oh, that is fantastic. Thank you so much. We were literally just talking about getting a deep freezer last night. We toyed back and forth with the idea, but it looks like that's settled now," Sonya said.

"Yes, so you both have our contact information. You can feel free to reach out to either one of us for whatever you need or any questions you have. We both feel that we're leaving the house in great hands," Halston replied.

He grabbed the paintings that were stacked behind the kitchen door before he said his final goodbye to the Bartners.

"Oh, wait. Halston, those paintings are beautiful. Who is the artist that designed those?" Sonya inquired.

"Kelly painted these. This one is a portrait of us that she painted and the rest are some paintings she's done over the years," Halston replied.

"Oh, great. I'm sure she probably doesn't want to part with them. Just in case, Isaac and I host a quarterly art gallery and we're always looking for new artists to showcase. Something like this would go for a few hundred dollars easily, probably more," Sonya said, as she studied the paintings.

Halston quickly did the math in his head. That was a quick $2,000 if all the paintings were sold at $500 each. He already received Kelly's blessing on doing whatever he wanted with the paintings. So, he didn't feel like he owed her an explanation. Plus, he didn't expect to get the wedding ring back from her. Although she promised she would give it back to him because of his uncertain financial state, he had yet to receive it. He had to start making moves that worked best for him and not think about Kelly.

"Hmmm, I'm sure she would be honored. Just let me know when and I can be there for the art gallery. I'm not exactly sure how it works, but she left these for me. Ultimately, it will be my decision on what happens with the paintings," he replied.

"Oh, well I'd say that settles it then. Our next show is in two weeks. If you don't mind, we'll just need to take a photo of each of the paintings and then you can bring them on the day of the event. We have room for three this go-round. We'll let you know what the board says on the top three and let you know if that works," Isaac said.

"Sure, that sounds perfect. I'll be there and I'll wait to hear back in the meantime," Halston agreed.

Although it wasn't exactly a nine-to-five, the paintings and the money from the house would at least help tide him over until he had a solid plan and steady stream of income.

What do you mean you're not trying to get alimony?" Omar asked.

"It's just not me, man. I don't think I can do it," Halston said.

"Get outta here, man. This should be a requirement for you to stay here. If you don't do it, you're out," Omar laughed.

"I'll only be here for a couple of months anyway until I can find an apartment. The money I got from my split from the house isn't quite enough for me to get a new house yet. This market is so crazy right now," Halston replied.

"Are you listening to yourself right now? She makes more money than you, by a long shot – your words, not mine. She hasn't given you your ring back and let's not even mention the bullshit with Devin and the child that's not yours. It's easy money, literally," Omar ranted.

"I don't know. I'll think about it, alright. All of this is happening so quickly. I need time to process everything,"

"Whatever. Seriously, what's your game plan with getting back on your feet financially?"

"I'm still ironing everything out. This pandemic is spreading quickly, so a lot of these companies aren't hiring right now. I'm thinking about doing this gig that my ex-coworker told me about, but that's more of a last resort."

"Yeah, it's getting scary. There are a few cases in Texas now. Again, you can stay here as long as you need. I'm just trying to help you walk through a plan. Hmph, what's the new gig with the old co-worker?"

"She used to flirt with me a lot at my old job, but things are platonic between us. We met for lunch a few weeks ago. She was pretty vague, so I need to get more details from her."

"Have you banged her yet?"

"What? No, man I haven't banged her. I'm technically still married."

"But you want to bang her. I can tell. I say go for it. What do you have to lose? Even if Kelly finds out, what can she say? She cheated first. You have to stop subscribing to this good guy bullshit," Omar continued.

"We?" Halston asked, with a raised eyebrow.

"You know what I mean, smart ass. I'm changing. I haven't cheated on Melina. I really like her."

"Well, even if you were right, I think it would be best to keep that to myself. That doesn't seem like something I should disclose if I'm trying to get alimony," Halston cautioned.

"Now, you're thinking. That is a good point. Just don't tell her then. As a matter of fact, wait until you get the alimony, and then, boom. Tell her then," Omar shouted.

"Oh, my God. There is no hope for you, man," Halston laughed heartily.

"None at all. What's Miss Yet-To-Be-Banged's name?" Omar continued.

"Julia. I'll give her a call this week."

"Well, if you want to get a head start and call her tonight you can. I'm going to Melina's tonight, so you'll have the whole place to yourself," Omar replied.

"I thought we were going out for drinks tonight," Halston said.

"We'll have plenty of time for that. Call Julia and you can even invite her over if you want. Just don't get any love juices on my furniture."

"I'm not bringing her over here. I might give her a call. We'll see. Sounds like you and Melina have been together almost as long as you and Simone. It's been about five months now. This is going for the record," Halston joked.

"Haha. Laugh now. Yes, she's really cool and I'm trying to do right this time. Plus, the sex......oooh. It is a-maz-ing. Damn, I'm getting hot just thinking about it. I'm about to get in the shower and get ready to go see her. Make yourself at home playboy."

"Thanks, man. I really appreciate you letting me crash here for a little bit."

"You got it, man, Now, call up Jennifer or whatever her name is."

Halston was grateful to have such a good friend like Omar, who allowed him to stay at his place until he got back on his feet. Things had to turn around for him soon.

He sat there for a moment and then pulled out his phone. He stared at it and scrolled through some old texts between him and Kelly.

"Nope. That's done," he muttered aloud.

Halston stopped at Julia's phone number.

Hey, I think I'm ready to learn more about that gig you told me about. I still haven't found anything steady, he typed.

He placed his phone on the couch, as he anticipated a quick response.

Silence.

Two minutes passed.

Then three.

Another seven.

Halston arose from the couch and poured himself a glass of Simply Orange juice from the refrigerator. He decided he would go get some groceries tomorrow. It was the least he could do while he stayed with Omar, rent-free. He knew what type of food Omar liked, since they were friends for so long.

Ding.

His text alert sounded.

Halston walked over to his phone and checked the unread message.

Hey there, sir. Sure, I can talk to you about it. It's better that I show you rather than tell you. I can invite you over and show you over dinner this week, if you feel comfortable with that, she said.

Dinner? Halston thought.

It sounded good to him. After all, he knew he was done with Kelly even if they were still legally married. What did he have to lose?

Oh yeah, dinner is cool. It's a long story, but I'll fill you in. How does this Wednesday work for you?

I'll be ready to hear all about it. Yep, Wednesday is perfect. 7:00 pm? Julia replied.

"Alright, boss man. The place is all yours. Make yourself at home. If tonight goes as well as I hope, I'll see you tomorrow," Omar said.

"Have fun man. Thanks again. Let me know if you need me to pick up anything," Halston replied.

"Anytime. See you man."

Halston laughed to himself as the hollow sound of Omar's door echoed throughout the house. It was a nice house, but a true bachelor pad, void of much decoration or furniture. Halston and Devin had always given Omar grief about his seemingly immature ways with women. Now, here he was separated and technically homeless.

Omar's life was turning around. He was becoming more of a man in Halston's eyes. He always thought of his friend as more of his little brother, but his little brother found a way to teach him a few lessons about life.

et's try something a little different today, Halston," Sharon suggested.

"Ok, I'm game. What's that?" Halston asked with a hint of curiosity.

Halston was about to begin his eighth session with Sharon. He thought he showed progress, although he wasn't sure about the end goal of his therapy. All he knew about therapy was it was supposed to make you less on edge and more in tune with your inner self, whatever that meant. Halston had a hunch that his luck was about to turn.

"I think that our sessions have been great. I've learned a lot of your triggers. What we haven't really uncovered is how they make you feel today.".

"Ok, I think our sessions have been great too. I enjoy coming here and I feel much better about myself since we've started our sessions."

"Yes, I agree with you. Healing is multi-dimensional. I'm not looking for you to flip out or break down, but part of healing is walking through the valley of your pain. I want to get into how you, Halston, feel today."

Silence.

Halston looked down and then stared back at Sharon squarely

in her eyes.

"I don't know. I mean, I do know but I feel like I can never let my guard down. The funny thing is it's not the divorce for me. It's the fact that I was a father, only to have that privilege swept away in the blink of an eye. That hurts the most," he replied, with a listless look in his eyes.

"Have you considered adoption?"

"I haven't thought about it until recently. I'll be 31 next month. I guess I still have some time, but we'll see."

"I was adopted. It's funny how because of my experience, I look at the world differently, especially when it comes to children."

"Oh, I'm sorry. I didn't mean to sound insensitive. That's great that you were adopted."

"I didn't tell you that for sympathy, only to give you a perspective. Halston, I think that because of your unique experiences, specifically within your marriage, you may view life through a different lens."

"Could that be a bad thing?" Halston inquired genuinely.

"I think only you know that answer. Follow your instinct and listen to what feels right. I get a kick out of society always praising female intuition. Don't get me wrong, there's some truth to that myth. However, men are often just as intuitive. I sense that you're aware of the right things to do," Sharon assured him.

"Maybe so. I'm still bitter. I'm better than I was, but I know I have some work to do. My friend Omar is a big reason why I'm here. I started coming after I moved in with him for a bit once Kelly and I sold the house. All of this has been a humbling experience, to say the least."

"That's a good friend. Speaking of, that's another topic we've merely scratched the surface. A divorce cannot only have a profound psychological and physiological impact, but a financial impact as well. How was that part been for you?"

Halston sensed her attempt to pry deeper into his current state of well-being.

Plus, there was a growing sexual tension between them that seemed to escalate with each session, despite never crossing the line.

Halston cleared his throat and snapped back to reality. He day-dreamed about Sharon slowly opening the next two buttons of her mauve-colored blouse to reveal her perky breasts. The sun shone right above them, like a beacon atop mountains, through the slits in the blinds in her office.

"Um, it was ok. I mean, it was a challenge for a while. The pandemic slowed things down a lot, but it's better now. I've been doing a lot of independent consulting. It has its ups and downs. When it's good, it's good. So, I've just been saving in the meantime. I saved while I worked odd jobs and staying with Omar for a while helped me too," he said.

He wasn't exactly sure what she was trying to uncover, but he decided it was best to keep the details about his financial status vague.

"Oh, the pandemic. I think that has changed all of us, hasn't it? That's great that you were able to get back on your feet despite the odds being stacked against you," Sharon replied.

"Yes, it really has and I'm blessed that things are continuing to look up," Halston said.

"I cannot begin to tell you how mundane it felt to only be able to take appointments with my clients via teleconference. I did what I had to do, but it was quite grueling on both sides," Sharon admitted.

"There's nothing quite like human-to-human interaction, even with all of the technology at our fingertips. Isn't that amazing how that works?" Halston questioned.

Sharon paused to gather her thoughts. She was turned on by Halston's deflective interrogation. There weren't many times that she was rendered speechless, unlike at that moment.

"I couldn't agree more. Well, we have come to the end of our session. Next week, let's talk about your relationship with Devin. I'm proud of you Halston. You've made some great progress today. I think uncovering some of these things will only help in the future," Sharon concluded, as she rose from the chair.

Although Sharon was completely turned on by Halston, she had to keep control of the situation. She walked towards her desk to take a sip of water, as if to give Halston a cue that he should leave her office.

"Ok, sounds good. I'm mean, not exactly but I will be ready," Halston smirked.

"I know. It's all for your healing," Sharon smiled back at him.

"That's what I pay you for, right? I guess this is the hard part. The dreaded homework assignment like those old high school days. You have a great rest of your day," Halston said as he prepared to exit her office.

"Thank you, Halton. You as well," she smiled generously.

·

"Halston, it's Isaac."

"Isaac, it's great to hear from you. How are you doing? Everything going well with the house?"

"Yes, certainly. We love it," Isaac replied.

"Great news. I'm glad to hear that," Halston said.

"Sonya and I wanted to reach out to you again to get your information for those paintings. The gallery will be next Thursday evening at 7:00 pm. Will it be an issue for you to be there at that time with the select paintings we discussed?" Isaac replied.

Halston sighed a silent breath of relief. He hoped Isaac's call was about the gallery. He still had no real job prospects and could use the money.

"That sounds great. Yes, I will be there. Thanks for getting back to me," Halston said.

"Of course. Your ex-wife was really sitting on a gold mine. Well, it's all yours now. Our contacts haven't crunched the final numbers yet, but I'd say the total for all of the paintings should be just under $5,000, if that works for you," Isaac revealed.

If that works?

Hell yeah, it works.

Halston's heart started beating fast. He quickly toned down his excitement before he responded.

"Sure, that sounds great to me. Is there a specific dress code I should follow?"

"Ah yes, thank you for reminding me. I just texted the flyer to you, which has all the details. Feel free to invite any of your friends. The more the merrier for these types of events," Isaac answered.

"Perfect. I just saw it come through. I'll see you then. Thanks, Isaac."

"No, thank you. We're glad you're allowing these pieces to be a part of the show. It's going to be a nice event."

"I love the flyer and I'm looking forward to this. Thanks again for the opportunity, Isaac."

"Anytime. Talk to you soon."

.

"Well, that sounded promising. I just made a Moscow mule. You want one?" Halston asked Omar.

"Thanks, yes I haven't had one of these in forever. It wasn't exactly a job proposition but it's the next best thing for now."

"Let me guess. You decided to listen to me about alimony and that was your lawyer on the phone. Am I right?"

"Man, no. Listen, that's not it. That was Isaac, the husband of the couple that bought the house. I'm going to showcase Kelly's paintings at the event. It's next Thursday."

He brushed off Omar's silly proposition, but he was grateful for the light-hearted banter during such a tense time.

"Oh, nice. I'm there, man. Wait, is Kelly ok with you selling her paintings?"

"Yep, she's gonna have to be. She already said she didn't want to take them with her when she left. Since they're in my possession, I'll decide how I get rid of them," Halston said in a matter-of-fact tone, as he took a sip of his drink.

"That's what the hell I'm talking about. Make her ass pay. I wouldn't miss this shit for the world."

He was so excited that he finished the last of his drink in one swallow.

"You are a trip man. I can't say I disagree. Being the nice guy hasn't gotten me anywhere up to this point."

CHAPTER 28

re we still on for tonight?

Halston checked his phone and smiled before he responded. He was ready for whatever tonight. Although he was still a married man, he didn't care about the spiritual or legal ramifications. He decided he would do whatever felt right to him.

Yes, I'll be there. Looking forward to it.

Good. Be ready to eat. I'm cooking dinner for us. I'll send you my address.

Nice. I didn't know you knew your way around the kitchen, Halston replied.

Oh, you've got jokes? You'll see just how much I know my way around the kitchen when you get here. See you soon, silly.

5:07 pm.

Halston put Julia's address in his GPS to find out his commute timing. She was just under 30 minutes away from him. He decided he would leave in about an hour to make room for the traffic.

His clothes and things were in Omar's guest bedroom. The living arrangement with his friend wasn't bad. Nonetheless, he had to get his own place soon. He was too grown to live like college roommates with Omar.

A knock sounded on the bedroom door.

"Hey, what's up man? Come in," Halston said.

"Oh hey, what are you getting out clothes for? Got a hot date?" Omar asked in a hopeful tone.

"Not exactly. I'm going to Julia's house for dinner. She's going to show me whatever this money scheme is that she's started."

"Hmm, sounds sketchy….and freaky. Best of luck to you on the "meeting".

"Whatever man. What are you up to?"

"I was going to ask if you wanted to try that new taco spot downtown but we'll go another day."

"Oh yeah, Taco Majesty. I forgot about that place. I've been wanting to try that place too. Maybe this weekend or next week?"

"Yep, that sounds good. We can try Saturday afternoon then. Well, don't let me hold you up from getting ready for your date, big man."

Halston showered and went through three different options of clothes to wear to Julia's house before he settled on some gray jeans and a burnt orange polo. He thought it would be a nice mix between presentable and casual.

6:02 pm.

Right on time.

He grabbed his wallet and his keys before he walked out of the house.

Halston set his GPS to navigate to Julia's house and turned on a new podcast, *Scared Money Don't Make Cents*. The show had two guys, Damon and Evan, one a former accountant turned entrepreneur and the other who was more of a regular guy that made several dumb financial mistakes before he amassed his wealth.

"Alright, let's get it started. It's Tuesday, so you know what time it is. We're touching a sensitive topic for some today," Damon said.

"Oh really? What's that, Damon?" Evan asked.

"Divorce. We're talking about the things you should never do with your money during and after a divorce. We're going to save you from making some catastrophic mistakes. Stay tuned…."

•

Divorce seemed to be all around Halston. It was like that feeling of getting a new car and everyone on the road suddenly has the exact same make and model. Maybe he was just oblivious to it before. He started to turn it off and switch to another podcast or music, but he continued to listen.

"Now, Damon you've been married before, right?" Evan asked.

"Yes, and happily divorced," Damon replied quickly.

"Ok, well you've made that crystal clear. I'm married now but we were both married before each other. What's a big thing people miss when getting a divorce that sets them back financially?" Even asked.

"Man, where do I start? I'd say most people, including myself at that time, don't realize marriage is a business. As harsh as it sounds, it's a legally binding agreement. If that's broken, that means you must look out for yourself," Damon answered.

"Well, you're right about that. Plus, there's almost always one person in the marriage that makes considerably less income. If that person isn't careful, it's so easy for them to get screwed and find himself or herself in a financial setback," Evan added.

"Ugh, that's enough of this," Halston mumbled.

They were hitting too close to home, and he could feel it impacting his mood. He knew he had to set himself up better financially, which was why he finally decided to meet with Julia to get a jump start on the situation.

He decided to listen to the rest of the episode when he was in a better headspace.

"In .6 miles, take the ramp to get on President George Bush," Siri sounded.

He had just under twenty minutes left before he arrived at Julia's house. Thankfully, the traffic was lighter than he expected.

He started one of his Spotify R&B playlists to listen to for the duration of his commute. Finally, he arrived. Halston had a few minutes to spare so he took his time getting out of the car. He wanted to be punctual but also didn't want to seem too eager.

As he walked towards her front door, he admired the landscape and character of the house. Surprisingly, it looked better than he imagined. Two tall shrubs nestled beside beige pillars that guarded gray brick steps up to the front door. He guessed that it was a one-story house with high ceilings. It looked colonial, yet modern and frankly out of the budget he suspected she made at their old job.

He smelled a pleasant, savory fragrance as he advanced towards Julia's front door. Mmmm….wait. He hoped it wasn't spaghetti. He wasn't superstitious but he always grew up hearing that he shouldn't eat a woman's spaghetti unless it was his wife's and even then, beware.

Halston dismissed his heebie-jeebies and pressed her Ring doorbell.

"Halston! Welcome to my humble abode. Come on in," she ushered.

Julia pulled him close for an embrace and quickly pulled away, as not to seem inappropriate. She wanted to hold him longer, but she thought it would be best to keep her manners with a married man. Plus, she wanted to exercise caution since she wasn't sure if he was skittish about physical contact, due to the spread of the pandemic.

"This is….nice. I see someone must have really come up after leaving the Axl Corp," Halston laughed as he did a quick once over of the immaculately decorated home. The ceilings were high and the fan she had hanging from the center point of her living room ceiling had to have cost her a pretty penny.

"Come on in. I wouldn't say all that. Let me just tell you that if you agree to what I'm going to show you tonight, you and your wife can have a hefty stack of extra money to throw at whatever you wish. I just moved into this house a few months ago. What Bosniac didn't know is I started working on the side. It was inevitable that I was going to quit soon anyway," she admitted.

"I'm just glad you'll probably have a chance to sock it to his sick ass. He pisses me off just thinking about him. It smells amazing in here. What did you cook?" Halston asked.

"You will find out soon enough, but I'm glad it smells appetizing. It's my first time trying this recipe. I hope you don't mind being my guinea pig. Let me get you something to drink. I have some fresh sangria that I made, water and tea," Julia offered.

"Well, what kind of man would I be to pass up sangria? Thank you, I'll take a glass of that," he replied.

"Coming right up. The food will be done in about five minutes. Make yourself comfortable. So how is life as a new father now? Honestly, I was shocked you were able to get you out of the house on a weeknight," she chuckled.

"Hmph. Some things have changed. Kelly and I aren't together anymore. We're in the process of getting a divorce and Matthew is actually not my son," he sighed.

"Wait. What? Damn, I'm so sorry, Halston. Let me add a double shot of vodka to this sangria," Julia said before she handed him his glass.

"You are a hoot. Thanks, this is delicious.".

"Wow, I can't believe it. Let me give this one last quick stir. Have a seat at the table and I will bring your plate to you. So, is it too much to ask what happened? I understand if it's too fresh or too personal to talk about."

"I guess now is as good a time as any. I'll have to get used to telling it but long story short, she cheated on me with my best friend. To add insult to injury, our baby was not my baby. He was conceived during their affair," he uttered.

A certain sense of simultaneous power and defeat poured over him like warm honey. He felt weak and euphoric releasing the truth about the demise of his marriage, even if Julia was one of the first people to know.

"That is unbelievable. I'm sorry, well…, not really. I have to ask, was this a retaliation affair? Women are good for that," Julia said.

"Nope. Sometimes, I wish I had. I was faithful the whole time and it still ended up in shambles. Oh well, I guess that's life, right?" Halston shrugged.

"I don't know what to say then. You know what? We're going to hopefully enjoy some good food and I'll show you how to make some good money. How about that?"

"Cheers to that. Let's do it," Halston replied with a genuine smile.

He felt bad for giving Julia such a hard time when they worked together, even if she was persistently flirtatious.

"Alright, we are having baked lobster ziti, a strawberry fields salad with my homemade vinaigrette and French bread tonight. I pray you aren't allergic to shellfish," she said as she placed the salad on the table.

"Wow, look at you. I didn't know you cooked this much. Everything looks and smells great. I'm not allergic to shellfish either. I love it. Thanks again for having me over."

"Yeah, I guess I didn't exactly present myself as Suzie Homemaker when we worked together. I cooked sometimes back then but I didn't feel motivated to do it most days. That's all changed now. I feel like I'm back to my original self, if that makes sense."

Halston watched as Julia placed the baked ziti on the table, which was still bubbling from the oven.

Red sauce.

Damn.

He felt uneasy for a moment, but it wasn't exactly spaghetti. He told himself it would be okay, at least he hoped.

"Change is a good thing especially if it makes you feel better."

"You can say that again. After what I have to share with you tonight, I think you'll be excited about your new change on the horizon too. Let's dig in. I'll serve you; it's just the hostess in me," Julia commanded.

"Ok, thank you. I won't object since it's your house," Halston laughed.

"Alright, give it to me straight. I can take it. Don't pull my leg if you really don't like it," she pleaded.

"Julia, no bullshit. This is amazing. I need the recipe for this ziti and the salad is amazing too. I love the banana peppers. Spice is my thing. Wait, is there a bit of cilantro in the salad too?"

"Yes, uh….is that a bad thing? I know it may seem a little odd, but I love it."

"Not at all. That makes two of us. I love cilantro in my salad."

"Ah, thank God. I can breathe now. I'm so glad you like it and I remember you like spicy food too."

"Hmmm, impressive. You have a great memory. Great cooking skills too. So, what is this mystery profession you're into now? Don't tell me it's Only Fans," Halston joked.

"No, but I hear some people are really cashing in on it. Maybe I need to add that in as an additional stream of income," Julia replied sarcastically.

"Ingenuity. I love it," Halston added, between bites.

The food was so delicious that he had to be mindful to pace himself to not look too greedy.

"Here goes. I just ask that you keep an open mind with what I'm about to tell you. In a nutshell, it's borrowing money from people via social media and putting it back before they even feel it," Julia said nonchalantly.

"Wait. What? That's illegal. You've got to be joking," Halston said.

His facial expression resembled the moment when you unwrap a gift on Christmas morning that you never remotely insinuated that you wanted.

"I know that's what it seems like on the surface, but it's deeper than that. Look, you buy a laptop with money that you receive via Cash App, Venmo, PayPal or any of those types of services. Then you get the money out of your account with three withdrawals over a month's time. It's important that you don't withdraw the money from your account all at one time," she paused.

"Ok, I'm guessing that's so it's harder to trace the money? Can't they just trace the sender's account and ultimately trace the illegal act back to the recipient?" he asked.

"Great question, but no. They're basically ghost accounts. They're manned from a machine on their side. I'm telling you, it's kinda like the Illuminati but without the weird sacrificing your soul part," she assured him.

"If you say so. I'm guessing that after you withdraw all of the money, you purchase the laptop and use that to do the elaborate account theft you're about to tell me about?" Halston asked.

"In so many words, yes. You pay for it in cash. The money they give you is enough to cover the cost of the laptop, warranty, taxes – all of it," Julia answered.

"What about the account? Are you just doing this willy nilly from every platform or just certain ones?"

"Facebook and Instagram are the cash cows. It's easier to do it on there. Snapchat is a little harder to crack and Twitter is the holy grail. That's where the most money is if you can get anyone to take the bait from there. Trust me, the money you'll make from the other platforms more than make up for anything you miss out on from Twitter."

Julia refilled their glasses of sangria as they neared the end of their meal.

"I'm trying to follow and be patient for the innocent part of all this," Halston laughed nervously.

"I know, man. It sounds weird but it's legit. I've been doing it for about six months now and it has literally changed my life. Oh, I do have dessert too. I hope you like cheesecake. I layer mine like a parfait."

"Hell yeah. I love cheesecake. You have really outdone yourself with this dinner tonight. Thank you again. I'll have to cook for you too."

"Anytime. You're very welcome. Let me have your plate. Oh and just to let you know, the company uses clickbait for what they believe will be most enticing to the user. They study these people for a long time before you get them as clients," she continued.

"Wait. Clients? Aren't they more like victims or targets?" he asked, with a genuinely perplexed expression.

"Well, yes they are targets but a certain amount of money is withdrawn. We keep the money and they get reimbursed from their financial institutions usually within seven business days. We typically don't try to bait anyone on the first of the month when their rent or mortgages are due. There are some morals involved. It's not a completely savage occupation. Typically, some of the older people fall for the ones on Facebook. That's where the bread and butter comes from. Plus, I hate to sound cryptic, but if this so-called pandemic really spreads like the CDC says it could, we'll all be in the house anyway," she ranted.

"How will that help the situation?" Halston inquired.

"People will have more disposable income. Think about it. They'll save money on gas, healthcare, eating out, everything. So, when we take the money it's even less of an inconvenience than it was before. Plus, they'll probably get it back faster," Julia explained.

"I see you've got it all figured out," Halston laughed.

"I'm just laying out all of the possibilities," she rebutted, with a witty smirk.

Julia lifted the small pitcher of sangria from the table and moved it over to the counter. She placed it too close to the edge and accidentally bumped it when she turned back around. She saw Halston's eyes widen as he jumped up from his seat to run towards the pitcher.

"Woo, got it. That was a close call," he panted.

"Oh my God, Halston. Thank you so much for saving that. I'm so clumsy. I would have been devastated if that pitcher broke because it used to be my grandmother's. You are a lifesaver," she exclaimed as she threw her arms around his neck and squeezed for dear life.

The intoxicating aroma of her perfume mixed with the fragrance of the meal made Halston breathe in her essence longer than he intended. He returned the tight squeeze and hugged her even harder. He felt her exhale deeply as he wrapped his arms around her waist.

Julia lifted her head from his shoulder and met his eyes with hers.

"I'm sorry. I didn't mean to…um…."

Julia tried to pull herself away from Halston's embrace but he wouldn't loosen his grip.

"No, it's ok," he whispered.

Halston grabbed Julia's neck with his hands? right underneath her jawline and pulled her towards him to kiss her. He felt her hesitation for a moment before she went all-in, and their tongues dueled each other to fight for whose would be on top.

"I've dreamed of this day in my mind for so long," Julia breathed heavily in between kisses.

"Oh yeah?" Halston asked rhetorically as if he didn't know.

He knew damn well she wanted him and they both knew it was obvious. The only difference is he didn't care anymore. Halston knew she was a pretty girl, with high, supple-looking breasts (which he was now validating with his hands), a tiny waist and a firm, mini basketball-shaped behind. He kept one hand firmly pressed against the small of her back and placed the other one firmly on her left cheek.

Julia moaned as she lifted her leg to wrap around his waist. She helped Halston unbuckle her belt and slide her jeans down.

He lifted her blouse and exposed her lavender-colored lace bra. Her panties matched perfectly, which turned him on even more. His penis was engorged with so much blood that he was barely able to take off his pants.

Julia sucked on the side of his neck while she unzipped his jeans. She was pleasantly surprised at the large, cucumber-sized member that poked her through his black boxer briefs. She couldn't wait to please him and make him feel like he deserved.

Halston pulled down his boxers and then slid her laced boy-shorts to the side. He slid two fingers inside of her love land and then licked the wetness from his fingertips.

"Shit, I can't wait for it. I want you right now," she said as she slipped his boxer briefs down to his ankles.

Halston's rock-hard penis bounced back from Julia removing his underwear.

Julia's nipples hardened at the sight of him standing at attention to greet her. She pulled him to direct it inside of her.

"Wait. Wait. I'm sorry, do you have a condom?" she asked.

"Dammit. No, I didn't bring one. I didn't think we would…." Halston's voice trailed. He could barely speak.

"Can I just put the head in for a little bit?" he pleaded.

"As tempting as that sounds, we can't do that. Hold that thought for just a second," she said as she hopped off the kitchen counter.

"Okay, shit," he muttered to himself.

Julia sauntered back into the kitchen with a Magnum condom in her hand.

"Looks like you're in luck. I think you'll be able to fit this one," she said as she sat on the counter again with the condom between her legs.

Halston smiled and got on his knees to grab the condom with his teeth. He then dove headfirst between her legs and lapped his tongue around her clitoris and the walls of her vagina, tasting her every drop. He picked her up and wrapped her legs around his waist as he walked with her straddled around him towards her bedroom.

He could feel her dripping against his pelvis as he lowered her on the bed. He continued to feast on her and undulated his tongue as if he vied for a gold medal at the Olympics. This type of sex, with such urgency and passion, was something he hadn't experienced in quite a while.

Julia moaned as Halston explored her. She squeezed the back of his neck with her thighs until she had to push his head away. She had already climaxed twice and felt overly stimulated. Most men couldn't even make her have one orgasm, let alone two. She brought his face up to hers and kissed him.

"Lay down on your back," she commanded.

Halston did as he was told without uttering a word.

Julia swung her perfectly shaped posterior right on his chin as she went to work on his throbbing penis.

Halston moaned in pleasure and commenced to feast on her again from behind. They moved in a syncopated rhythm of ecstasy.

Julia grabbed the condom from the bed and handed it to Halston.

"Do you mind doing the honors?" she whispered.

"Of course not," he muttered, out of breath.

Halston put the condom on quickly and inserted himself inside of Julia while she sat on his lap, cowgirl style.

She loosened the pens from her hair and then placed her hands firmly on Halston's thighs. Julia rocked back and forth, then up and down. She was amazed that Halston seemed to grow even more while he was inside of her.

Damn. This is even better than I imagined, she thought to herself.

Meanwhile, Halston shared the same sentiment. He kept thinking about how amazing she felt, even with a condom. He slapped her ass as he thought about how good she would likely feel if he were inside of her with no barrier.

They continued exploring various positions as they kissed, groped and created friction against each other until they both reached an explosive climax. At that moment, it was like they were spiritually connected on a higher level.

Despite how surprisingly wonderful the sex was with Julia, Halston reminded himself that he couldn't spend the night. He sensed she may have wanted him to stay. Nonetheless, he had to keep the upper hand in the situation. He decided to lay there for just a few more moments and accidentally fell asleep.

He didn't wake up until shortly after 5:00 am.

O oh, don't you look dapper, Halston. I love the ascot. It's such a nice touch isn't it, Isaac?" Sonya asked as she smirked at her husband.

"I will admit, it does look nice. If you can't tell, Sonya has been pressuring me to wear an ascot," he laughed.

"Well, thank you both. Isaac, I'm not trying to get you in any trouble. Believe me, I don't wear ascots on the regular. I just wanted to step outside of my comfort zone a little bit tonight," Halston said.

"See there, babe, stepping outside of your comfort zone is a good thing. We won't hold you, Halston. We've already heard a lot of buzz about your paintings. I think you'll probably get even more than we discussed for them," Sonya said.

"Really? That's great news. I guess I can't take too much credit since Kelly painted them," he replied, with a sigh.

"You said she didn't want them and she said to do what you wish with them, right?" Sonya asked.

"True, that is correct," Halston laughed.

"Guess what? They're yours. I personally hope you get all you can for them. They're gorgeous. Her loss, your gain. Enjoy the evening," she shrugged and lovingly tapped him on the shoulder.

Halston saw Omar and Brandy walk in from the distance. He

waved at them but there were too many people in the way for him to make a clear-cut path towards them.

Omar winked at him and nodded his head as if to say "good job" for the paintings. He loved the fact that Halston was sticking it to Kelly any way he could, even it was because of desperation.

Halston walked through the crowd and eventually bumped into Omar. He was glad to see his friend look so happy with Brandy. Although Omar said he would come to the art gallery, Halston was still slightly surprised to see him.

"Man, this is a pretty big event. This place is packed. Congratulations," Omar exclaimed.

"Thank you, man. I'm glad y'all could make it out. Brandy, it's good to see you again," Halston said.

"Thanks, and it's great to see you again too. I love the ambiance here. This place is beautiful. How often do they host these events?" she asked.

"According to Isaac and Sonya, it's a bi-annual event. I look forward to the next one. It's something different than I'm used to, but I'm ready for new experiences. I may as well start now, right?" Halston replied.

"I hear that," Omar chimed in.

"Oh, I can't believe it," Halston gasped.

Omar traced his friend's gaze to determine what had him so flustered. It only took a few seconds before he spotted them: Kelly and Devin together.

"Oh my," Brandy muttered.

"Hey man, if you want to me run interference…." Omar ranted.

"Nope, it's unnecessary. This is an open event. I don't think Isaac and Sonya purposely invited her without telling me. She, or should I say they, must have heard about it decided to come," Halston concluded nonchalantly.

Omar was impressed and surprised at his friend's calm demeanor about just seeing his soon-to-ex-wife and ex-best-friend out for a night on the town together.

"Do you think we should maybe move around a bit to avoid

them?" Brandy whispered not-so-softly to Omar.

"I have no idea. I guess if he's okay with it, I am too. I feel caught in the middle of these two, like some high school kids," he complained.

"Tell me about it. So do I," Brandy agreed.

"Oh shit, I guess we don't have much time to think because here she they come. That's bold, even for Devin," Omar replied, with an expression of disgust on his face.

Meanwhile, Halston stood there unphased by it all. Omar and Brandy glanced over at him to gauge his reaction as Devin and Kelly appeared to make a bee-line in their direction.

"Halston, hey man. How's it going?" Devin asked with Kelly by his side.

Halston looked at Kelly, who looked like she wanted to crawl underneath the building's foundation, and back at Devin before he responded.

An uncomfortable few seconds of silence ensued.

How's it going?

Motherfucker, you're standing there with my wife. We're not even divorced yet and you have the audacity to show up here and ask me how I'm doing?

Halston envisioned grabbing one of Kelly's paintings and smashing them both over the head with it. He decided against the brilliant idea to avoid causing a scene. Plus, he had full intentions of making money from her paintings and didn't want anything to jeopardize that.

"Devin. Kelly. Good evening," Halston answered.

"Hi, Halston," Kelly chimed in with a nervous smile.

Is she wearing the shoes I bought her?

Halston noticed Kelly was wearing the eggplant-colored stiletto pumps she was dying to have a couple of years ago. *How poetic.*

"This is a really nice event. I didn't know you'd be here, Kelly. What a coincidence," Brandy replied.

She tried to look genuinely surprised that Devin was her date for the evening. Of course, Kelly didn't divulge that information. Omar filled her in but she didn't want to let on that he told her anything.

"Yeah, we heard about it last minute and decided to stop by," Devin continued.

"Cool, well I think Brandy and I are going to get some wine," Omar suggested.

"Lord knows I need a drink after this interaction," Brandy mumbled as they walked away together.

"Ah, wait. Is that my painting on the wall behind you? Wait, that one is mine too and that one in the back over there," Kelly inquired in an agitated tone.

Halston never witnessed her look so confused, other than when she accidentally revealed she was cheating on him with his then-best friend.

Good.

You deserve to suffer.

"Yes, all three of them are your paintings. I think they look exceptionally nice under this lighting. Don't you think?" Halston asked, with a smirk that could have sliced through her soul.

"I suppose, but the more important question is I don't recall giving you permission to have the paintings here," she rebutted.

"You don't remember the verbal agreement? You told me I could do whatever I wanted to do with them. So, this is what I decided to do. Why let such beautiful art go to waste?" Halston said.

"I guess you have a good point," Kelly smirked with a sly, defeated smile.

Halston saw Sonya from across the room. He sensed that her demeanor revealed she saw Kelly walk in with Devin. He smiled back as she winked at him from across the room.

"You two have a good evening," Halston replied curtly as he walked towards the refreshments table.

Although his heart was still broken, he was elated that at least for that night, he had one hell of a one-up on Kelly.

CHAPTER 29

I knew it!" Omar exclaimed.

"You always think you know everything. How did you know?" Halston laughed.

"I'm me. How could I not know? You walked in that next morning with a different kind of swagger. Imagine if she had shown up to the art gallery last night. That would have been epic. You're getting your mojo back and I'm here for it," Omar said.

"I don't know about all that. It was hot like fire, man. I'll tell you that," Halston admitted.

"Ooh wee. You deserve all the fire you can get. You get a fireball. You get a fireball and you get a fireball. I mean, you know, without the burn from an STD. Safe fire, of course."

"It was a night. A really good night," Halston replied, as he played flashbacks through his mind.

"So, what is the end goal with her? Is it a friend with benefits kind of thing or do you think it's too early to tell?" Omar asked.

Halston was slightly taken aback that his friend asked about an "end goal". This came from a man who had more than his share of one-night stands. Brandy must have really changed him.

"Look at you. End goals. I guess we're really growing up, huh? I don't know, man. It's really just strictly business and I guess a little pleasure in there too," Halston said.

"Yeah, I remember you telling me about that. Did she give you a lead on a job?" Omar asked.

"Ah, I guess you can say that, in a way," Halston trailed.

"Wait a minute. Don't tell me she has you roped in some *Breaking Bad* type of stuff," Omar replied.

"Well, not exactly. It's basically borrowing money from people through social media platforms and then their bank gives it back to them," Halston replied.

"Do you hear yourself right now? The sex couldn't have been that good. That kind of stuff can land you in jail. If you go to jail behind that shit, I'm not bailing you out," Omar ranted.

"Look, man. I'm not asking you to bail me out. Things are good right now, but this house money is going to run out soon. I haven't gotten any real job leads, even when I get an interview. I appreciate you letting me stay here, but we both know I can't do this forever. I gotta do something," Halston countered his friend.

Halston didn't even fully believe in the new money-making scheme Julia was slowly convincing him to do. However, he knew he couldn't sit back and let the circumstances fall where they may. He had to take control of his own life.

"I understand things are rough right now. I'm not giving you a deadline to be out of here either. I hope you know that. I just want you to think about this clearly and not get yourself into a sticky situation," Omar replied.

"Thanks, man, I really appreciate that. I'm leaning towards it but I haven't made a final decision yet. Who knows? I may not even do it. If I do, it won't be a full-time thing. Just enough to stack up some money for a house until I get something steady. You know how crazy this housing market is right now. I want to be prepared," Halston sighed.

"I get it. Be careful, that's all I'm saying," Omar responded.

"I will and I appreciate that. It's Friday night man. I'm sure you and Melina probably have a hot date planned," Halston said.

"Nah, last night worked out well. That was our date night. She's hanging out with the girls tonight. If you're free, do you want to go to Taco Majesty? I heard that place is really catching on, so it might be harder to get in soon," Omar said, as he turned on the TV to catch the news.

"Yeah, that sounds good. I could use some tacos right about now. I've seen a lot of people posting about it on Instagram. Looks like a cool spot. Let me go jump in the shower. I'll be ready whenever you are," he said.

"Sounds good. It's 5:15 now. Let's wait til 6 to let the traffic die down," Omar suggested.

"Coming up, our top story this evening about rising cases of the nation's new deadly virus coming to Texas, what medical experts are calling it and how its threat could change your daily routine soon," the news anchor announced.

"Damn, I thought it was letting up, but apparently not," Halston said as he took a seat to see the upcoming news segment.

"You and me both. This can't be real. It's like we're about to live in the days of the apocalypse," Omar added.

"Kiely, what are the latest developments on this catastrophic new virus?" Blake, the lead news anchor, reported.

"Yes, Blake, and what a new series of developments it is. This deadly virus has now been dubbed the Coronavirus; a highly infectious disease caused by the SARS-CoV-2 virus, discovered in 2019: COVID-19. It is spreading like a raging wildfire. Just this week, there were 16 cases in Texas; now that number has quadrupled. Although there are no known cases in the greater Dallas area, the CDC has asked that everyone takes careful precautions as to not spread the virus," she continued.

"Wow, those numbers are astounding considering this has all happened in less than a week. What are the warning signs for symptoms and are there any precautions people can take for preventative measures?" Blake asked.

"Right now, people should be alerted by any excessive coughing, sneezing, fever, or sudden body aches, amongst other symptoms. The Coronavirus mirrors common flu symptoms. The CDC recommends that people stay away from large gatherings of people, especially indoors, remember to wash their hands and wear face masks in public settings," she said.

"Um, wow. Ugh, I guess that kinda throws a wrench in our plans for tonight. Wait, I have some masks in my closet that have never been used. Let me grab those and we can still go. I'm going to get in the shower too," Omar said.

"Yeah, good thinking. Looks like this stuff is moving closer and closer to us. I'm not ungrateful, but why do you have spare masks lying around in your closet?" Halston asked with a perplexed expression that formed on his face.

"It was Brandy's idea. She wanted to spice things up a bit and play doctor," Omar laughed.

"Hey, do what you do. Are you sure the masks are clean?" Halston teased.

"Man, yes, they're clean. I'm about to get ready," Omar replied.

Halston replayed the newscast in his head while he was in the shower. In just a few short months, the virus spread faster than anyone could have imagined. He was grateful that it hadn't hit Dallas, but he wasn't too optimistic that it would miss hitting even closer to home.

Matthew.

What if he got sick?

He hated that he was so concerned. Although it was technically Devin's child, he already started to form a bond with that child. The thought of Kelly and Devin together made his stomach turn, but he sincerely didn't want any harm for Matthew.

The thought of a pandemic brought on another fear; not having a steady job.

He decided his best option was to take Julia up on her proposition, especially since he didn't have to go into an office to make money.

I must admit, I didn't expect to hear back from you so soon," Julia said.

"Yeah, I gave it some thought and it's the strongest iron I have in the fire right now. I'm still a bit skeptical about it, but I trust you," he said.

"Everything has gone well for me. I can connect you with a few people on the team who are more seasoned if that helps sway you. Have a seat, I'd say we're past subtle pleasantries at this point," she smiled.

"True, that is a good point. I would have invited you over to my place, but I'm still staying at my friend Omar's place. Nonetheless, one day soon…," Halston replied.

"You don't owe me any explanation. If you start this and do it as well as I know you can, you'll have your own place in no time," Julia assured him.

"That's what I'm hoping."

They both tried to ignore how much they enjoyed each other sexually. Halston wanted to have sex with Julia again. He was confident he would have his chance.

"Good. So, let's get you started. Do you have a preferred method of receiving your money, Cash App, Venmo, Zelle, either one of those? I personally recommend a mix of two, which helps diversify the income stream," she smiled.

"I'd say Cash App and Zelle," Halston replied, with a tinge of hesitation.

"Alright, I can begin to send the funds for the laptop over to you in the next week. Remember to make the withdrawals over a few transactions, not all at once. Pay for everything in cash when you get to the store," she continued.

"Wait. Won't that look suspicious for me to just slap over $1,000 down in cash for a laptop? Are there not any special debit cards for this gig?" he asked.

"Great question, but no. Remember, the less traceable you are, the better. You don't want to be connected to any transactions that can be linked back to a financial institution. Let them get involved when we take the money from the not-so-innocent people on our list," she said.

"List? Is there a list of people that I'll be tasked to take the money from? Is there a certain time that I have to take the money from them?" Halston inquired.

"You just won't let up, will you?" Julia laughed.

"I just want to be fully aware of everything I'm getting myself into," he said.

"I got you and that's commendable; sexy even. Here's the deal: you will start off with a list of seven. Everyone gets seven people right off the bat. If you happen to know the person, you must report it immediately. You want to stay away from people you know at all costs. Of course, there will be some unlucky distant cousins that may slip through the cracks.".

"Not that I want to do this to anyone I know, but why is that so off-limits? Is it only because of the moral compass of it all?"

"If you're thinking about sticking it to your ex-wife, I like your thinking. Yes and no. As I said, people can recoup this money back within a few business days under most circumstances, so there's not a terrible loss. You wouldn't want to do something like that to someone you really care about. However, if an enemy of yours just happens to appear on your list, who are we to intervene with vengeance?"

"Hmmm, ok. I'll keep that in mind."

"So, if you're serious about this, I will add you to the virtual group chat. There are no email addresses, obviously for tracking purposes. The virtual group does have a wealth of information, training decks, objection handling and everything of the sort."

"Ok, so there's got to be a catch. I'm sure I just can't jump in this for free. How much does it cost?"

"You beat me to the punch. The entry fee is $350, which is re-coupable, granted you can close the loop on your first list of seven people within three months. So, remember those numbers, seven in three. That's your golden ticket to get an even bigger list and more money."

"Ok, I'm ready. How do I submit the fee?"

"Not so fast, cowboy. You'll submit the money after the next interest meeting, which will be Tuesday of next week. There will be a section during the call where any new prospects can pay the membership fee. At that time, the leader of the meeting will walk you through the steps to submit the funds. Then, I'll submit your Cash App and Zelle info to the area leader. After that, you'll be set to start receiving the cash for your laptop," she finished.

"Wow, ok. This is all moving so quickly. I'm all in, but I'm sure I'll have more questions along the way," he said nervously.

"Don't worry. I was the same and I had a lot of questions when I started too. You'll be fine. If I can do it, you can surely do it."

"Thanks for the vote of confidence. Can I ask you a question?"

"Um, at this point, I'd say we're way past any awkward question phase. Go ahead. Ask away," Julia laughed.

"Is your house and the furniture a result of the work you've been doing?" Halston said.

"I'm going to take that as the compliment I believe it is. Yes, I had been saving for a house. I eyed this one for a while. When the previous bidder's loan fell through, I knew I had my chance. I stashed away the cash from the job the whole time. I love a good consignment deal, so some of the furniture pieces were expensive hand-me-downs from strangers so to speak."

"Nice. You've done really well for yourself."

"Can I ask you a question, sir?"

"Sure, fire away."

"Do you find it hard to believe that a single woman can afford nice things?"

Silence.

Halston didn't know how to respond. He didn't mean any harm by his question. However, he did know the ballpark of what she made when they worked together. That salary couldn't have afforded her the house and lifestyle she appeared to have now.

A lump formed in the back of Halston's throat as he quickly scanned his mind for a logical, yet gentle response.

"I'm pulling your leg, silly. Don't answer that. Just kiss me."

Julia straddled him on her couch and unbuttoned his shirt.

Halston was pleasantly surprised. He wrapped his arms around her waist firmly, as he kissed her back passionately. He sucked on her bottom lip and felt her nipples harden through her blouse. He knew she wasn't wearing a bra when he walked inside her house and had a difficult time staying focused on the business at hand.

Julia kissed him and grazed her fingernails across the back of his neck as Halston pulled her in close.

"Damn, I've been wanting you," he admitted.

"Oh yeah?" she replied, as she panted between kisses.

"Yeah. Really bad," he replied.

"That makes two of us then," Julia said.

"Mmm, that's good to know," he moaned.

Halston picked her up while she was still on his lap and sat her down on the couch. He got on his knees before he her and removed her shirt so he could devour her breasts like two ripe melons on a hot summer day.

Julia moaned in ecstasy as he nibbled on her nipples between each lap of his tongue.

"Damn, come here," she said.

Julia pulled Halston's face up to hers and kissed him passionately.

She pulled him on the couch with her and flipped him over on his back. She pulled his pants and underwear down to his ankles and kissed his inner thighs. Julia could tell by the way his penis jumped with each kiss that he enjoyed her seductive teases.

She then engulfed all of him in her mouth and looked him directly in his eyes.

"Ah, Julia. Shit, wait," he said.

Halston started mumbling a series of phrases that didn't make sense. Then, he gathered his senses and pulled himself away from Julia.

He pulled her on top of him again, as he sat on the couch.

"I came prepared this time."

Halston pulled a condom out of his jeans pocket.

"A man with a plan. I love it," she replied, as she rocked back on his lap and squeezed her breasts.

Halston slipped himself inside of her while she straddled him.

Julia started off slow and then rocked her hips swiftly back and forth like she was riding a bull at the rodeo. She grabbed his shoulders and thrust her hips in a circular motion. She held on for dear life as Halston stood up with Julia still inside of him.

She was thoroughly impressed as he pumped swiftly while he stood up and wrapped her legs around his waist. Julia seemed to get wetter with each pump and thrust until Halston felt her juices smeared all over his pelvic area.

"It feels so tight. Damn, Julia," Halston said as he backed against the wall.

He still stood inside of her as Julia clawed at the top of his back.

"I don't want to cum yet. Please don't make me cum yet," Julia pleaded.

"Just let yourself go. I don't want to cum either, but I can't hold it," Halston said.

They both moved harder and faster until the heat of their friction started to burn.

"I'm…Halston, I'm about to cum," she exclaimed.

"Me too," Halston moaned and kissed her.

He exploded inside of her. His knees weakened as soon as he released.

Her head fell limp on his shoulder as he eased down onto the couch.

<h1 style="text-align:center">CHAPTER 31</h1>

ey, it's me, Halston. I'm calling to give you an update on the status of the filing. I filed, so if you sign the new papers, everything should be good to go in the next 60 days. Call me if you have any questions," he said as he hung up the phone.

"Boom! Just like that. Man, I would pay to see the reaction on her face when she hears that voicemail," Omar fumed.

"I'm just glad it's almost over with now. This divorce should have been finalized months ago."

"True. I think that's the last box, man. I know you're Big Bank Hank now with the new job but if you ever need a place to stay, mine is still open."

"Thanks, man. I really appreciate that. Here's a little something for letting me crash at your place for all that time."

Halston handed Omar a black and gold Diesel watch that he knew Omar wanted. The watch was originally $550, but it was on sale for $475. That still wasn't low enough for Omar to make the purchase. He decided he would either save a little bit more or just wait for the price to go down.

"Whoa man, are you serious? No way. I can't take this. This is way too much," Omar exclaimed.

"Nope. You keep it. You wouldn't let me give you rent money, so I figured this would be the next best thing. Enjoy it," Halston replied.

"Thank you. Damn, I'm speechless," Omar gasped.

Halston had been working the new job for about three months and it was one of the best decisions he ever made. By next month, he would have more disposable income than he did when he was married to Kelly. He was glad he decided to listen to Julia and saw it as fate that they reconnected.

Now, he was able to have his own place and freedom again. He was grateful for Omar helping him, but he was glad to officially be a bachelor on his own terms. Plus, he enjoyed the satisfaction of delivering an element of surprise to Kelly. He was certain that she used his perceived financial situation as a means to have an upper hand. Those days were over.

"Thanks again for helping me get the rest of the stuff the movers couldn't pack up."

"Anytime. I know the market is crazy right now, but I'd say you'll be quite content in this apartment in the meantime. This place is decked out. I love it. Well, let me make my way back to my side of town before the traffic builds up."

"Yeah man, get out of here. It's almost 5:00pm. That traffic is going to be thick if you're not on the road in the next 15 minutes."

"Alright, I'll holler at you soon. Don't do any freaky things I wouldn't do in this new place."

"I'll be sure to do just that. See you, man."

The hollow sound of the front door closing jolted Halston's memory. The last time he heard a similar sound, he was preparing to move out of the house he shared with Kelly. Now, the echo symbolized something different: euphoria. He felt like he finally had a fresh start.

His moment of Zen was interrupted by his phone ringing. He had a special ringtone set for Kelly (that he still needed to change), so he immediately knew it was her.

"Hello?" he answered in a professional tone, as if he was a telemarketer.

"Oh, hey. Halston. How are you?" Kelly asked with genuine interest.

Halston could sense her uneasiness. He knew she must have listened to his voicemail before she called.

"I'm doing great. I can't complain. How are you?" he replied curtly.

He really didn't give a shit how she was doing, but he was in a good mood. Nothing could bring him down.

"That's nice. I'm good, just been crazy busy. Look; I got your voicemail and I'm sorry it took me so long to get the filing done. I've been all over the place lately. I didn't mean to have you carry the brunt of that, financially. I know how things were with the job search," she replied.

"Oh, That's a thing of the past. I'm in a much better space now, so it's all good," Halston said.

"Ah, really? Congratulations. I knew it wouldn't take you long to find something you liked. Where are you working now if you don't mind me asking?" she inquired.

Hell yeah, I mind you asking.

"I'm a financial advisor at a new startup company. I basically help them diversify their portfolio," he stated.

"Oh, nice. That sounds interesting. Sounds like you really like it. Um, and about the other night, Devin and I are not a couple. I just thought you should know that. He just asked if he could come with me to the art gallery that night," she explained.

"That's ok, you don't owe me an explanation. I understand," he responded.

He knew she wouldn't dare ask him how much he made from her paintings. He wasn't willing to supply her with any information on his own either.

"Well, I guess it's really final. I guess I'll see you once everything is ready to be finalized. I don't want to hold you up but for what it's worth, I'm sorry again," she said.

Halston could hear a tinge of a crack in her voice. He always felt a soft spot when she cried. However, he couldn't get weak now. He had to keep his eye on the prize: building a new life without Kelly.

"Thank you, I appreciate that. I'm sorry things happened the way they did too. I think we'll both be alright.".

They said their goodbyes and Halston continued unpacking his apartment. He took out his Bluetooth speaker so he could play music from his phone. He settled on a 90's throwback Hip Hop playlist, something edgy enough to keep him out of his feelings.

He turned on his MacBook before he organized his kitchen. As soon as he placed it on the counter, he received an email alert. He had a new list that came in for him to sift through. His list grew a little each time and this was the longest list he ever received: 16 people.

Halston started sifting through the list of people to make sure there wasn't anyone he knew included. Then, he opened the files to review the demographics of the first two people on his list.

"Stay focused," he whispered aloud.

He was already working ahead and had plenty of time to review his list. For now, he needed to get his apartment together so he could be in a good headspace to work.

As soon as he unpacked his last kitchen box, his phone alerted. Two more alerts came in quick succession after the first one. He stopped putting his plates in the cabinet and walked over to check his phone. At this rate, he figured he may not be able to get as much work done setting up his new place as he planned.

Halston walked over to the bar to check his phone. He had three unread texts, all from Julia.

Hey, have you checked the latest list they sent out?
Your wife's first name is Kelly, right?
Call me when you get a chance.

Halston combed through his list again to see if there were any names that he knew. He didn't see anyone that he recognized and certainly didn't see Kelly on his list. He would have been shocked if she was included on Julia's list.

He dialed her to find out what was going on.

She picked up on the third ring.

"Hey, Halston. Sorry for the back-to-back texts. Did I catch you at a bad time?"

"No, you're fine. I just moved into my new apartment today. I'm just getting it situated but that will be a work in progress."

"Nice! Ok, look at you. I take it that the job has still been treating you well. Congratulations. I'd love to see it soon."

They both towed a delicate balancing act of maintaining their friends with benefits status and working relationship without catching feelings. It wasn't working out too well for either of them but they both avoided admitting how much they cared.

"Thank you. I'll have you over as soon as I can get it in a presentable state."

"Sounds good. Look, I don't want to hold you up from getting your bachelor pad unpacked. Did you have a chance to look through your list yet?"

Everyone on the team received their lists on the same day, so everyone knew when new "clients" were available.

"I briefly scanned it before I got your text. I didn't see any familiar names. You mentioned Kelly. That is my soon-to-be-ex-wife's name. Is she on your list?"

"I'm almost certain she's on it. Let me check again. I think I saw Pointe as the last name too. You know I had to check first because I know how separations go. Things can be off one minute and back on the next."

"Well, after what she did that's definitely not the case for me. I filed for divorce last week since it took her too long and I finally had the money to get it done."

"Alright, it's sealed then. I hear that. I've always been an on or off type of woman myself. I hate that limbo shit," she replied, as she attempted to mask her excitement of the news of Halston's pending divorce.

"Yep, my thoughts exactly. So, what's going on with the list?"

"Alright, let me search for her name again. Lisa, Timothy, Devin, Mya, Kelly – there it is. I found it. That's her; Kelly Pointe."

"Wait a minute. Ok, so she's on your list and I don't know too many people named Devin. What's his last name?"

"Olford. Why? Do you know him too?"

Halston paused for a moment.

He was speechless.

This couldn't be possible.

"Hey, you still there?"

Julia waited for him to say something, anything.

"Yeah, I'm sorry. Damn, Devin Olford is the guy that Kelly had the affair with and he's the father of her child. He used to be one of my best friends. What are the chances of this?" Halston asked.

"You've got to be kidding me. Between the two of them, that's a $3,500 payout. I wanted to present a proposition to you, but it sounds like it will be an even sweeter deal for you than I realized."

"Ok….what do you have in mind?"

"Look, I know you're trying to get back on your feet. Things are going well, but how sweet would it be for you to have the payout for Kelly and Devin? My list is larger than I expected this time anyway. I'll be out of town at the end of the week, visiting my sister. So if you don't mind taking two "random" people from my list, I'll give you the payout for Kelly and Devin."

"I couldn't do that. I mean, I don't mind taking two from your list to lighten the load, but I don't know about taking the payout from Kelly and Devin. You would have worked for that on your own."

"Just consider it a divorce present or a house-warming gift. I'm sure I might need you to return the favor down the line. So, what do you say?"

"Ok, I'll shut up and accept the gift. Thank you."

"Alright, that's what I love to hear. The only thing I have to be careful about is if one of them shares it with the other first. It must be timed just right. I'll have to tweak the strategy for it a bit, but I'll make it work and I'll keep you posted."

"True, that is a good point. I'll think of some things that could probably throw them off if you don't think there's enough to hook them in their profile. Let me know."

"Ok, good thinking. If you don't mind, go ahead and send me anything you think will help. Something tells me I'll need anything I can get for them."

"Will do. I can probably get it to you by tomorrow if that works."

"That's fine or you can wait until Monday or Tuesday if you want. I likely won't dive into it until then. I said I'd be quick though, so you get back to setting up your place. We'll talk soon," Julia said.

"Ok, sounds like a plan. Talk to you soon and thanks again," Halston replied.

"Sure thing. Anytime."

Halston smiled to himself at the thought of getting revenge on the two people in his life who hurt him the most. Let the games begin.

Halston's divorce from Kelly had been finalized now for just over a month. He was glad to have received the money from Devin and Kelly being scammed by Julia. It was a difficult feat, but he was ecstatic that she could pull it off. The money drove him even more.

He began to collect payments hand over fist and felt as if he would soon be able to purchase his own house, another one of the goals he set after splitting from Kelly. He didn't want just any house. He wanted something better than what they built together.

Nonetheless, all his efforts led him to the emptiness he felt at that moment. Today would have been their seventh wedding anniversary. Seven, the number of completion. How appropriate, considering the series of events that led to the demise of their union.

Halston felt restless and lethargic. He decided not to respond to anyone's texts or phone calls that day. He simply didn't have the energy.

He worked a little on his most recent list and started with a woman named Sherry, a massage therapist.

She seemed innocent enough but not gullible by any means. Her demeanor seemed light and fun from her profile photo. She donned an infectiously genuine smile and wore her hair in a shoulder-length bob with golden highlights.

Halston sent the introductory message, disguised as a duplicate account from one of her close friends.

Hey, Sherry. Are you ready for this weekend? It's going to be one to remember.

Halston waited impatiently for a response.

Yes, it is! I'm trying to get my outfit together. I can't decide between these three dresses.

Sherry surveyed all three dresses across her bed as she waited for her friend, Donna, to respond. Little did she know, Halston hacked Donna's account.

She snapped out of her daydream when she heard her notification sound again. The alert was barely audible, as she danced to Bruno Mars playing from her Bluetooth speaker.

Try this link. There are some great options I found here.

"Hmmm…" Sherry uttered aloud.

She nearly clicked on the link but something about the message didn't feel right. Donna hardly ever responded with links on social media. Plus, she didn't comment on the dresses Sherry displayed, which was unlike her.

No movement or response from Sherry's end. Finally, Halston saw she was typing a response.

Bingo.

The rest would be as easy as pie, or so he thought.

Sherry's typing ended and no response was sent. She didn't even click on the link.

Great.

Halston was somewhat exhausted from the back-and-forth that ensued to successfully cross Sherry off his list. He attempted to move on to the next person, but his head wasn't in the game. On top of all of that, the city was set to be declared as a code orange status by next Friday, which required all restaurants and bars to implement a 9:00 pm closing curfew. He figured it was the perfect night to visit one of his favorite new bars, *Coyote Wild*, before the incoming pandemic would shut them down soon.

He was already starting to feel a little woozy, but he decided to cap off the night with one more old-fashioned. His slurred speech was even more apparent as he attempted to speak.

"I'll take one more," he muttered.

"I think you said that will be one more, love. You got a friend taking you home tonight? I don't mean to pry, but this is your fourth one," the bartender responded.

"I'll be good. Thanks for the concern. Fill me up," he insisted.

For the first time during the night, Halston really examined the bartender's eyes. Honestly, he couldn't help but lust for her perky breasts that overflowed from her taut red blouse. Her eyes stirred his inner turmoil even more. Something about the way she looked at him reminded him of Kelly. The intensity of her gaze and even the color of her eye shadow were reminiscent of his now ex-wife.

"Alright then, handsome. Here you go. Just a heads-up, we'll be turning the lights off in this place in about 15 minutes," she warned.

Although she wore a face mask (a red one that perfectly matched her blouse), as Halston did, her voice seemed much clearer than his.

"Thanks. I'll be sure to get out of here before then," he responded quietly.

His mask coupled with his tipsiness made his response barely audible. The bartender's expression revealed she still understood him.

Halston surveyed the bar and noticed he was one of only three people left, besides the bartender and two other workers. He took his time with the last few sips and savored the less-potent whiskey at the bottom of the glass. As soon as he placed his glass on the bar counter, a rolling clap of thunder arrived that shuddered the various bottles of alcohol behind the counter.

"Dammit. Just what I needed. I just got my hair done and this is the day weatherman actually gets it right," the waitress mumbled.

"Tell me about it. My hair is gonna be ruined too," Halston replied sarcastically, as he ran his palm across the back of his close-cropped haircut.

"Oh, you've got jokes, mister. Well, I'm afraid the joke's on you because it's closing time. You've got precisely seven minutes before we're locking the doors," she rebutted.

"I was actually just about to make my way out," Halston replied as he slid a $50 bill on the counter.

"Let me close out your tab and get your change. I hope you're not too shit-faced to drive."

"I'm perfectly fine Ms.? I don't think I got your name," he replied.

"The name is Janet… 'Ms. Jackson if you're nasty'," she replied, with an intense eye-roll and a few hard chews of her gum.

"Mmmm, is that right, Janet? Well, the 'principle of pleasure' is all mine to meet you," he rebutted.

"Clever," she laughed. "My name really is Janet, but I'm only pulling your leg about the Jackson part. What's your end game, man?"

Janet was intrigued by Halston's rugged good looks and witting charm. Underneath his charismatic exterior, she saw a man who seemed to have been dealt a trick deck of cards. Nonetheless, she was intrigued to learn more about him.

"Sir, we are closing up here. If you don't mind closing out your tab and heading out as soon as possible," Kevin responded in a stern tone.

Kevin was 6'3" with broad shoulders, bulging biceps and a waistline that would make Prince envious. His exaggerated prison build made him look more like a caricature than a real threat.

"I got it man," Halston replied, as he sarcastically threw up his hands as if to surrender. "Looks like there's a pretty nasty storm brewing outside. I just wanted to give the lady here a little southern charm and offer my umbrella to walk to her car. That's all."

"Janet, do you know this guy?"

Kevin totally disregarded Halston's statement and directed his gaze solely on Janet.

"It's fine, Kevin. He's harmless, I think. Thanks for checking on me," Janet said.

"Well, I'll get out of your way and let you finish up here. You have yourself a great night now. Keep the change," Halston interjected, as he descended from the barstool.

"Wait, I left my umbrella in the car and the rain has already started. If you're not a creep, I'll take you up on the walk to my car," Janet replied cautiously as she peered beyond the bar to view the rain falling outside.

The intensity increased as the raindrops danced more fervently on the tin roof of the bar. Only she, Kevin, and Halston remained inside the bar now. She noticed Kevin purposely moved slower to make sure she was okay.

"I promise, I'll just walk to your car and be on my way," he vowed.

"Alright, thank you. I really appreciate the gesture. It's getting nasty out there," Janet sighed.

"Sure thing. You're welcome. Just let me know when you're ready."

"Kev! I'm outta here. The guy at the bar is walking me out," Janet yelled.

Kevin pushed through the double doors before he responded. "Ok, you just yell if you need anything. I'll be here for a while," he replied, as he directed his gaze to Halston.

His eyes gave a piercing nonverbal warning to him.

Halston hustled to get his umbrella out of his back seat. The steady rain quickly sobered his buzz as he swung open the back door to grab his umbrella. He was already fully drenched by the time he popped it open.

"Oh my God. I feel so bad. This rain is ridiculous. Thank you. I have a couple of clean towels in my car. You can't drive home wet like this."

"Don't feel bad at all. I would have felt worse leaving and knowing you were caught out in this. Ready to make a run for it?"

He could feel the building's cool air on top of his head. His jeans stuck to him and the water from his button-down shirt dripped over his tall leather boots.

"Yeah, let's go for it. The red Acura is mine," Janet replied.

Halston tilted the umbrella more on Janet's side. The rain swept underneath the umbrella as they ran in unison strides towards Janet's car. Her blue, form-fitted blouse barely covered her midriff. He felt the flesh of the side of her torso as he gripped her defined physique. Although he innocently pulled her closer to keep her dry, he enjoyed how she felt in his hand.

"Take your time," Halston stated.

Janet quickly fumbled for her keys in her purse.

"Sorry, it would have been smart if I had these out ahead of time. Get in the passenger seat," she urged.

"Ah, ok. I'll be good to drive home though. I'm not too far from here," he replied.

"No. Get in," Janet demanded.

She started the ignition as Halston hurried to the passenger side. He exhaled deeply as he placed the umbrella between his legs.

"Well, that was an adventure."

"I know, right. You can say that again. Reach in the back seat. There should be two towels back there."

"Thanks. I guess this will help. Planning on taking any beach trips soon?"

Although Halston was grateful that Janet had dry towels in her backseat, it seemed a bit odd.

"Well, if you must know, I moonlight as a bartender but I really work as a lifeguard," she replied, with an intensified tone of sarcasm.

"Touché," he laughed.

"Here, let me do it. What's your story, Mr. Halston?" Janet inquired, as she folded the towel to find new pockets of dryness to soak up the moisture.

"I don't think you have that kind of time," he smirked.

"Hmm. Try me," she replied.

A moment of silence arose as the soundtrack of the beating rain tapped against the windshield. They locked eyes as Janet pressed a dry corner of the towel on Halston's inner thigh.

Halston moved in to connect his lips with Janet's. They tasted like honey-infused almond milk and he devoured them. He gently squeezed the side of her neck beneath her ear as he continued to feast on her lips like the last slice of pecan pie at Thanksgiving.

Janet squeezed the inside of his thigh as the moisture between her own thighs competed with the rain outside. She inhaled his woodsy, earthy scent. The trace of whiskey on his lips only made his kisses that much sweeter. She guided his free hand around her waist.

Halston took the nonverbal cue to begin unbuttoning her blouse. He could see the top of the curve of her full breasts peeking out of her matching lace bra. The beautiful sight hardened the growing mass inside his wet jeans even more. He moved his left hand up the back of her blouse to unfasten her bra.

Janet shuddered as his touch invoked a shiver down her spine. She unbuckled his belt first and then his shirt, exposing his chiseled chest. She was pleasantly surprised to see he was even more in shape than she expected.

They both finished removing each other's shirts with ferocious passion as Janet removed her pants and climbed over the console to sit on his lap. Halston slid his pants down and reclined the seat. The wetness from her love land seeped through her matching blue lace boy shorts and lubricated his thighs. He slid them to one side and slowly inserted himself inside her.

That initial thrust felt like heaven. Janet could hardly compose herself. She moaned in ecstasy as she rocked back and forth on top of him.

"Wait. Wait. Here, put this on," she panted.

Janet handed him a condom. She cringed at the thought of having to press pause on the steamy moment, but she wanted to be safe.

"Ok, alright. I'm ready," Halston replied.

He thrust himself inside her again as she gripped him tightly with each stroke. He sat up to pull her closer and devour her breasts. The more his tongue lapped against her nipples, the faster she bucked in unison with his intensified strokes. He squeezed his arms tightly around her waist as she dug her freshly manicured nails in the back of his neck. The harder he pulsated, the louder she moaned.

"I'm about to…..ah. Don't stop, please," she begged.

"Me too. I'm….just waiting for you," he barely spoke.

"Go. Go. Right now. Give it to me," she demanded.

Halston felt all the energy in his body rush to his throbbing member. A puddle of wetness settled on his thighs as he thrust harder and faster. It felt like ecstasy. Despite the quick and dirty circumstances, there was something euphoric about their encounter. As the last of his juices escaped him, there was a very realistic sensation he felt as she slowly raised from his lap.

That's when he realized it. The condom broke.

CHAPTER 33

Halston awakened with a pounding headache. The sun greeted him through a thin slit in his living room window. He slept on the couch and didn't quite make it to the bed. He stripped down to his underwear and his wet clothes were balled up on top of one of his bar stools. He couldn't remember the last time he had that much to drink.

His phone sounded an alert for a low battery, which surprised him. He assumed his phone was dead. He stumbled over to his phone and quickly plugged it into the charger. Walking was a more challenging feat than he expected.

Hey, it's me – Janet. Call me when you can.

Suddenly, last night flashed through his mind.

The condom broke.

He knew she must have got home safely, but he couldn't remember what happened afterwards.

He prayed that he didn't just make a huge mistake before he dialed Janet.

She texted him over an hour ago.

He hoped he would still be able to reach her. Halston walked towards the refrigerator for some water to help soothe his swirling headache. His anxiety heightened as he awaited for her to answer the phone.

One ring.

Two rings.

Three rings.

She finally picked up on the third ring.

"Well, hello there sleeping beauty. Sounds like you made it home safely," she uttered.

"Hey, Janet. I'm sorry it took me a while to respond to your message. I just woke up a few minutes ago. Are you alright?"

"If 'you're alright' is your way of finding out if I'm pregnant, you have nothing to worry about."

"Ah, thank God. Thank you. Last night was amazing by the way. I don't remember much, but I do remember that."

"You're not too bad yourself. You may not remember this part, but you followed me to the CVS to get a morning-after pill. So, we're all good. Last night was a thrill, in more ways than one."

Halston silently rejoiced that he hadn't gotten Janet pregnant. Although his chance of having children was slim, he didn't want to test it with random women.

"Ok, I think it's slowly coming back to me now. That's not usually how I operate. I don't even remember getting inside of my apartment last night," he confessed.

"Oh, I'm not surprised. You were pretty wasted. Hey, I know we started things off a bit quickly and this pandemic is looming over our heads but let me know if you ever want to hang out again sometime," she proposed.

"We can make that happen soon. I'm fresh out of a divorce so I'm damaged goods, just so you have fair warning."

"Ah, now that explains it. No offense, but I've seen guys like you come through the bar more times than I can count – drinking their sorrows away. You be careful with that. We all come with a little damage. That doesn't scare me."

"You're right. I guess we all carry baggage."

"Well, I don't want to keep you. I need to run some errands before my shift tonight. I need to think of another means of income since this might be my last full week coming up. I guess the threat of this pandemic is getting real," she sighed.

Halston fought back the urge to tell her about his job. After all, it would be a perfect way for her to quickly supplement her income.

He had to stay focused.

She was nice but they only had sex once and it wasn't like he was interested in her for anything more than that. Plus, it might be too complicated to explain to Julia since all referrals were passed through the company.

"Ah, that's a bummer. I hope all of this will just blow over soon. I'm sure it won't impact you at work too much. I'll keep an eye out for you too," he falsely assured her.

"Aren't you the sweetest? Thank you, I appreciate that. Take care of yourself."

"Anytime. Indeed: you too. Talk to you soon."

Halston smiled as he remembered the risqué sexual escapade, he had with Janet last night. He was beyond grateful that he didn't get her pregnant. What about an STD? He was sure he was 'bug-free'. At least he hoped he was.

He decided to lay down on the couch to get a little more rest before he tackled his list. Within a few minutes, he fell into a sound sleep.

"Halston," he heard a voice call out to him.

The voice sounded eerily familiar, yet unrecognizable. Nonetheless, he could tell by the tone that it was a female voice.

The sky above him was purple, with faint, glowing hints of orange. He sat alone in the jacuzzi on the balcony as he watched oversized cards float in the sky above him. As a few of the cards descended closer to him, he noticed they were tarot cards. Right before he had a chance to investigate what was on each card, the voice called out again.

"Hey, I'm sorry to keep you waiting. I'll be there in a minute," the woman said.

"Alright, the tub is getting cold," he replied, with a snicker.

"It is not. It's a hot tub, silly. Guess who? I guess I didn't fool you, did I?" the woman joked as she walked behind Halston and placed her hands over his eyes.

Kelly.

That's who the woman was.

Her voice was clearer now, although she still sounded unlike herself.

Halston was unable to speak for some reason. He was paralyzed in the moment.

Kelly disappeared for a moment and returned with a bottle of wine.

Halston turned to face her and noticed she only had on her bikini bottoms.

"I figured I'd get the party started a little early. I hope you don't mind," she said as she popped open the wine bottle and poured the overflow on top of her glistening, plump breasts.

Kelly flashed a sinister smile as she carefully stepped into the hot tub to join Halston.

"Ah!" Halston exclaimed aloud.

He leaned towards the coffee table and picked up his phone to check the time. Less than 30 minutes had passed but he felt like he slept much longer.

Halston didn't attempt to go back to sleep. He felt like the dream would just return. He couldn't understand why he had several variations of the same dream over the last two years. The scenario was slightly different but one thing never changed: Kelly always tried to harm him in the dream.

He started picking up things around his apartment and then he sat down to focus on his list. He really had to focus to make sure he was able to get all his money on time. At that point, he didn't even need it to get by. Halston's savings was at a nice, healthy five figures and for once in his life, he felt like he was in control of his destiny.

Ding.

His phone alerted again.

He didn't think it was Janet again. Maybe it was Julia.

He opened his phone to see the message was from neither of them.

It was from Sharon.

He smiled from ear to ear when he saw her name on his phone. She was the one woman he could see himself in a relationship with after his divorce from Kelly. Although they only had a few sessions together, her impression and impact lasted.

Hey, it's me – Sharon. I'm just checking on you and hope all is well in your world, mister;).

Halston grinned and slipped into another daydream before he responded to Sharon.

CHAPTER 34

Halston never forgot the first day he visited Sharon for their initial session. The most profound words often come from a stranger. During one of the darkest days in his depression from his and Kelly's separation, he ran into an elderly woman at a small café who referred him to Sharon.

The lady could sense his disgruntled state.

Halston didn't want to be bothered. He wanted to steep and stew over his disastrous situation while drinking his Chai Tea Latte, in peace.

Nevertheless. She was insistent on giving him her two cents.

"Hello, young man. How are you?" she greeted him.

"I'm okay - just fine," Halston replied curtly.

"Are you really? You don't seem fine. Look, I don't mean to pry but here I go. I don't know your situation and I don't need to know, but…." she ranted.

"Thanks for your concern, ma'am. I'm truly ok," he assured her with shaky conviction.

"Well, you just take this card and use it when you're ready. She's an excellent therapist. I wouldn't recommend her if I hadn't tried her out for myself. My soul says you need to speak with someone to pour out what's on your heart and you need to do it quickly. You have a good day now," she said as she tapped the table and slid the business card just before his fingertips.

Halston sat there dumbfounded.

He was angered at the lady's accurate perception of him. Nevertheless, he knew she was right. He was a steeping kettle about to blow.

Looking back on all their sessions, Halston wondered if it was really fate that collided their worlds.

There was a strong attraction between the two of them and things took a heated turn during their last session. Halston remembered feeling light on his feet and particularly confident that day. He didn't have a care in the world. Perhaps finally getting a stream of steady income (whether legal or not) played a substantial role in his demeanor that day.

As the state of the looming pandemic was uncertain, Halston remembered Sharon giving him some hand sanitizer when he entered the room.

"Hello, Halston. Come on in. Well, here we are. Our last session. The time has passed very quickly," Sharon smiled gleefully.

"Yes, it has. I, um, did some deep searching about my friend. My ex-friend, Devin," Halston sighed.

"Did you? Ok, that's good. That's fantastic. Thank you for digging into your feelings about him. Before we delve into that, how are you?" Sharon asked.

"Oh, I'm sorry. I guess I just cut straight to the chase, huh?" Halston laughed nervously.

"It's ok, I just want you to acknowledge and recognize how you feel right now in this very moment before we get into the potentially heavy details."

"Thank you. Well, today has been a great day. It's been a great week, actually. I'm taking things day by day and I know we'll probably get to this later, but I'm proud of myself for not being triggered by something that disturbed me. Look at me, I'm being terribly rude. How has your week been?"

"No, you're fine. It's been a great week for me too. My sister came into town, so I got to spend some quality time with her. I bought a new record player this week too. That was exciting. I'm curious to hear about your trigger that you managed to dodge. Please, do tell," she insisted as she crossed her legs.

Halston tried not to gawk at her as he glanced at her shapely, well-toned legs peeping out of her maroon sweater dress. He pictured her crossing her legs again, with the dress much shorter, reenacting the iconic Sharon Stone moment from *Basic Instinct*.

"It was a couple of days after our last session. I decided to try a new pizza shop near my new apartment. That's when I saw them together, my ex-wife and Devin."

"Oh, ok. What did they appear to be doing together? Did you speak to them?".

"They didn't see me. At least I don't think they did. They looked like they were out on a date. I don't think I mentioned that I did see them a little while before that at an art gallery. I didn't expect to see either one of them, but we kept it cordial."

"How did it make you feel when you saw them and more importantly when it appeared that they were on a date?"

"Honestly, I was pissed.".

"That's perfectly normal considering the circumstance."

"Yeah, I guess. Can you believe they were going to the same pizza place? The irony. Anyhow, I envisioned attacking them or better yet, smashing the window of their car with my bare hands. The element of surprise has always excited me. I went through this whole fantasy of the shards of glass exploding everywhere. Of course, there was some blood; it dripped down my hand. I heard the screams of people watching, wondering what was wrong with me. It was a whole ordeal in my head, you know? Then, I just snapped out of it," Halston concluded.

"Just like that? You just snapped out of it?" Sharon asked, seemingly in disbelief.

"Yeah, I even surprised myself. I swear I envisioned the whole thing in my head. It felt so real, I could taste it," Halston admitted.

"That is commendable, I must say, to have thought of a plan so vividly in your mind and have the restraint to avoid carrying it out.

It's very impressive. I honestly can't say I would have been able to hold back like that," Sharon replied.

"Really? I'm shocked. I mean, I just assume that therapists and people in your profession always do the right thing," Halston said.

Sharon could see that he was genuinely surprised by her response.

"Well, thank you for the compliment. I have not always been the best at controlling my emotions. Can I share something with you?" she inquired.

"Sure, of course. Go ahead," Halston replied.

He felt somewhat relieved that he wasn't in the hot seat now.

"Ok, I've been married before and I was cheated on. I guess I felt it and I just knew my husband was cheating on me. So, against my better judgment, I followed him one night. He told me he had a business dinner and he'd be coming home late. That's the age-old lie, you know, the oldest trick in the book. He was not a great liar because he told me the restaurant he was going to for the 'business dinner'," Sharon said.

She took a brief pause to gather her thoughts and her breath before she continued.

"So, I walked into the restaurant after I saw him and her both walk into the restaurant. I waited about ten minutes and acted like I had left something inside the restaurant from dining there earlier. I walked towards the restroom and spotted them at a cozy table together. I was furious when I walked out of that restaurant. I walked to his car in the garage where it was parked in the valet. I kept a switchblade in my purse for safety then. That night, it turned into a weapon of mass destruction to puncture his two back tires," she sighed.

"Really? I can't remember if I mentioned this before but I did throw a brick at my ex-best friend's car the first time I met up with him after I found out my wife cheated with him. I get it. There's definitely no judgment here," Halston laughed nervously.

"I guess we've both had our struggles with cheating partners," Sharon replied.

"Yes, that's so true. Thank you for everything, Sharon. These last few weeks have been tremendously helpful for me."

"I'm really glad to hear that. It's been more than a pleasure having you these last few weeks as well. I have really enjoyed it," Sharon replied, as she cleared her throat.

An awkward silence filled the room.

"Thanks, I'm glad to hear that. Can I share something with you too?" Halston asked.

"Yes, of course. Go ahead. Forgive me for interjecting my personal rant. This is your time," Sharon smiled as she eased back into her chair and recrossed her legs, this time throwing her right leg over the left one.

"I think you're beautiful. I know that could be crossing a line and you don't have to respond but I just want you to know," he revealed.

He felt like beautiful was the safest word to use, but he honestly felt like she was sexy, with a wonderfully sculpted body and he desperately wanted to be inside of her. Nonetheless, 'beautiful' was the PG-13 version of the fantasy he avoided sharing until today.

"Oh, wow! I was not expecting that. Thank you. You are incredibly handsome yourself. Look, I don't want to get myself in any incriminating situations here. I must keep things professional. I'm sure you understand," she replied.

"Yes, I'm sorry. I know we don't have much time left in today's session. If you want to stop here, I totally understand. I didn't mean to make anything awkward," he said.

"No, I don't want you to stop there. Today is your last session and although this discussion means it probably impedes me from having a client relationship with you in the future, that doesn't mean we should pass up this electric connection we're both apparently feeling," she smiled.

Halston smiled back with a mischievous grin, even though he was speechless for a moment. He did not expect Sharon to respond that way. He hoped for the far-fetched chance to have sex with her, and he even fantasized about it a few times. However, he didn't think it was a real possibility – until now.

"Ok, I can't say I disagree with that. I'm glad we're both on the same page," Halston said as he stood up and moved towards Sharon.

He slid his hands around the back of her neck, just underneath her short-cropped auburn bob, as he leaned in to kiss her lips. He was intoxicated by her delicious scent and the invigorating taste of her lips. They were soft and supple, even better than he imagined.

"Damn, I've been wanting that for so long," she sighed, as she pushed him off of her and rose from her chair.

Halston looked perplexed. He didn't understand why she pushed him away.

Sharon moved towards her office door and turned both locks to make sure they had complete privacy.

"Now, where were we?" she asked, as she leaned against her desk.

Her eyes spoke to Halston without opening her mouth. They said, "Come devour me."

He graciously obliged.

He slid off her black pumps and slowly massaged each of her feet before he traced his fingers along her calves, before he finally rested on the outside of her thighs.

She smelled even sweeter with her legs open for him, on top of her desk.

He slid his head underneath her sweater dress and moved her panties to the side with his teeth. His left hand held them in place as his tongue lapped around her clitoris like he was attempting to catch dripping ice cream from a cone on a hot summer day.

"Yesssss," she purred, as she grabbed his ears and grazed the back of his neck with her fingernails.

Halston reveled in her wet pond of ecstasy and pushed her thighs against his face so hard that he could barely turn his head left or right.

Sharon slid back and loosened the oversized black leather belt around her sweater dress that accentuated her hourglass physique. She struggled to loosen her legs from Halston's grip and slid her black lace panties down to her ankles.

Halston allowed her to stand from the desk as they kissed passionately. He unbuckled his belt and Sharon helped him get out of his polo shirt.

She was pleasantly surprised when she saw him without his shirt. She could tell he was in shape, but she did not expect him to be so ripped. She reached into her purse and pulled a magnum condom out. Sharon hoped she wasn't being too presumptuous with his size.

Damn, she thought to herself.

Once she saw his erect bulge through his boxer briefs, she knew he would have absolutely no issue filling the condom. She wanted him even more now.

"Sit down on the couch," Sharon commanded him.

She slipped her sweater dress down to her ankles, leaving only her bra on her body.

Halston removed it as soon as she lowered herself onto his lap. He took each one of her breasts and flicked the nipples with his tongue before he stuffed and sucked them like there was no to-morrow. He was pleasantly surprised to find she had her left nipple pierced.

"I can't take it anymore. I can't wait to be inside you," Halston admitted.

"Well, what are you waiting on big boy? Let's get this session started," she laughed.

Halston secured the condom on his erect, throbbing penis.

Sharon sighed with pleasure as he slipped inside of her. She started moving in a rhythmic gyration on top of him – slow at first and eventually, she picked up speed.

"Wait. Slow down. I just want to hold it in you for a minute," Halston requested.

Sharon did as she was told and stopped moving.

Halston could feel all her muscles welcoming his manhood with a warm hello even though she wasn't moving.

"Damn, you feel so good," he whispered.

They started kissing each other again as Sharon couldn't keep her composure any longer. She began to ride Halston like she was trying to tame a raging bull.

"It's so deep," she exclaimed.

"It's so wet and tight," he replied.

Halston stood up while he was still inside of Sharon to preserve his stamina. He knew he wouldn't be able to last long if she kept riding him so vigorously.

Sharon kissed the right side of his neck as they stumbled back towards her desk.

Halston laid her on her back and delivered slow, intentional strokes before he couldn't contain himself and started moving faster to match Sharon's rhythm.

She pulled him in deeper with each stroke and he couldn't get enough. Right before they were both about to climax, she stood up and bent over the front of her desk.

Halston entered her from behind and grabbed her breasts.

Sharon met each of his thrusts and matched him for an equal push against his pelvis.

They both throbbed and slapped against each other's skin until Halston felt Sharon explode and drip all over his pelvis and thighs.

He climaxed shortly after and exhaled deeply as he collapsed on her back and kissed her neck.

Mmmm, this salmon is to die for," Julia said as she took another bite of the meal Halston prepared.

"Thank you. I'm glad to hear you like it. I tried a new recipe. It's only my third time making it like this," he replied.

"Well, you say I can cook but I can get used to this kind of eating," she laughed.

Julia took another bite of the mashed potatoes and green beans from her plate, as Halston walked over with his MacBook.

"You are not going to believe this," Halston said excitedly.

"Oh yeah, what's that?"

"Look through this list and tell me if you see any familiar names that stick out to you."

Ok, let me see. Hmmmm……wait. What? Bosniac is on here. That is hilarious. If only we could go after him, right?" Julia joked.

"We can. What's stopping us?"

"Are you out of your mind? I know we did it that one time for Kelly and Devin, but that was different. I only suggested it because I knew that was personal to you. That was so different," Julia continued.

"I appreciate that. I really do. Look at it like I could return the favor to you. That could be one I give to you," he suggested.

"Hey, I appreciate the kind gesture, but I think that's too risky.

You had those couple of hiccups last week where the people nearly found out your real identity. You have to lay low. I know you're knocking it out of the park, but I've been doing this longer than you have," Julia cautioned.

"So, what are you trying to say?"

Halston leaned back and glared at Julia in disbelief.

"Halston, I'm not trying to imply anything. I'm telling you, it's not a good idea. You know he's a vindictive asshole. If it comes back and he's able to pinpoint that it's you, everything you've built will be in jeopardy. Look at you. You won't even be in this apartment much longer and you'll be in your own house, outside of corporate America. Do you really want to throw all of that away behind a little greed?"

"Greed?"

Yes, I didn't stutter. Greed. Give me one good reason why you can't just swap his name out with someone else, other than you want the thrill of getting even with him?" she asked.

"I guess. I'll just drop it," he replied curtly.

"Don't get all salty with me, mister. I'm just looking out for your best interest," she replied.

"I know. I see your point," he laughed.

Halston was surprised that Julia wasn't onboard with his idea to stick it to Bosniac. After all that he had done to them both, he thought the idea to scam him would be a no brainer for her. Obviously, she decided to play good cop instead.

"I'm glad you see it my way. Seriously, this food was amazing. I don't mind washing the dishes since you cooked. That's the least I can do. I'll get out of your hair after that," she promised.

"You're not bothering me," Halston replied.

Deep down, he was agitated and did want her to leave. Nonetheless, he played it cool. He suspected she could see through him but he didn't care.

"I'm glad but I do need to get going. I need to start on my own list. I'm a couple of days behind. Plus, I have a load of laundry waiting for me when I get back home. Everything was delicious. You have a good night. I'll talk to you later," Julia said before she kissed him on the cheek and left his apartment.

Even though she flirted so hard with him when they worked together, she had a much more nonchalant attitude towards him now. That made him want her even more but tonight, he did want his space.

"Alright, I'll talk to you later then. Let me know when you make it home," Halston said, as he barely looked up from his laptop.

"You gonna come lock the door?" she asked, as she leaned against the wall.

"Oh yeah, I'm sorry," he replied, as he advanced towards the front door.

"I care about you man. Just remember that."

"I know and I care about you too."

Halston kissed her before she walked down the hallway. He locked the door and exhaled deeply before he sat back down at his computer. Deep down, he knew Julia was right. Regardless, the money drove him away from better judgment. He always hoped for the day that he could get back at Mr. Bosniac. Now, he had the perfect opportunity.

•

Halston blazed through a profitable summer and stacked up more cash than he imagined. It was almost Thanksgiving now and although he cared about Julia, he was more focused on gaining financial freedom. As a result, their situation-ship began to suffer. They didn't argue but they grew distant.

He managed to not partake in purchasing any fancy cars or clothes, but he was determined to get a nice house on his own. Halston spoke with the same realtor that Devin used for his house. He felt like he was getting closer to his dreams and his healing from Kelly.

As he pulled up to the house he saw online, it looked even better in-person. He sat in the car and admired the architecture from the outside before he reached the front door.

The realtor greeted him as soon as he stepped inside.

"Halston?" he asked.

"Yes sir, that's me. It's nice to meet you, Zach."

"Thank you, it's nice to meet you as well. May I interest you in a bottle of water?" Zach asked.

"Oh sure, thank you. This floorplan is amazing. When Devin told me about you, I knew I would be in good hands. He was so picky when he bought his house but after I visited, I could see that his selectiveness was well worth it," Halston replied.

"Tell him I said thanks for the kind words. Hopefully, this home will be to your liking. As you can see the high-vaulted ceilings are a nice touch. Plus, the open concept with the distinct sections is something that's hard to find in this area. If you're a man that likes to spend some time in the kitchen, you'll love this island with the gas stove and plentiful counterspace," Zach continued.

"I do like to cook a little bit. The kitchen is very spacious. What year was this house built again? 2015?" Halston inquired.

He knew exactly what year it was built. He knew the stats of the house better than Zach probably did but he didn't want to seem too eager.

"Yes, a man that knows his information. It was built in 2015 and the asking price is just a hair lower than the going rate for other homes in this neighborhood. The previous owners had to move out quickly due to a new job opportunity, so they are very eager to sell," Zach said.

"Ok, I get it. They left behind a good one. Do you mind if I view the bedrooms too?" Halston asked.

"Sure, you probably saw the guestroom to your right as you entered. Plus, there is one more room downstairs. The master and the office room are both upstairs."

Zach followed behind Halston as he perused the rest of the house.

Halston was thoroughly impressed. He was excited at the possibility of finally having his own home, after his divorce. It truly signaled a new start that he desperately wanted and needed.

"Here we are in the master bedroom. There's almost enough

room in here for two king-sized beds. Everyone goes wild about the tub too. I guess the vintage look is making a comeback."

"Ah, I see what you mean. Yes, I must admit, I fall into that group as well. I love the stand-alone, vintage tubs like that. Well, this is a beautiful home. I'm sure I'll need to act fast. Do you have a card or contact information that I can reach back out to you?" Halston asked.

"Yes, of course. Sounds great. Yes, please give me a call. As I've mentioned, this is a hot one so let me know as soon as you decide," Zach cautioned.

"I will do that. Thanks, Zach. It's been a pleasure man. Well, I will sleep on it tonight and you'll hear something from me either way by tomorrow morning."

"Sounds like a plan to me. I look forward to it."

They both walked downstairs and Halston did another visual once over before he moved towards the front door.

"Alright, take care man," Halston replied, as he walked outside.

Something about Zach seemed familiar, but he couldn't quite determine why.

The midday cool breeze greeted Halston as he stepped out of the shade and opened his car door. He started his car and gazed at Zach's business card for a moment.

Brinton.

Zach Brinton.

Halston repeated the full name in his head.

Zach was on the latest list he received.

H alston?"

Halston heard the distant, yet familiar sound of a female voice. He turned around and didn't see anyone he knew.

He was at Whole Foods picking out some vegetables to make soup and get some other things he didn't need but wanted. A smile formed involuntarily across his face as he remembered the time he couldn't afford to buy anything he wanted in the store, let alone the necessities.

"Halston?" You looked deep in thought back there. I didn't know if I was going to have to run to catch you or not."

"Lynelle? Well, look what the wind blew in. I apologize. That's what I get for coming in here when I'm already hungry. How are you?"

"I'm great and yourself? You look very well," she replied.

"Thank you and so do you. What are you up to these days? I haven't seen you since the Halloween party. I can't believe it's been so long."

"Yeah, I know. I've been holding up well; taking it day by day. I'm enjoying my freedom and my singleness, surprisingly."

"You can say that again. I wanted to reach out to see how you were doing but I didn't want to make things more awkward. I guess we both knew how each other felt at least to some degree," Halston sighed.

"Yeah, I can't believe it but I guess the truth really is stranger than fiction. I have to ask you a question if you don't mind."

"Sure, go ahead. What's that?"

Halston moved towards the bench in the deli area for them to have a seat. Although he anticipated a quick store visit, he wanted to make time to speak with Lynelle. After all, she was a totally innocent party in the demise of her marriage, just like he was.

"Did you know? I mean, did you ever feel like something was going on between them?"

The question punched him hard in the gut.

He quickly ran through all the doubtful moments he had about he and Kelly's marriage in his mind.

"Did I think there was a possibility she would cheat on me? I've thought about it a few times, like I think any normal married person would after the first couple of years. I didn't see what happened coming. That was a surprise indeed."

"At least I know I'm not crazy. It was pretty much the same for me too. You know what they say about women's intuition. I guess my radar was focused somewhere else because I didn't think he was cheating with Kelly either. Mmmm, who would have thought this is where we'd be today?"

"You know what? I just remembered that I used to have this weird, recurring dream about Kelly and me. We are away on a vacation or a honeymoon and right before she tried to kiss me or hug me, she would always do something devious. It felt creepy like she was about to kill me or something. I guess it was just my mind playing tricks on me. I haven't had that dream in a while," Halston replied.

"Wow, that is creepy. I'm glad you don't have that dream anymore. I hate to be that vindictive person but all I can say is karma is not kind. They both will have to answer for their actions," she said.

"Did you ever have a moment where you lost your cool about the whole situation with him?"

"Oh, if you're asking if I broke his car window like you did, I didn't do that," she laughed.

"Ouch. I guess I stepped right into that one."

"You did. I loved it. In all seriousness, my lowest point was about three months ago. I heard through the grapevine that they are a happy little family now. I had a tracker on his car and for a long time I didn't use it, but something got into me that night. I pulled up where he was – I guess maybe her new house. I got out of the car and stood there at the front door with my gun. I stood there for maybe two minutes, but it felt like an eternity. It was pitch black outside and I wasn't thinking rationally but I was completely sober, not an ounce of alcohol in my system. I planned to blast whoever came through that door squarely between the eyes."

"Whoa, that's intense and highly understandable. I've had similar thoughts of doing the same thing to them."

"Yeah, I couldn't live in that place anymore. I had to snap out of it. I started picking up new hobbies, exercising more, anything that would get my mind off him. I'm out of that house now and that helped tremendously," she said.

"I can understand that. Clearing the mental space is a serious thing. I started seeing a therapist. I don't see her anymore but she's great. Her name is Sharon. I can send you her contact information if you're interested in speaking with a professional," he replied.

"I'd like that. Yes, please send her info. This has felt like a few therapy sessions in one. Thanks for listening, Halston. Don't be a stranger. My number is still the same. I'll let you get back to your shopping. You take care of yourself."

"You take care of yourself too. We're going to be alright."

Halston stood up and gave Lynelle a tight hug.

They both exhaled together in unison.

"Yes, we are and we'll be that much better for it. See you soon, Halton."

"Definitely. Sounds good, Lynelle. Good seeing you and you're right. We will be better for it all."

Halston awoke to the feeling of small, steady droplets of water falling on his head. His eyes felt incredible heavy, and he was barely able to open them. A faint stench of damp cardboard and sewage filled the room. He kept feeling like he was in a dream. However, his physical limitations confirmed it all too real.

He tried to stand up from the chair he sat in but quickly found out his hands were bound behind his back. A single red laser beam shone on his forehead.

He panicked.

As Halston surveyed his surroundings, he realized he was in some type of abandoned warehouse.

He had no idea how he got there or more importantly, who put him there. The last thing he remembered was going out on a late-night run for some ice cream – Rocky Road. How appropriate.

That's when he remembered it. A man walked up to him and asked him if he had jumper cables to start his car. The details after that point were extremely fuzzy.

The rusty chair that he sat in was placed squarely in the middle of the abandoned room. The place had to be no larger than a 1000 square-foot apartment.

Drip.

Drip.

Drip.

The water continued to fall on his head. He feared to look up at the ceiling above him to see where it came from. He didn't remember there being any rain last night.

"Hello?" he called out.

Silence.

"Hello. Shit. Who's there? Who's doing this?"

Still no response; only the echo of his voice resounding from the damp room. He moved his body from side-to-side, in hopes of wiggling the knot loose that kept him tied to the chair.

He then stood up and walked, awkwardly with the chair scraping the ground, to nowhere in particular, searching for a way out.

"I wouldn't try to make an escape if I were you. You are here to learn a lesson."

Halston looked upwards in the direction of where the distorted voice came from. He couldn't tell if the person was male or female. Their voice sounded somewhat groggy and scratchy, much like someone who had just recovered from tuberculous.

"A lesson? Who are you? What are you talking about? Get me out of here now," Halston commanded.

"You're a bit haughty to be in such a compromising position."

The red dot continued to follow Halston wherever he moved.

Although he was infuriated about his current state, he realized it might be in his best interest to have a seat and play nice with whoever the lunatic was that captured him.

"Seriously, what do you want from me?"

"What do I want from you? Now, that's a loaded question. It's really tragic that what I want, you have no ability to give to me."

"Is it money? I can get it for you. I just need a little time depending on how much you need," Halston said.

He could feel his wallet still in his back pocket when he fidgeted in his seat. Whoever the person was must have not intended to rob him.

"It's not your money that I'm after; it's you. It's answers. It's justice; all of which you have no damned clue how to give me, do you?"

"I'm really sorry for whatever I did. I promise I will make it up to you. I don't know how or what it will take but if you let me go, I'll make it up to you. You have my word," Halston pleaded.

"I have your word. You know, people like you make my stomach turn. You have the perfect life, the perfect wife, the perfect job and none of it really seems to satisfy you. I know a lot more about you than you think I do. I've been watching you for a long time," the unidentified person sighed.

Halston tried to look closer in the direction of the person's voice. He could only see a figure dressed in black, with a ski mask. The red dot continued to loom over his forehead.

Heavy footsteps filled in the uncomfortable silence.

Halston could barely see the person's eyes but nothing else.

"I'm not perfect by any means. I'm not married anymore. I'm divorced. Look, I'm not trying to hurt anyone. If I did anything to offend you, I promise I didn't mean it."

"Shut up. Shut up. Shut the absolute fuck up!"

Halston bit his tongue and did as he was told. He could literally feel his blood boiling.

"Let me tell you a story. I had a brother once, an older brother. He died recently and do you want to know how he died?"

Silence.

"Speak up!"

"I'm really sorry to hear that. Um, yes, I do," Halston replied nervously.

"Good because you're fresh out of choices, so you have to listen anyway. He was always troubled, even when we grew up. He never quite seemed to find his worth outside of hanging with the wrong crowd. He was hooked on drugs, got clean and was sober for a few years. The whole family was ecstatic. You know how those journeys sometimes go. The joy didn't last because he kept....he kept having setback after setback... after setback. Granted, none of it was really his fault but it was all how he chose to react to it. Do you know what the last straw was for him?"

"I'm sorry, I don't. I really hate to hear that about your brother," Halston continued.

He tried to pull out his best reverse psychology sympathy tactics, but to no avail.

"His last straw was you."

"Wait. What? I think you've got the wrong guy. I'm pretty sure I never even met your brother," Halston pleaded.

"You didn't meet him but you drove him to end his life. Does the name Jeff Thompson ring a bell to you? Of course not. It's such a common name, right?"

"I'm sorry. I don't believe I know him."

"You don't know him because he was just a random person on your list. I confiscated his computer from his home right after he died. I searched for anything that could give me a clue as to what pushed him to take his life. There were a few messages back and forth with you and your fake profile. He begged you to give him the money back and you lied. You promised him that you would get it to him the next day and then the next day, but you never did. His last message to you said 'I'm on the edge and I really need this money to survive. You don't understand. I don't have a few days to wait.'"

Halston paused before he responded. He honestly didn't remember the dialogue with Jeff. Nonetheless, he thought it was very possible that it was true. After all, it sounded like the interactions he had with many people he had taken money from.

"I'm sorry. I can't say I recall that."

That was all Halston was able to muster to say.

"I'm pretty savvy with computers. All I had to do was find the spot where the message came from. Once I found that, I came straight to your apartment. It was like poetic justice because you didn't even know it was me. I looked you directly in your eyes, but you were too drunk or high off your ass to even recognize who I was. It took you over five minutes just to fumble for your keys and get inside your apartment."

"I do remember that night. I was in a bind. I was just doing some things to get some quick money. That was all. If you just let me go, I won't tell anyone. I'll pay you and get you whatever you want," Halston replied.

"Did I ask you to speak? You can't bring him back. It's over. Oh, but before it's lights out for you, I guess it would only be right to reveal myself."

Halston waited nervously. He wasn't sure if these were the last few moments of his life.

"Does it ring a bell now?" the previously unidentified person asked, with the voice distorter removed and the mask off.

"Are you serious? You can't do this. I get it. I've lost people too and it hurts, but you can't do this," Halston ranted, as he recognized the person who orchestrated his capture and now threatened to kill him.

"I'm sure it's all coming back to you like a fucking flash before your eyes. It's over. Say good night, sucker."

"Wait. No. Please don't do this. Please…."

Halston glared towards the direction of the red beam and heard the gun cock. It was the last sound he consciously remembered hearing before his demise.

The shooter snickered as blood trickled down the front of Halston's face.

Halston took his final breath as he slumped over in his chair.

ulia sobbed uncontrollably as she flat ironed her hair. She wanted to look her best for Halston, even though he wouldn't be able to see her in the flesh. Her sleep pattern had been thrown off ever since he died and last night she barely slept for a couple of hours.

She felt silly that she never expressed her true feelings to Halston. She chose to believe that he felt the same way about her.

Neither one of them crossed the line of expecting more from each other. Perhaps if she had pushed harder, asked more questions and been more present, she could have stopped him from getting killed.

"I love you," she said aloud as she finished teasing her hair in the mirror.

Julia zipped up her boots and walked into the kitchen to have a glass of water. Her throat was sore from crying all night.

The blender still sat on her counter from the day before. She realized she hadn't eaten anything since breakfast yesterday – an apple that she barely finished and a handful of walnuts. She forced herself to make a smoothie to prevent her stomach from rumbling through the service.

Halston always loved pineapples, so she added a few chunks in her smoothie for him.

"I can do this. I can do this. I can do this," she chanted to herself.

Julia grabbed her keys and her smoothie before she walked out of the door. She didn't even make it to her car before she realized she forgot her purse. The door remained ajar as she marched briskly inside to grab her purse.

The door closed abruptly when she grabbed her purse from the bedroom. She eased back into the living room slowly, with her hand on the gun inside her purse. No sleep, plus her typical paranoia created an intoxicating cocktail for her mental state.

As she peered around the corner, she noticed that her umbrella was on the floor. She exhaled deeply as she realized no one was in her home.

Thank God.

Julia peered out of her window and grabbed her umbrella. The sky was overcast with a shade of gloomy gray beneath the light blue patches. The picture was apropos for the occasion.

After a couple of near breakdowns at red lights, she finally made it to the church.

10:37 am.

Although she arrived early, the parking lot was already packed. It was a testament to the great man she knew Halston to be and a sign of nosiness from people who couldn't wait to get inside of a funeral service for a man who had been murdered.

She reluctantly got out of the car and advanced towards the front doors of the church. Her breath escaped her as she entered the building and saw a large headshot of Halston on an easel.

Her legs felt immobile as she moved inside the sanctuary. All the people sitting inside looked like irrelevant ants filling space.

Devin caught her eye as he turned around from his seat.

Julia waved and smiled at him. She was thankful that Halston had such a loyal friend. There was no question in her mind that he set up everything up for the funeral.

"Don't you want to go up there and view the body? They fixed him up nicely. He almost looks like himself. I'll save your seat, if you want to go up there," an elderly woman whispered to Julia as she took her seat near the back of the church.

"Hmmm, I'll pass. I mean, thank you but I would like to remember him as I knew him," Julia responded.

She attempted to mask the perplexed look on her face but didn't believe she succeeded.

"Ok, I get it. You're one of those people. Suit yourself. As for me, I wouldn't want to cheat myself out of the memory. That's all I'm saying."

Julia looked at the elderly woman squarely in her eyes and cleared her throat as if to say, *You can shut up now.*

Although her curiosity almost pushed her to view him lying in the casket, her desire to not be haunted by him won. She scanned the packed sanctuary and studied everyone's emotional state. Some were sobbing, others looked on blankly and some seemed to survey the attendees just like she did.

Her heart beat so forcefully that she could almost hear it echoing in her eardrums. Julia sat there in a daze, occasionally wiping tears that formed at the corners of her eyes. She felt like she couldn't fully grieve Halston; not at that moment at least. She was merely his ex-coworker in the eyes of anyone that knew her, but only she knew she was much more than that.

Finally, it was time for the eulogy. She made it through everyone's remarks, including Kelly's dramatically distraught resolution, and a couple of mediocre song selections (besides her friend Durant's excellent performance) before it was time for the eulogy.

The minister walked smoothly up to the podium as he began his message.

"Ah, to behold a man. We all knew Halston in different facets but one thing I think we can all agree on is that he made you feel welcome. He made you feel important. Halston made you feel like you were the only person in the room whenever he spoke with you. He was calm but the intention behind his words hit with full force. As we gather here today to….."

The rest of his words sounded like gibberish to Julia. Her head started to swim and her stomach felt light. She was glad her seat was at the end of the pew so she could quietly tip out and excuse herself to go to the restroom.

She sauntered into the restroom and was elated to find she was the only person inside. She simply didn't have the energy to muster up another fake smile or hello.

There was a stack of thick paper towels in a quaint straw tray that sat on either end of the sink. Julia grabbed a couple of paper towels and let some cool water run on them. She then placed them across her forehead for a moment.

A conversation she had with her sister a few weeks prior resonated inside her head.

Girl, don't you get involved with that man. It's those quiet ones that get you every time. Watch yourself. Those types of situations rarely end well.

If only she knew then how true her sister's words would be now. Had it not been for this catastrophe, she thought they could have worked. They could have been their own secret Bonnie and Clyde.

Mr. Bosniac.

It hit her.

What if he did this? What if Halston went against her warning like she was almost positive he did? What if there were others on his list that he shouldn't have taken or others that could have been connected to the people's money they took?

It could have been Kelly as well, or even his ex-best friend Devin.

"Shit," she mumbled aloud.

Julia dabbed her forehead once more before she exited the restroom.

Two ladies entered and nearly hit her with the door.

She heard one of them say, "I just still can't believe it. Who could have done such a heinous thing to him?"

The other lady replied, "There's no telling. I know everyone says he's so good but those are exactly the type of men you have to watch."

"Excuse me, ladies," Julie said.

Her facial expression revealed she heard everything they said.

Julia glanced at Halston's photo on the easel once more and took a moment to ingest her surroundings as she found her way back to her seat. She decided she would sit through the rest of the funeral service, but she would not attend his gravesite or the repast. She came to pay her respects to the man she loved; nothing more than that.

Durant stopped her right before she walked through the double doors of the sanctuary again.

"Hey, stranger. It's nice to see you here. I'm sorry about what happened to your co-worker. I only met him once but he seemed like a nice guy," Durant sighed.

"Look at what the cat dragged in. It's so good to see you and it was even better to hear you amidst those painful song selections," she laughed.

"You're still crazy as ever, I see. Thank you for that vote of confidence."

"You're welcome and yes, he was a great guy. I still can't believe it. How did you know him?"

"I'm friends with his friend, Omar. When everything happened, Omar reached out to me that next day to sing. I believe the other singers are members of this church. I heard Halston was involved in some type of pyramid scamming scheme. I hope that's not the reason for what happened," he revealed.

"Oh really? That's crazy. Hopefully, that's not the case. You know how everyone talks and likes to make up things. I thought Omar was the one that organized everything for the funeral. That makes sense that he wasn't able to pick all of the singers."

Julia gave her best poker face against Durant's comment about Halston's rumored scam involvement. She hoped he couldn't see right through her.

"Right, I don't know a dead person without some type of false rumor looming around their legacy. Yeah, well I don't mean to sound insensitive, but I need to collect my money from the church and my stomach is talking to me. I haven't eaten all day so I'm about to get out of here. Let's catch up soon."

"Yes, that sounds great. Let me know when you're free. Get some food. I'll see you soon."

Julia waved and quietly entered the sanctuary again.

Sweat beads formed on her forehead. She wiped them away and attempted to remain calm.

The pastor's eulogy was uplifting, yet generic. It was the type of message that many pastors give to people they may have known in passing, but not in great detail.

Julia continued to zone in and out during the rest of the funeral service. Finally, it was time for the procession. The officiating funeral company began removing the flowers displayed around Halston's casket.

"Mmmhmmm," she moaned quietly.

As everyone in the first two rows began to file out behind the casket, the reality of his death sank in deeper. Julia watched Kelly and Devin together, without the love child they created. Although she despised her more than spoiled sardines, she was glad that she at least had the decency to not bring the child she created from an affair. Kudos to her.

Omar passed by her next. He scooted over to give her a hug.

Brandy waved at Julia from Omar's right side, as she stood next to him.

"We're really going to miss him, huh? I still can't believe this."

Omar's voice croaked and the residue of tears nestled in the whites of his bloodshot eyes.

"Yes, we really are. It's going to be hard without him," Julia replied solemnly.

Although he didn't know the full extent of their relationship, Omar's condolences came from a different place. His words meant more than anyone else's that day.

Julia was now antsy to leave and regretted sitting at the back of the sanctuary. She watched all the people spill out and resisted the urge to slide in with the crowd before it was her turn. As everyone slowly moved past her, she specifically looked for Mr. Bosniac.

She wished she knew if Halston followed through with going

after him from his list. If she knew him half as well as she thought she did, she was almost positive the answer was yes. It was possible Mr. Bosniac could have been there and already exited from the other side of the sanctuary.

Finally, it was her turn to leave. Her knees buckled as she caught another glimpse of Halston's picture in the foyer.

"Goodbye, Halston," she whispered.

Someone touched her on the small of her back. The unfamiliar sensation startled her and made her jump. She turned around to see it was James.

"Oh, it's you. Hey, James. I didn't expect to see you here. It's good to see you. I just hate it's because of such a somber occasion. Um, how have you been?"

"I'm sorry. I didn't mean to startle you. It's great to see you too. I didn't know Halston that well, but from the few times I interacted with him, he was always a stand-up guy.

"Yes, he really was. You're the only one I've seen here from work, but I'm sure there may have been others that I missed. I just kept to myself in the back," Julia replied.

"I thought I saw you when you came in. You weren't the only one here from work. Mr. Bosniac was here, but I saw him leave early."

"That was nice of him to make an appearance."

She kept her comments limited regarding Mr. Bosniac, as not to allude to any unnecessary information to James. Besides, she had a feeling James would volunteer any information he had anyway.

"It was. Well, I'll let you get out of here. I'm not going to the cemetery, but I wanted to at least stop by the service," James said.

"Same here. I'm going to get out of here too. It was good to see you, James. You take care of yourself."

"Thank you and oh, you take care of yourself too."

Julia strode down the steps of the church and turned the corner to get to her car. She felt like someone was behind her but didn't see anyone in her immediate vicinity. Several people still congregated outside of the church, so it wouldn't have been far-fetched for anyone to be close to her vicinity.

"I made it," she said aloud, as she sank into the car.

She sat there for a couple of minutes, frozen.

Before she pulled out of the parking lot, she glanced over at her purse in the passenger seat. She reached inside to grab her phone and lift the silent mode. A new friend request and an unread message appeared in Instagram notifications.

She opened the app to read the notifications and was shocked at what she saw.

A friend request from Halston.

How the hell could this be?

She opened the unread message, which also came from Halston's account.

You're next.

A car horn beeped and shook her out of her daze.

James smiled and waved slowly at her as he drove past her car and eased onto the street.

Carlos Harleaux is an author, poet, publishing consultant and podcaster. He is a native of Houston, TX and now resides in Dallas, TX. His other novels include the *Fortune Cookie* novel trilogy series (including *No Cream in the Middle* and *When the Cookie Crumbles*), *Only for One Night* (co-written with Akela Renae) and *A Swipe in the Wrong Direction*.

He enjoys transporting his readers to an alternate universe that is as relatable as it is entertaining. Tune into the accompanying Trigger Pointe podcast and the Brown Liquor & Cigars podcast on all digital streaming platforms.

Visit peauxeticexpressions.com for his entire book catalog and introspective blogs.

www.ingramcontent.com/pod-product-compliance
Lightning Source LLC
Chambersburg PA
CBHW021148110726
47900CB00002B/479